W9-CCN-304

MIDDLE MAN

Also by David Rich

Caravan of Thieves

MIDDLE MAN

A LIEUTENANT ROLLIE WATERS NOVEL

David Rich

DUTTON

DUTTON
Published by the Penguin Group
Penguin Group (USA) Inc., 375 Hudson Street,
New York, New York 10014, USA

USA | Canada | UK | Ireland | Australia | New Zealand | India | South Africa | China
Penguin Books Ltd, Registered Offices: 80 Strand, London WC2R 0RL, England
For more information about the Penguin Group visit penguin.com.

 REGISTERED TRADEMARK—MARCA REGISTRADA

LIBRARY OF CONGRESS CATALOGING-IN-PUBLICATION DATA

Rich, David Neal.
  Middle man : a Lieutenant Rollie Waters novel / David Rich.
     pages   cm
  ISBN 978-0-525-95323-4 (hardcover)
 1. Suspense fiction. I. Title.
  PS3618.I3327M53   2013
  813'.6—dc23   2013000697

Printed in the United States of America
10 9 8 7 6 5 4 3 2 1

Set in Haarlemmer MT Std with Microgramma Com
Designed by Daniel Lagin

PUBLISHER'S NOTE
This book is a work of fiction. Names, characters, places, and incidents either are the product of the author's imagination or are used fictitiously, and any resemblance to actual per-
sons, living or dead, business establishments, events, or locales is entirely coincidental.

For Harriet and Bernie

God bless the King—I mean the faith's defender!
God bless—no harm in blessing—the Pretender!
But who Pretender is, or who is King,—
God Bless us all! That's quite another thing.

John Byrom

MIDDLE MAN

1

Snowflakes appeared in Havre, Montana, then disappeared when they hit the ground. The headstone had been pulled out of the ground and laid faceup. It said: ETHAN WILLIAMS 1979–2004. He had been a father, a husband, a son, but none of that was mentioned even though the Army would have paid for the listing. The headstone was probably going to become obsolete as soon as we opened the coffin, but the family might not get a chance at a replacement: My job was to find the money, not the bodies.

A police cruiser pulled up to the curb near the cemetery entrance. The cop did not get out. Our car was parked on the opposite side of the small cemetery, near the exit.

Sergeant Will Panos shrugged. "Had to notify them." He shifted his gaze across the grave. "Who's the smoker?"

The family was clumped together, with one exception. "Must be the father. Met all the others."

"They all keep looking at you."

"It's the uniform." We wore our service uniforms; this wasn't an occasion for dress blues, according to Sergeant Panos.

"Got my eye on the widow. Does that make me a bad guy?"

"That isn't what makes you a bad guy, Will." We had been working together for weeks, traveling around the country and to Iraq, and I had not discovered too much about him that was bad. He was the only one who thought he was a bad guy. I figured he was the expert. Sergeant Will Panos had a fleshy face and saggy eyes. His skin was pockmarked, dark and rough. His nose was crooked from fighting. It was the face of a tough guy, a slob, a bruiser. His face lied: Will Panos was a refined, meticulous, careful man who navigated Marine regulations so precisely that I wondered if he had written them himself.

The widow, Kristen, was a pretty woman, wary, about thirty, short, with her dark roots pushing the blond hair away. Her parents and a sister and the sister's husband huddled together in their winter coats near the foot of the grave. I had met them last night at Kristen's house. She had papers to sign. We had waited thirty minutes for Ethan Williams's father, but he never showed up, and no one found that noteworthy.

The smoker stood alone, smoked his cigarette to the stub, tossed it down and lit another. I walked over and introduced myself. Up close, he looked ragged. Random patches of his beard had evaded the razor. He was too young to look like that. "Marine Lieutenant Rollie Waters, sir." He didn't reply, so I said, "Are you Specialist Williams's father?"

His eyes narrowed and he seemed to hiss. "You don't fool me," he said.

"I'm sorry we have to do this." I just wanted to get away from him. The smell of liquor cut through the tobacco on his breath. Watery film covered his eyes and he could not hold my gaze.

"You've never been sorry for nothing," he said.

Kristen stepped in close to intervene. "I realize I didn't introduce you two. Lieutenant Waters, this is Ethan's father, Jim."

The father pointed at me and said, "That oughta be you in that grave and we both know it." His right hand turned up and I saw something black in it, and a second later the blade popped out the side.

Kristen said, "Jim! I'm over here." He looked at her. "Put the knife away, Jim. There's no danger." She moved closer to him.

"Mrs. Williams . . ."

She was half his size and the blade looked like it would go all the way through her even with the puffy down coat she wore. Jim noticed me again and his eyes narrowed as if they were going to take over the hissing, but they wavered. He was afraid. Kristen put up one hand to stop me from making a move, and put the other on Jim's shoulder. I stood still.

"Jim, give me the knife. This'll be over soon." Her voice was soft and understanding, as if they had been partners in some harrowing experience. She put out her hand. He retracted the blade and put the knife in his pocket. He was back in this world. Kristen checked with me and I nodded that I was okay with that.

Jim spat on the ground next to me, then shuffled a few feet away. Kristen waited for my reaction.

"Usually people wait until they get to know me before they do that."

"He's just . . . it's been hard," she said. She stood silently beside me for a while. "How many of these have you done so far, Lieutenant?"

"I've lost count." I glanced toward Will. He was watching us jealously.

"Lots of tears? Fainting?"

"Some."

"The sergeant is acting as if I'm going fall to pieces."

"He's seen what happens. . . . He's a good man." I waited too long to give the recommendation and it sounded forced to me, but she ignored it.

"This one will be different," she said in a way that made me believe her.

I wanted to believe her. This job, my first for SHADE, had cloaked me in respectability. The families treated me like a black-swaddled Keeper of Some Holy Secrets; they feared and resented me. Being mistaken for someone I'm not has always been a private pleasure and I always enjoyed feeding the misconceptions about me. But this identity, Exhumationist, a joke at first, became an open wound. I started thinking that one day I would unzip a body bag and find myself inside.

Kristen rejoined her family. They were not crying either, yet. A preacher had tagged along, ignored by all, stationed on the opposite side of the grave from Jim. I glanced at the man working with a rake about one hundred yards to my right, on a small rise. He was Mack Rios, a Marine sniper I brought along as a precaution: Millions in cash is a temptation for everyone, even the bereaved. The small white tent where we would open the coffin stood between us. Exhumation is a private business. This one, even without tears, felt no different from the others.

I wished it did.

The first time we dug up a grave and unzipped the body bag

and found money, I got that thrill that comes from being right. Hard work rewarded. We had to count the money even though the game was still going on and counting brought questions, which deflated the good feeling. We expected to find twenty-five million dollars in each grave: The first had one million; the second had a million and a half. Something was wrong. We did not understand what it was.

The snow stopped. The winch operator signaled to Will that he was ready. Will nodded. The winch spun. Everyone stared dutifully at the hole in the ground as if they did not know what was going to emerge. But the grave seemed to be two miles deep. The creaky chains rolled up slowly. Maybe the winch man was holding out for overtime. I snuck in behind Jim Williams and grabbed his right arm into a quick hammerlock and slipped my hand into his pocket and extracted the knife. He hissed once more.

At last the casket floated up from the grave and hovered like an alien drone that we had foolishly unearthed and activated. It swung hypnotically and Kristen flinched. It almost hit the preacher, whose eyes were closed, but no one interrupted his reverie. Each exhumation was like a combat patrol. This was my third exhumation, so I felt like a veteran: weary but addicted. I tried to watch the family without staring. I wanted to know what they were hoping for. If I was wrong, if the body was in the grave, then hope was crushed forever. If I was right and the grave contained a body bag filled with money, then hope, which I knew I had revived when I contacted them, would rise up and slam them to the ground and stomp on them, probably as long as they lived. I wanted to watch them to see which choice they thought they preferred. But this was only the third grave and it would take thousands to make a good sample.

The explosion was small, a flash and a pop, but so was the tent. Dirt pelted us, speeding through the strips and bits of white canvas swirling around us. Beyond the tent, Mack Rios went down with the first shot. The second shot hit Will Panos, who had jumped in front of Kristen to shield her. He yelled, "Damn, damn, damn," and tottered and brought her down when he fell. A hand pushed me in the back and I bent forward to maintain my balance. Jim Williams said something like "You, damn you . . ." The rest was drowned out by the third shot, which went through his neck.

For a moment I thought the silence was complete, but the creaking of the chains holding the coffin kept a steady beat as I ran up the hill to Mack. He was dead, shot in the face, lying on his back with his rifle just inches from his left hand.

I stood up and looked back toward the grave. At first, the area was diorama still. Then the spell expired and figures began to move as if wound up by the slow ticktock of the gently swinging coffin. The shots had come from the big, peaceful field of headstones lined up like seats in an auditorium beyond the grave site. A shooter could have hidden behind any one of them, but no one was out there now.

The sirens were close by the time I got back to the graveside and Will Panos. His wound cut across the front of his right thigh. He was trying to stand. I pulled him down and kneeled next to him. "How is it?"

"Not bad," he said while wincing, because the only bullets that don't hurt are the fatal ones.

Kristen had crawled out from under him and gone over to her parents. The flashing lights from the cop cars coated the scene in glimpses of red, so it took me a moment to realize the back of her jacket was smeared with Will's blood.

"Get the attention of the first cops. Howl if you have to," I said. "I'm going to try to get out of here with the money."

I left Will and went to the winch operator and pulled him up. "Lower the coffin to the ground. Right where it is. Now," I said. He was staring at Will, still on the ground. "Just do it. Do it now. Where's the crank?" He pointed to a tool chest next to the winch. I pushed him toward the controls and he went to work. I meant for him to drop the thing, but he lowered it as if the world's last bottle of bourbon were inside. As soon as the casket was on the ground, I put in the crank to pop the lock, then wedged the crowbar in the middle to lift the top. The winch operator sat there as if waiting for further instructions.

The cops were getting out of their cars. An ambulance was pulling up. I was not sure how I was going to get out of there with the money, but I knew I did not want the local police claiming it. I lifted the top of the casket and reached inside and unzipped the body bag and I flinched. The skin was thin as fancy stationery and the hair was sparse and the remains of a man wore a Marine uniform. From behind me Kristen said, "Who the hell is that?" I stared at her and might have kept staring at her while I tried to comprehend the situation, but I saw cops coming toward us. I zipped up the bag and closed the lid.

My father, Dan, dead now, though not departed, the former and forever Minister of Collateral Damage, had sniffed out the plot by a bunch of officers to ship millions home from Iraq in body bags in the early days of the war. Dan only knew about one shipment. Retrieving it and relocating it came as naturally to him as burying nuts is to a squirrel. He stole it, but he did not want to spend it. The money lay hidden for years until about six months ago, when the plotters dug up the grave Dan had already looted and found nothing but stale air. Dan's last, and only, gift to me was a clue about where he had hidden it.

Colonel McColl and his gang killed Dan and followed me while I followed Dan's clue; I found the money and used it as bait to kill them for what they had done to him. That brought me to the attention of Major Hensel. He had just formed SHADE, which is short for Shared Defense Executive; it's a division of the Defense Intelligence Agency. "Concerned with national security issues involving the military," according to the Major, who is the only one who would know. That is how I came to have the job these past months hunting down the other money-seeded graves McColl had boasted of.

I didn't burn Dan's body with the intent of ridding myself of him forever, though I thought that would be a side benefit. For any decent father, a son avenging his murder would have put the matter to rest, but that sort of decency eluded Dan even in death and he has been stalking me relentlessly, with the same irresponsibility, unpredictability, and irritating selfishness that he perfected in life, dogging me with stories I had heard many times and stories I had never heard before.

Though I studied desert combat, small arms combat, mountain combat, survival techniques, counterinsurgency, tai chi, aikido, yoga, petty thievery, breaking and entering, and other arcane street lessons, Dan studies was my major, my minor, my hobby, my relentless affliction. I hated him while he lived and avoided him as soon as I could, but his death defeated my hatred. Dan fascination, long unacknowledged, often denied, found no new poison after his death and so flourished.

Dan accompanied me out of Havre to the Canadian border, going on about the scene at the grave before the shooting.

"Nice of the old man to save your life like that."

"He was a great guy."

"I'd have done the same."

I laughed.

"Tough having to put your son in the ground and then having to stand there again to find out if you did it right the first time."

That's when I knew the purpose of this chat: Dan had been robbed of the grand stage my graveside would have provided him.

What stories would he have concocted on the spot? My last letter: He would pull a few pieces of paper from his pocket, hold them a moment, then shake his head and put them away. He could recite it by heart: a letter foreshadowing my tragic death and revealing to him the ways he had always inspired me. Funny stories would follow, oozing fatherly wisdom in the face of the stubbornness of impetuous youth. If I left an attractive widow, the show would be directed toward her. Whatever tears and laughs he evoked would be in service of that conquest.

Dan spoke up at that thought: *"I would not."*

"Because you had already succeeded, or because you had already been turned down?"

"Because at some point she would start feeling guilty and ruin all the fun."

But he would not feel guilty.

Canada looked just like Montana. A thin white coating over a flat sheet spreading to the horizon like an exposed bed you could never roll out of. The snow started again, just enough to make a dusting on the road and on the windshield. I pulled onto the shoulder about fifty yards before the border and parked myself on the hood of my car. I took off my jacket and enjoyed the bite of the cold air. I wanted to linger, to clear my mind so I could begin to understand the puzzle of the graves. Dan receded, but just a moment later a border guard emerged from the small station on the left, which looked like a drive-through coffee stand. He wore a parka with an American flag on the sleeve and a Homeland Security patch.

"You waiting for something?"

"Yes."

"What's that?"

"A revelation."

He looked around for a moment, stared as if he could see the North Pole, brushed snow off his coat. "Well, trust me on this; I been working this station fifteen years and unless you're waiting for Santy Claus, you're facing the wrong direction." He tapped on my roof and gestured with his gloved hand. "If this isn't government business then you gotta move along."

When he got about ten yards away I said, "Truth is, I'm waiting for Ethan Williams."

His head slowly tilted and his eyes got squinty as if I had asked him to complete a tough math equation. A car was coming up from behind me. The guard considered hustling back to his post. Instead, he put up his hand to stop the car. It slowed down and stopped next to him and he leaned down. I could only hear his end:

"Hey, Bill. You got anything I need to know about . . . ? When you coming back . . . ? It's fine. No problems . . ." Bill drove across the invisible border and the guard returned to me.

"Who'd you say?"

"Ethan Williams."

"You a relation of his?"

"No."

"Well, if you're waiting for Ethan, you better be patient. That boy died in Iraq years ago."

"You knew him?"

"I know about everybody here. Except you."

It took a day and a half to get to Chicago. Only Dan interrupted my guilty silence.

"This isn't on you. You didn't cause this."

"Man down, a good man. Another man wounded."

"It might have been worse if they hadn't been there."

"How?"

"Did I ever tell you the story about the time I fell in love? Beautiful woman, lived up in San Francisco."

"Before I was born?"

"I think you were staying with someone in Arizona and I didn't want to interrupt your life. It wouldn't have been fair to drag you away." Fair to him, he meant. "A beauty she was, and rich, too. Her father was a financial wizard on the East Coast. She ran an art gallery. The walls lined with paintings I couldn't look at and the floor filled with rich friends I couldn't take my eyes off of. All of them eager to spend their money. For me, it was like being the house at a craps game; I could make a deal every time I blinked my eyes. The biggest problem was keeping track of them all. Sometimes I would hide from people trying to give me checks, which you know made them increase the size of those checks. She was perfect; I don't think she cared what deals I made. And then, suddenly, she broke it off. Not only did the checks stop coming in, everybody wanted their money back. I was devastated. At least I convinced myself of that, at first. Played the part. Of course that helped me with all the investors who suddenly needed their money back. I was too distracted to bother about such small matters. But I must have bought into my show of distress because they seemed to believe me."

"How long did that last?"

"Couple of weeks. But I could never believe anyone's tears, not even my own. I felt lousy, but it wasn't about the woman. I felt lousy because I didn't feel lousy about the woman. I was relieved it was over. Love was a burden I did not like to bear. That was not easy to face. But once I *admitted that I disliked being in love, I was elated and left town imme-diately with all the money."*

"Who did she catch you with?"

"She didn't catch me with anyone. Her sister confessed. Unsolicited. More of a boast than a confession."

"Your story does not help me. There's no correlation with my situ-ation. A woman caught you cheating; a sniper killed two men and wounded another on my watch. Not the same thing."

Even in death, Dan did not argue or explain, though I would have welcomed either. *"Okay,"* he said.

I knew what I had to do and did not want any orders getting in my way, so I ignored Major Hensel's calls, but I left the battery in the phone. When he knew where I was, he would know what I was doing. Dan's story was like a thorn in my shoe: The irritation lin-gered. I had to let go of the idea of Dan dispensing wisdom. Dan did not dispense, not anything of value. Dan led you toward the truth and stood there watching you find ways to ignore it, twist it, disguise it. That was his thrill in life. As a shadow he was the same, only more so, though I suspected the thrill was gone.

The humiliating possibilities outlined in Dan's story slouched in front of me like criminal candidates in a police lineup: relief, ex-citement, delight, elation. Whichever I chose incriminated me. But even if I put aside the guilt and ache of losing my man, I could not place any one of those snickering partners with me at the scene. I longed for change, longed to be released from the drudgery of in-terviews and paperwork. But longing for change does not cause change.

The plane felt like a cage. Behind me, a young boy started to cry in a throbbing rhythm that matched the drone of the engines. The woman in the aisle seat woke herself with a snoring snort. She wiped drool from the side of her mouth and looked past me at the dull black outside the window. She closed her eyes again and her head tilted back sharply, as if she had been hit. Below, a cluster of lights looked like the marking of a drop zone. The exit row was just three in front of me.

All I had to do was admit that I was relieved and I would not mind whatever condemnation came along with it. I would be free. That temptation, posing as my shadowed reflection, winked at me in the window, tempted me to open it up. But I did not want to follow Dan's lead. I never did. Love was a burden he did not want to bear, as was the truth. Dan was a ghost and had been a ghost for many years before he died. I was not ready to become a ghost. I was not ready to open the window and get sucked out.

I was released, not relieved. Released from the routine and administration that my first job with SHADE had devolved into. Released from the lies and paperwork and permits required to retrieve the dead. The bundled emotions were easier to carry than any single one of them would have been. I could open the bundle and inhale the vile mixture whenever I got too sure of myself.

The list of graves was wrong. I was certain we had followed the right path to obtain it, but the list was wrong, and hoping the next graves would have millions inside them would mark me as an arrogant, ignorant mark. I closed my eyes and rewalked the steps that led to the list, trying to understand where I went wrong.

Major Hensel had sent Will Panos along with me to Iraq: to spy on me, I thought. But Sergeant Panos proved to be the perfect partner, documenting the search and quoting regulations no one ever heard of, with enough gruff authority and self-assurance to inject doubt into the nastiest obstructing bureaucrat. Unfortunately, the men and women we interviewed were the most innocent, pure, untainted sample of humanity on the planet. Colonel McColl was their saint. No one ever saw any money in Iraq, but each one swore to do his or her all to help us.

McColl served in Baghdad from March 2003 until August 2004. More than one thousand Americans were killed in that time. The problem could not be attacked that way. The grave Dan dug up provided our best lead and most frustrating dead end. Master Sergeant Brian Kenny signed the death certificate. But Brian Kenny died days later. To those who worked with him, it was inconceivable that he was involved in anything criminal. Brian Kenny had signed many forms just like that one before he died. Too many. Will and I sat at computers in a windowless room at Camp Pendleton. I don't know what Will was looking at. I was looking at lists of the dead as if they were assembly directions written by foreigners.

"We can't dig up all of them, Will."

He kept staring at his screen and said, "Do you think he was murdered? Brian Kenny, I mean."

"One way or another."

"You know what I mean."

"The report said an IED blew up the vehicle. Four men died. How many lived? It's the difficult way to go about eliminating one guy."

"The driver lived. Lamar Davis. Lost his right leg." Will didn't have to check his notes to recall the name. "He says he didn't know Sergeant Kenny except to say hello when he got into the vehicle." I returned my eyes to the lists on my computer screen, but my mind wandered to Baghdad, trying to picture Sergeant Kenny deciding to go into town. Why? "Maybe if you called him," said Will.

"Who?"

"Lamar Davis. Maybe he'll be more talkative with an officer. Maybe he remembered something."

I called from my phone, which blocked the ID. Lamar Davis answered the phone, saying, "I told you not to call me at work."

A bad start. I explained the reason for the call. He did not want to be called about that, either.

"Look, here's everything I know. I drove from the Green Zone to the airport on October fifth, 2003, and dropped off a general and two majors. Four soldiers filled up the vehicle for the ride back.

About five kilometers along Route Irish, I saw a car stopped in the right-hand lane and pulled to the left; about five seconds later, there was a blast. That's all I remember."

"You mean October fifteenth," I said.

"Screw you. All you guys. You think I don't remember the day? You changing the truth? October fifth, fourteen hundred hours twenty-one minutes, 2003. That's all I know. I never said more than hello to Sergeant Kenny or any of the others. And I didn't overhear anything they might have said to each other. Don't call me again."

Will could hear Davis's tone and the hang-up. "Sorry," he said. "I thought it was worth a try. We can still search for every death certificate Sergeant Kenny signed and check who had an open casket and . . . Why are you smiling?"

"What day did Sergeant Kenny sign the death certificate?"

"October twelfth."

"After he was dead for a week. Check it. Check the date Lamar Davis drove over the IED." He checked. It was October fifth. "Which means someone else filed that paperwork. And it was probably a master sergeant, right?"

"Right."

And so we found our way to Chicago in February, an exotic treat for me, a desert child, but a torment for Will Panos, a native. Will visited his sister and mother while I went to the Triple A, a bar featuring gooey wings, northwest of the city on a strip of Milwaukee Avenue lined with restaurants. There, at three P.M., I found the owner, Frank Godwin, Army master sergeant, retired, perched, short legs dangling, on a barstool the size of a love seat next to the waitress station, copping feels with his gooey hands and barking greetings to his customers. He wore a Blackhawks sweater that made him look like an Easter egg with a flat top.

Godwin pushed away his most recently finished basket of wings and we shook hands and I caught a waitress watching for my reaction to that experience. Her name was Nita. Godwin was gregarious at first, pegged me for a salesman, and I let him think that while we talked about the weather and the reputation his place had all across the country.

"A friend in Arizona told me about it," I said. On the slight chance that he had heard about who brought down Colonel McColl, I was Mickey Taylor, formerly a Marine warrant officer. His smile disappeared. He sent Nita away and tried to force the smile back. Strangers from the military worried him. I told Frank that Colonel McColl had died and watched his reaction closely. He knew.

"I didn't know," he said. "When?" Godwin looked up at one of the thousands of flat-screen TVs plastering the place. Someone was running and being chased. He asked, "Were you there?"

"If I were there, the Colonel would be alive." The bartender brought me a beer and another Diet Coke for his boss. I could see the dark fingerprints of barbecue sauce on the bright red of his sweater.

We toasted to Colonel McColl, the great man. "A great man, a great soldier. If we had more like him, we'd run the whole damned world. I'd follow that man to hell." He talked until he could get the tears started.

Behind the bar, in a glass case, was a display of Third Army patches: a large *A* in a circle, usually red. That was the only military reference I saw there. When I finished my beer, he said, "Well, thanks for letting me know. How long you in town for?"

"That depends on you, Sergeant." I looked around dramatically, then leaned in close to him. "It's time. We have to know if you're in." And I did not back up.

"Slow down. In what?"

"The Colonel started the ball rolling. The plan is going forward. Are you with us?"

"Could you back up a few inches?"

"The Colonel told me you were solid." He was boxed in and squirming like a child who wanted to get out of his high chair.

"I don't know what you mean."

I stepped back and just stared at him. The bartender watched from the other end of the bar, waiting for Frank's signal for help. But Frank still thought he could wriggle out of this on his own. "I don't know what the hell you're talking about. Maybe it's time for you to go back to Arizona."

"The graves, Frank. We have three of them. We need the other three." I thought he would be more comfortable giving me a partial list, especially if I already had half on my own. Arrest was my worst option. He could play dumb while investigators played with handwriting specialists decoding the death certificates. Besides, I had no authority to arrest him.

I was certain we had the right guy. Godwin served at the airport in Baghdad; he served under McColl in the first Gulf War; he knew the procedures; he had the means and the motive, which was the desire to do as McColl told him to. Most revealing, though, was the squirrelly aura of fear surrounding his roundness. Godwin knew where the graves were.

Will Panos had exhausted the possibilities with his relatives. He told them he was leaving town then hid out at the Holiday Inn bar. "How will you break him? And when?" He sounded like a man who was on the run. Chicago made him nervous because it reminded him of his life as a civilian. He wasn't sure of the rules. Camp Pendleton was home and refuge for him.

"I'm going to make him realize how scared he is," I said.

"I thought you weren't going to threaten him."

"I'm going to make him realize how good it would feel to share the knowledge. Relieve the burden."

The Triple A filled and emptied. Trays of wings crashed. Bouncers tossed young sports fans. Women came in packs and left in pairs with men. Frank balanced on his stool, commanded the floor, as only a master sergeant could. I would have paid him to turn off just one of the TVs so I could stop seeing and hearing the excited propaganda from ESPN for a few minutes while I camped out the next few days at the bar, ignoring the chicken wings, flirting fuzzily with Nita the waitress. She got impatient with me. "Are you married or something?"

"I've got to take care of something first. Then I can concentrate on you." I was concentrating on making Humpty Dumpty crack.

"I checked. No one ever heard of you," said Frank.

"Did you tell them why I'm here, Frank?" I knew the answer. "Are they coming around to take care of me? No, they're not. Because you can't tell anyone why I'm here. If you do, they might decide they want the information from you, or it might mean you intend to steal the money for yourself. Even if you have enough brains not to try it, how long until they come to the conclusion you've gotten greedy? Even the Colonel, even the great Colonel McColl couldn't last once word of the money leaked out. The guy who killed the Colonel isn't going to stop there, Frank."

"Why would he come after me?"

"A lot of good men have been busted. The Colonel's people. Someone is talking. Someone is handing them over. Word is getting out. Why am I here? You're the man with the secrets. At least the Colonel sent me. I wouldn't want you to have to face the guy who killed him."

He pushed the basket of wings away and stared at a TV showing a hockey game. Someone in a Blackhawks jersey that matched Frank's checked someone hard into the boards from behind. A fight started. The two players threw off their gloves, and each one grabbed the other's jersey with his left hand and they pounded each other with short rights. The referees circled to make sure no one else interfered. Eventually the fighters fell to the ice, the enemy on top of the Blackhawk. "That guy never wins a damn fight. He's useless," Frank said.

"What does he lose?"

Frank turned to me and his mouth fell open and his eyes flashed with the self-indulgent outrage of a sports fan given a nit to pick. He thought I had taken the pressure off. "It's all about positioning and strategy and . . ."

"I thought it would be a relief for you to get rid of the secrets, Frank. But play it your way." I left.

When I came back the next day, I brought along my suitcase: Frank's last chance. An older man with white hair, red nose, and yellow fingers was boring Frank on the subject of baseball. I stood a few feet away to let Frank ponder my appearance and it was clear he did not hear a word the old man was saying. I left the suitcase in the middle of the floor and joined them at the bar. Suddenly, Frank was fascinated by every word from the old man's mouth. The focus was the Cubs.

"They're two players away. Two players. The question is which two," he explained.

"I heard they're moving to the American League," I said. The man jolted upright and his jaw hung open. "I'd like to speak with Frank alone for a moment, please."

"What about the Sox?"

"Let me buy you another, Joe," said Frank, and he signaled the bartender. "He's just putting you on. He's a big joker."

"You had me. I never thought of that one. They just need two players . . ." The bartender delivered his beer, but the old guy was talking too much to touch it.

I stared at Frank and this time he met my eyes and smiled as if he had outmaneuvered me. Frank was not much of a tactician.

The old man kept talking and I started in, too. "The Colonel financed this place for you, didn't he, Frank? He was a loyal guy, but he didn't do that for everyone who worked for him. He couldn't. You were special and we both know why."

"I don't think it's the pitching or the defense . . ."

"But the Colonel had pressures on him, didn't he? You must have seen that. He could get paranoid. Didn't you worry, Frank? Worry that you knew something he didn't want anyone to know? I know you did."

"There's speed and there's power and then there's brains . . ."

"Worry that someone like me would arrive. Someone, though, who didn't come to ask for your help. Give me the names, Frank, and I'll be gone."

"But that's three guys . . ."

"Joe . . . Joe!" Frank was a sergeant again, barking. Joe stopped talking for a second. "Go away. Go over there. I'll send over some wings." Frank's voice was trembling. Joe just shrugged and nodded to me and left with his beer.

"Who are you?" Frank was defeated and relieved to surrender, and he could not look at me now. He put both hands on the bar and used it as support as he slid forward until his feet touched the floor. I followed him down the corridor, past the restrooms, to a small office, just a desk and chair and one filing cabinet and a safe about three feet high. The only photo on the wall was of Frank and Colonel McColl. McColl had his arm around Frank's shoulder.

"That's the day he shipped home. I never saw him again. I called him once to ask for a loan for this place and he sent me a package with fifty thousand in cash." I looked toward the safe, expecting the information to be in there. Instead, he squirmed around in his seat and managed to dig his thick fingers into his back pocket.

"You said six graves. There's seven."

The list was handwritten. Seven names and dates. He stared straight ahead, both hands flat on the desk in front of him.

"What are you going to do when the next guy comes along asking for the list, Frank?"

He was smart enough to be terrified. His body stayed still while he twisted his fat neck in a knot so tight, one of the chins almost disappeared. "Whatya mean? I'm gonna tell him I ain't got it."

"That's what you told me, Frank, at first." I didn't mind extending his state of terror. "Do you have copies?"

"No. No. I swear it." I did not answer just so I could make him say the next sentence. Frank needed to feel fear. "You don't have to kill me. I swear. Please."

I reached into my coat pocket, slowly, and watched his eyes follow my hand. I pulled out a folded sheet of paper. I set it on the desk in front of him. He shifted his eyes to mine. "I'm not gonna write a suicide note, that's for damn sure."

I laughed, caught off guard. Frank had principles after all. "Look at the paper. It's a list of six KIA and their hometowns. I want you to copy it out in your handwriting and keep it in that same back pocket. And I want you to wait until they work you over a little before you give it to them, so they'll believe it. I'll find out if you gave in too fast." He had to throw out the first two copy attempts because his hand shook too much.

After I watched him force the folded sheet into his back pocket, I was going to just walk away. But he spoke: "Who are you, really? Are you the guy who killed the Colonel? You are."

"You did the right thing, Frank."

"I knew you'd show up here. I heard about you." I didn't answer. "All those guys, the ones who didn't get shipped home, got buried properly, y'know. We saw to that. It's not like we left them in the desert."

"Were those orders, or did you think of that yourself? Someone's going to want to know where. Better start on that list, too."

"Am I gonna lose my place?"

"Get a good lawyer." I went back into the bar, picked up my suitcase, and left.

On this second trip to Chicago, Frank Godwin's perch at the bar was occupied by lovebirds, cannibals, I guess, munching on coated bird wings. The place was busy at just past midday. Nita the waitress smiled as she passed by on her way to deliver two pitchers and a handful of mugs. When she returned, she said, "I didn't expect to see you again. That's what Frank said."

"He won't like seeing his seat occupied."

"He won't know. He's on vacation. Beer?"

"Not right now. Who did he go with?"

She looked at me like I was crazy to ask her. Men at a table across the room were holding up their empty pitcher for her. About ten minutes later, she caught my eye and gestured toward the back. Outside, in the shade of an overhang, she leaned against the brick and sucked on her cigarette. "Did you come back here to ask me out?"

"Not this time."

"Why should I tell you anything about my boss, then?"

"You shouldn't." She spent a full minute squinting off into the bright parking lot. She flicked her cigarette high and far, and the glow was extinguished in the sunlight.

"He's got a cabin over on Lake Delavan. And, no, I've never been there. But he sure asked me enough. I'd go there with you."

"Some old military buddies come around before he went?"

"Looked like military. Yeah, two guys. I better get back."

She reached for the door. I grabbed her arm and turned her toward me and kissed her. She smiled and said, "You know why I like you?"

"Because I don't taste like barbecue sauce?"

"Exactly."

He reminded me of a boy with no friends, only a fishing rod and a bucket and a seat on the end of the pier where his feet could dangle just above the water. I was about eighty yards away, coming along the shore with the setting sun behind me elongating my shadow so it seemed to belong to an alien. I lengthened my stride just to see the effect. The choppy water was splotched with silver, and the air smelled wet and fresh with the last taste of winter fading. I could not tell if Frank was wearing shoes or not.

I had parked a few streets away from Frank's cabin and walked down the lane behind his, hoping to sneak through backyards to get a look. But a man was outside working on his motorcycle at the cabin directly behind Frank's and he looked like he would care where I went, so I walked down to the lake and found Frank by accident.

I was thirty yards away when Frank felt a tug on the line. He reeled in quickly, no need to play this fish, and a thin pan fryer, a sunfish so small and insignificant to make anyone toss it back, wriggled on the end of the line. Frank grabbed it, removed the hook, and tossed the fish in the pail. Maybe he had barbecue sauce in there.

"Nice catch, Frank."

He almost dropped his fishing rod. He squinted into the sun. He said, "Hey, you're back. It's not six. I'll be back at six."

One shot was fired and Frank toppled over into Lake Delavan like a kid making an awkward first dive. I dove for the cover of the trees just a few feet from the shore. Judging by the direction Frank had toppled, the shot came from behind him, up the lane where his cabin stood, which meant I would be out of sight of the shooter. I waited. I waited. I had no weapon and I was dealing with a good shot. He would be doing the same thing I was doing: scanning for movement. The only sound was a motorboat coming toward the pier. One fisherman sat at the tiller. He came close to shore, spent some time checking out the area, then decided that whatever had been shot wasn't going to benefit him and turned around.

The boat was almost to the middle of the lake when I heard the whistle, three quick notes, and then the footsteps in the leaves behind me. I turned slowly. A man wearing a ski mask was running toward Frank's house and had not seen me. I cut right so I would be directly behind him and tried to mimic his pace so I could keep him in sight. I had gone about fifty yards when the blow hit me behind the ear and I fell into the leaves, dazed. I made it to my knees and twisted around to see two men in ski masks standing over me. One held a rifle, the other a large automatic handgun. My eyes kept closing as I tried to stand.

One said, "Check his pockets."

"He has no gun. I can see that," said the other one. I thought he had an English accent.

"For a list," said number one. "I'll bet he has a list." His voice was high and light and full of hope. Someone kicked me in the head. I could feel them searching me.

I heard someone say, "It's the same as the one we got from Frank."

"That's good, then, isn't it?" The voice was very close. I forced my eyes open. The automatic was pointed at my head. The guy without the English accent was kneeling close to me. "Nice to see you, Lieutenant. You're very good. Very good." The emphasis was on "good" as if he were trying to prove his sincerity. His eyes were brown and intense and he looked cross-eyed because the mask spread out too far and covered the inner parts of his eyes. I could see his lips and his small teeth. "But I'm better than you."

"Just kill him and let's go," said the Englishman.

"He can't find me, can you, Lieutenant? He'll never find me. But I might need him later on." He stood up.

The Englishman said, "We have the list. You know we can't let him live."

The American answered him calmly, "I told you, I might need him."

The Englishman said, "If you won't do it, I will."

I tried to pull myself up, but the man behind me kicked me in the head again and I was out.

I thought I opened both my eyes, but only one worked. My lips were fuzzy and a heavy log lay across my chest, keeping me from drawing breath. I tried to roll out from under the log but hit a solid block.

I rolled the other way and was free. My face itched, so I scratched at it. The surface moved. I adjusted it so I could see with both eyes. The log next to me was wearing a mask. So was I.

He was shot in the back. I took the mask off him. He was in his twenties, shaved head, and a flame tattoo on his neck. I pried one eye open; it was blue, which meant he was the Englishman. The other man had brown eyes that I would be seeing for a long time. I put the mask back on the dead man and took mine with me.

I was walking away when I realized the American had called me Lieutenant. I was not wearing my uniform.

Frank's cabin was dark. A red Chevy pickup sat in front. The small porch was shaded by cedar trees on each side. I opened the screen door and banged it shut, then stood flat against the wall and watched down the lane toward the lake. I waited five still minutes but saw no movement and I heard nothing from inside.

I went in. The living room had a nubby brown couch and a TV and a stained reclining chair covered in something that looked like velour, from which Frank could dangle his feet, with a tray table beside it. The furniture was old and worn and drab and for a moment I felt sorry for Frank sneaking up here to settle back into his real self. Next to the TV, a stuffed marlin pointed the way to the kitchen. On the Formica table, there was a bowl of Cheerios, still half full of milk, spoon inside the bowl. The fridge held two six-packs of Hamm's beer, a block of cheddar, a pizza box. Two matchbooks and a clean ashtray sat next to the sink. One matchbook was from Applebee's and one from the Triple A. Frank's car keys and his wallet lay on the counter next to the sink. He had almost a thousand dollars in the wallet. Skimmed cash. There were two bedrooms, both with two twin beds, all with chenille covers. In one room, both beds had been slept in. In the other, just one bed was turned down. A Blackhawks poster, frameless, showing the team and the Stanley Cup, was tacked up next to the mirror in that bedroom. I assumed the one toothbrush belonged to Frank.

Outside, a white four-door sedan cruised slowly toward the lake: DELAVAN NEIGHBORHOOD PATROL painted on the side and a yellow bubble on top. The driver might have heard the shot, but he wouldn't be getting out of the car to look for a body off the end of the pier unless someone told him about it. Maybe someone told him to check Frank's house for strangers. I wanted to know.

The security car slowed down as it came even with the house. A man in a blue-gray uniform with a yellow patch on the sleeve got out. When he rang the bell, I stepped behind the door, and when he came in, I put my left arm around his throat and with my right hand I pulled his gun. I threw him onto the couch and cocked the gun and put it right up to his nose.

"Why are you here? Why are you here? Who the hell are you?" I was angrier than I realized and right away I felt foolish. The pain in my head and my frustration were taking control of me.

"I got a call. I had to come." His fear was real. He was young, early twenties. His eyes were blue; he was not the killer who got away. "I work for the security company."

"Did you see a guy driving away? Did you see who was staying here?"

"Frank lives here. I didn't see no one else but you."

"Keys in the car?" He nodded. I took his phone and his walkie-talkie and I left.

The Triple A was almost empty when I got back there. Nita stood at the bar, chatting with the bartender and sipping a cocktail. The bartender wasn't happy to see me, but Nita was. We went to the bar at the Holiday Inn. She knew the bartender there, too, and he didn't look so happy to see me either. Nita ordered a shot of Wild Turkey and a beer. I settled for just a beer. We moved to a table.

"Exciting night at the Triple A," she said.

"Somebody send the wings back?"

"FBI came in." I kept quiet because I knew the rest. I wanted to see if she did. She did. "They were looking for a guy named Rollie Waters."

"Did they have a photo?"

"Yes. Handsome guy. In uniform." I watched her while she ordered another drink. Lying to the FBI would have been foolish for her. The bartender and the other waitresses had all seen me. "I used to work here. But you make better money off regulars than you do off cheap businessmen. And the food is even worse than the Triple A." She waited, sipped, waited, then she said, "I had to tell them."

"I don't mind," I said. "It was the only way to handle it. Who else? Who else did you tell?"

She put her hand on mine. "Do you have a room here?" I shook my head. "I live just about a mile away. We can go there."

I looked at the bartender. He wasn't a big guy and I guessed he didn't have a weapon behind the bar, at least nothing he would use unless he was being robbed. He glanced my way and I nodded and circled my finger to order another round. Nita looked, too, and confirmed the order.

"You're not mad?"

"Not at you."

The drinks arrived. Nita clicked her shot glass against my beer and downed the bourbon. She sat back in her chair and waited for the punch in the gut, the follow-up, waited for me to try to ruin her night. She had decided to go home with me and her wide eyes challenged me to ruin it. That was easy. I decided it was best to handle this in public. "Frank is dead."

She was stunned. She grimaced and squinted her eyes. "Heart attack?" She said it hopefully. I shook my head even though she knew the answer. She widened her eyes to ask if I did it. I shook my head slowly and as I did, her eyes closed. She leaned back in her chair and lost her balance for a second and almost fell. When she righted herself, she said, "Who'd want to kill that fat fuck? All he wanted to do was eat and watch hockey and fish."

The waitress stopped by. "You guys all right?"

"Another shot," I said. The waitress went away. Nita took a long pull on her beer. "I want you to take your phone out and put it on the table. And I want you to tell me what time you called them so I can be sure what the number is. You can go outside for a smoke while I look."

"What are you talking about?"

"I also want you to describe them to me. There were two of them."

The waitress delivered the shot. Nita waited until she left to say, "You're nuts. What the hell's the matter with you?"

"You fingered me. Or so you thought. Maybe they hurt you. Maybe they paid you. Maybe both. I don't care. I care what happens now. You called them and told them I was coming up to the cabin, just like they told you to. Only they didn't go after me. They killed Frank, the fat fuck. Now give me your phone."

She looked at the floor. She looked at the window and at the TV showing a soccer game. I stared at her until she put her hand in her purse and slid the phone toward me. "They called me. It comes up private, no number."

I checked. The private call came in four times, earlier in the day. All the other incoming and outgoing calls were local numbers. "Describe them."

"Derek was a skinny guy, tallish. Shaved head. Flame tattoo running up his neck. He had an English accent. John was a little shorter than you, a little thicker. Dark complexion. I doubt those were their real names."

"Which one did you sleep with?"

She slapped me. I took it and smiled. She got up and I grabbed her wrist and stood beside her. The bartender had come around the bar, but he stopped when he saw us standing close together. "I need to know," I said.

"John. He was more my type. Just like you are."

No leads. Not many clues. I needed help. Major Hensel, who ran SHADE, had kept the reins loose and I ran as freely as I could. I hardly knew him and I resented how well he seemed to know me, so I kept communication to a minimum to test him, and to set a standard. But now I had reached the limit and knew I needed his help. I called him while I sat in my car in the hotel parking lot. His first words were "Do you know where Frank's killer is?"

"No."

"Then you should get away from there fast as you can."

And, by then, the local police were approaching my car from three sides.

From the tenth-floor corner office, I had a view of two parking lots and a toll road.

I counted the cars for a while and bet myself about which parking spots they would pull into. Black and silver were the predominant colors. Having completed my parking-lot accounting duties, I pushed the desk aside and began my tai chi, though I was not positive this was sanctioned executive behavior. Agent Hanrihan came in so soon after I began that I wondered if he had been watching. "Put that desk back," he said. I put the desk back and sat down in the big executive chair and put my feet up. "Get up. Now."

"It's time you learned to share. You'll have your turn later," I said.

"Get up or I'll pull you up."

I smiled at him and gave a look asking if he really wanted to try that: He didn't. I had been there all morning, and every half hour or so, Agent Hanrihan came in to scold me or question me. He wore a blue blazer and striped tie and beige pants, which made him look like a security man at an NBA game. Agent Sampson followed him in. Her light hair was pulled back tight and clipped into a pony-tail. I guessed she was about forty. Her face was lean and her skin was tight and smooth. She wore black slacks, a white shirt and a black jacket and heels that weren't too high. She carried a coffee cup with both hands.

"We've been looking for you. Why did you run away from Havre, Montana?" Hanrihan's blond hair fell sideways across his forehead, surfer-dude style, but it was a false impression: He wasn't laid back; he was a bully.

"I didn't like it there."

"Major Hensel told us you would cooperate." He pulled one of the chairs facing the desk close to mine and sat down. He moved his bangs aside with a vain, practiced gesture. Agent Sampson had assumed my spot at the window. "Are you aware that it is unlawful for the Army to operate on American soil?"

"I'm not in the Army."

"The military. A soldier in Havre had a rifle, a loaded rifle, which he was deployed to use. That is in direct violation of federal law."

"That soldier was shot and killed. That's a violation of the law, too. Isn't it?"

The local police had handed me over to these two in the morn-ing. The cops were extremely excited about the gun I took from the security guard, but the FBI prevailed. How did they spend the eve-ning? Hanrihan was in love with himself and Sampson acted like she hated him. At dinner they must have looked like a couple mar-ried too long: silent and distracted.

"We could arrest you right now, just for that. He was under

your command. Major Hensel told us as much. That's right. Your commanding officer threw you under the bus. Let's talk about Frank Godwin. Why did you kill him?"

"I don't know. Why would I kill him?"

"Maybe you thought he was behind the killing of your man in Montana and that's why you rushed away. To get revenge." He smiled with his mouth closed, and his breath blew noisily from his nose as if he had just exerted himself and was trying to hide it. My only job was to avoid saying anything until Major Hensel arrived. If I were in trouble for bringing along the sniper, it would be with him, not the FBI. Hanrihan went on. "Maybe you were trying to silence Frank Godwin. Maybe you were partners. You spent days conspiring with him just a short while ago. We know that. We have witnesses. Maybe you have a good reason. Maybe you were doing something for your country."

"Maybe we're all on the same side," I said. Hanrihan's face lit up with the fake innocence of a thief who is asked to watch a suitcase at the airport.

"Yes. Exactly. So tell us what is going on so we can all pull in the same direction. That's all we ask."

Hanrihan's hostility was just part of the package, but I could not understand why they were spending so much effort on me. Sampson kept looking out the window. This might have been her first corner-office experience, too. "It's sort of a long story," I said.

"We have time. Tell it all. We're on the same team."

"Well, I wasn't a good kid. I admit that. And one time, there was this woman and she invited me over and well, y'know, she was kind of attractive, at least I thought so. Big hair, big breasts. You probably know the type. Perfume. And her husband was always out of town, so . . ."

"That's Godwin? Godwin's wife seduced you?"

"No. Was Godwin married? He didn't strike me as a married guy."

Hanrihan was pissed off now. "If you don't cooperate, I'll arrest you. It's that simple."

"If I do cooperate you'll arrest me."

His eyes widened and he sat forward and did the thing with his bangs. "Are you saying you're guilty?"

"Of what?"

"You just said you would incriminate yourself." He spoke carefully, thinking he was reeling me in. Agent Sampson kept looking out the window.

"No, I said you're a bust-the-one-you're-with kind of guy."

Agent Sampson's shoulders went up as she suppressed a laugh. She said, "What was in the grave?" She was still looking out the window when she spoke, but she turned to hear my answer.

"How many cars did you count?"

"None. How many are there?"

"There were forty-two out that window."

"What was in that grave?"

Cops and child custody officials and officers and the master of all manipulators, Dan, had been questioning me my whole life, so I knew how to give answers that appeared to be born in ignorance. Sampson was on the right track, though Hanrihan regarded her questions as an intrusion.

"A body?"

"But it didn't belong to the guy whose name was on the grave,"

Sampson said. "Any idea who it was? The widow said you told her there was a mix-up and that's why you were digging up the grave. Is that correct?"

"Sounds like a mix-up to me. Unless you think she just couldn't recognize the corpse. Was it in pretty bad shape?"

Fortunately, Hanrihan felt the need to reassert his authority. "Who was the other dead man in Wisconsin?"

"I don't know."

"Why did you run away if you're innocent?"

It was such a complicated question, but there was no use mentioning that to Hanrihan. He wanted to wrap it all up in one big confession and would hear anything else as a lie. I welcomed the stupidity because it was pushing back Sampson, who was closing in on the real questions.

I said, "Ask her. Ask your partner."

"What are you talking about? What's he talking about?"

Sampson understood. She hesitated, deciding whether to explain it to him. It felt like she was measuring how much she hated him.

Hanrihan got impatient. "Hell, you don't understand him any more than I do."

Sampson said, "Why do you need snipers to dig up a dead body?"

That was the question I dreaded, so I answered Hanrihan instead. "I ran because I didn't want to talk to you."

"Why didn't you want to talk to the FBI?"

"I don't mind talking to the FBI. I didn't want to talk to you. And I still don't."

Sampson laughed. Hanrihan's eyes got wide and the skin on

his face pulled back. He showed her his bottom teeth, then he showed them to me. "Get up right now. You're under arrest." He stood over me and I jumped up fast so that we almost bumped heads. I put my hands forward for the cuffs, but he didn't have any. He just stood there breathing through his nose like an angry bull. Sampson came close and put a hand on Hanrihan's chest to move him back. "Calm down. You can't fight him and arrest him." Hanrihan brushed her hand aside. She didn't mind. I walked away, toward the desk. She was studying me. "Besides," she said, "he didn't kill Godwin."

"And how do you know that?"

"Godwin was shot from behind. And he was unarmed. Lieutenant Waters would have stepped right up and looked him in the eye and killed him up close. Now, you haven't answered my question, Lieutenant," she said.

"What was that?"

But before she could repeat the question, the door opened and Major Hensel entered.

Do you own a suit?"

"Not since I was about ten."

Major Hensel and I rode downtown in a taxi, neither of us speaking after that brief exchange. The clouds were still solid in all directions, light gray and unmoving. Occasionally, the cabbie put on his windshield wipers for a few moments until they started squeaking against the glass. It had taken Major Hensel only twenty minutes to spring me from Hanrihan and Sampson. If his silence was angry, I would find out soon enough. I hardly knew him. Even with the access this investigation gave me to personnel files, Major Hensel remained a cipher. The file I saw on the Camp Pendleton computers only contained his background page. He was born and raised in New York City and graduated in the top 10 percent of his class at West Point, served in Iraq twice, in Army Intelligence units. The details were vague: attached to CIA, JSOC liaison, attached to Defense Intelligence Agency. The file had no commendations, no senior officer reports of any kind. It looked like it had been heavily edited, but it was not restricted above the level that the file on any intelligence officer might be. Based on that, I began filling in the picture of a career intelligence officer on the fast track, suddenly stopped at major yet given control of SHADE. One night I told Will Panos what I had found out. "You looked at the wrong file," he said. "The Major graduated from Princeton and taught at the Defense Language Institute in Monterey."

"I read his service file."

"So did I," he said.

We were in Texas at the time, interviewing a bloated colonel who did not want to talk to us about McColl, because, he asserted, the dead can't defend themselves. We marched directly to the office we had been provided. Will worked the computer. No Arthur Hensel graduated from West Point or from Princeton. The service file that came up said he graduated from Middlebury College and worked as a civilian for DIA before joining the Army. Will found a medical file that listed him as wounded in action in Iraq with the 101st Airborne Division. He found more, each with a different story. When he went back to the service personnel file, it said Arthur Hensel was forty years old and had graduated from University of California at Berkeley. Another version said Arthur Hensel joined as an eighteen-year-old private in Arkansas and served in Korea and Okinawa. Will, who knew every form and regulation, wanted to start filing paperwork to get at the truth.

"His name got put on other people's files," he said. "It's a massive screwup."

But it was not a screwup. It was a plan, and a good one, better than some higher level of classification, which could be cracked.

Maybe he was not Hensel at all. I could not even be sure how long he had been in the Army, whether he was due for promotion or was passed over and kept on under selective continuation. The mystery gave me confidence in him because it meant he was in control of his story and when he did give orders, they would be precise and specific; when he spoke, I would be hearing what he wanted me to hear without emotion or pomposity, anger or resentment. And it gave me a goal: Someday I would find out who he really was.

Soon after the highways merged, the downtown skyline came into view, making the cloud canopy seem higher: Even the tallest buildings couldn't pierce it. The taxi crept past a few car dealerships, warehouses, office buildings, and factories with ads painted on their sides, a low building advertising Morton Salt. I figured Major Hensel had information for me about the Montana shooting or Godwin's shooting, so it would be a waste to try to fill the gaps myself. He occupied himself with his iPad. His belly filled his blue shirt and made the buttons work to keep it together. The suit, the shirt, the tie, made me think the Princeton identity or one just like it was true, but it could just as easily have been faked to throw the world off track. The thick temples of his eyeglasses blocked his eyes. I let my mind drift to salt and how it must be pretty much all the same, so the Morton people, way back, must have been brave to spend a lot of time and money giving salt a name. There must have been a salt war, though, with tears, bankruptcy, hope and deceit and stealing. Someone must have hated Morton and sworn revenge.

The cabbie dropped us in front of a men's store called Paul Stuart. The store was big and almost empty. Major Hensel looked over the salesmen and chose one with white hair and a mustache and told him to dress me like an investment banker, for work and for weekends. "Everything, shirts, belts, shoes and socks, the whole wardrobe. And, we'll pay extra to have any alterations done immediately," he said. "Whatever it takes. He's flying out tomorrow." That was news to me, but I nodded along as confirmation. "I'll be back," Major Hensel said, and he left.

I was fresh meat, but the salesman was polite and soft-spoken and patient. He had polished the act. "Congratulations," he said, "sounds like a promotion."

"Yes. I'm very excited."

"Which firm are you with?"

"Voster M.E.A.," I said. He nodded while he searched his memory for that firm. "Amalgamated," I added, as if to help him out. He didn't deserve it, but it just came out, and that lie was probably less hostile than claiming secrecy or, worst of all, answering, "The Marines." Voster M.E.A. was the name Dan gave to his enterprises, for private consumption only. After a successful venture, he would return to whichever girlfriend he had at the time, pop the champagne and toast to Voster M.E.A. Amalgamated. Loosely translated, Latin *voster mea est* means "yours is mine" in English. I looked it up once and it's pretty close to correct, close enough for the private joke.

The salesman led me over to racks of suits. "Forty-two long? Try this one on." He put a gray jacket with a white stripe on me and it felt like it fit pretty well. "What do you have right now, so we don't duplicate?"

I looked at him and shook my head and said, "I'm sorry. I don't own any suits. You'll have to decide."

He managed to mask any thoughts he had about that. "No problem. Step over here and we'll get you fixed up properly."

He moved me in front of the mirror and in that one glance I was fourteen again, in Dan's closet, trying on one of his suits. He had five: three had labels from a tailor named Tartaglia, one said Corneliani, one said Huntsman. I was wearing the dark blue tailor-made jacket, the sleeves hanging past my hands, and the shoulders down near my biceps, when I noticed that Dan had come in and was watching me. "You have good taste, Rollie boy," he said. "Had that one made in Beverly Hills. Hell of a tailor and a good friend." That meant Dan had not paid him, at least not the full amount. "With clothes, your best policy is to have just a few really good pieces rather than a closet full of junk." He did not have to mention that philosophy allowed faster getaways. I looked around and realized for the first time the closet was not full. It had always seemed like a thick forest to me. The conditions for poking around in Dan's closet frequently occurred: I was bored and he was out. I searched without pattern or plan for artifacts or secrets. Or money. Anything that would help augment my understanding of him, help me clear the mist. Dan always dressed well. He always looked sharp, so I always made sure I never looked sharp. For Dan, clothes were a uniform: jeans and cowboy boots, khakis and blue blazer, a fancy suit; he was careful to overdress just enough to contrast with and accentuate his relaxing charm.

Dan took the coat and hung it up. "Bet those boots almost fit you by now." I looked down; I was wearing shorts and his fancy cowboy boots. They were dark, like chocolate, on the lower part and black on the leg with a design that looked like wings. I admitted they did almost fit. "They're made from caiman. Know what that is?" I lied and said I did. "It's a sort of South American crocodile. I had to kill one once."

He smiled at the memory, or the smile was a reflex that helped him invent the memory. For a moment, I thought of trying to dart past him, but he filled the doorway, and I knew I wanted to hear the story whether it was true or not. "We had pulled our canoes up on the riverbank, it was an Amazon tributary, and grabbed our packs. There was a village just a quarter mile away through the forest where we planned to camp. A woman in our party lost her balance and fell into the river as she was hoisting her gear. The bottom was muddy. She was flopping around, struggling to get up. We all turned to the guide, he was an Indian, but he just watched her, so we figured it was no big deal. At least I did. Then the woman screamed. The caiman wasn't five feet from her. Still the guide didn't move. If this was a lesson, I didn't want to learn it. I took my pack off and threw it at the beast. It spun around and bit into the pack. I pulled my knife and moved forward into the water. The tail thrashed and hit me in the leg and that hurt. I almost fell. But I knew I would get only one chance. So I put my knife into its brain."

I remember looking down at the boots when he finished the story and starting to take them off. I didn't want to look at him. He said, "Don't worry. It's not that caiman. Y'know, I'll get you a pair just like them. Take you down and have you fitted."

I remember saying, "Will I have to kill a caiman?"

He said, "When you have to, you'll know it."

The desire to deflect the offer overwhelmed me. I thought I was hiding my expression well enough, but later I wondered. Could anyone ever hide his or her feelings from Dan? Those boots would have been heavy. I wanted them and I didn't, partly because I knew I would never get them and partly because of the burden they would have carried, the responsibility of ownership, and with it the identity shift that would happen whenever I pulled them on. I owned nothing that could not be ruined and forgotten, lost, tossed away without remorse. Jeans, T-shirts, hoodies, and work boots or basketball shoes constituted my entire range of attire. To walk out in fine boots, even if no one knew me, would have felt like a betrayal of myself. I would have had to walk differently and other changes would follow. I was adventurous, but not in that way. Coveting those boots opened one-way doors that led to places I was not ready to explore.

Dan did not come through on his promise and that time I was grateful in a way that went beyond the usual vindication of my understanding of the universe. More, I was complicit. He brought it up a few months later, but I made an excuse, knowing that would end the matter forever. Not owning anything that must be cared for or carried or coddled became a guiding principle. Just as Dan used clothes as costumes and cars and accessories to paint his many identities, I built my identity on the absence of those things. Years later, on the riverboat, not long before he died, I asked him if he had ever been to South America. He just looked at me and smiled and said, "Those were beautiful boots, weren't they?" After I started with SHADE, I went back to the house Dan had been renting in Phoenix. I gave away the suits and the rest of his clothing. The boots weren't there.

One of the suits was ready by the time Major Hensel returned with a leather duffel. He paid for everything with cash. The salesman asked for contact information for me, but Major Hensel pushed the card back at him and told him, politely, "That won't be necessary. We'll pick up everything in the morning."

We walked north. It was dark now and the clouds had descended, skewered in place by the tops of the tallest buildings. The lights backlit the clouds and made them glow. We stopped outside a restaurant called Tuskers. Major Hensel looked it over as if checking to see if it was the same place he remembered. We went inside: dark wood, leather chairs, hunting paintings and prints; it looked like it was designed by the same guy who designed the clothing store.

"I'll have a martini. Two olives," Major Hensel said. He hung back in open space and I sidestepped and slipped past a few dozen men dressed in suits very much like mine. Men outnumbered women two to one, at least, yet many of the women were clumped together like ingredients that did not blend well with these men.

The talk I heard was all of deals. "We're picking up all the options we can get."

Another guy waving at the bartender talked of "shorting that dog."

"The VCs are holding out," said the man standing next to him while he eyed a cluster of women.

"Screw 'em."

A fat guy said with delight, "I'm pulling swaps out of my ass."

I brought the Major his drink and one for me. "You're looking at a mix of investment bankers, bond salesmen, a few traders, and a few corporate finance people. The traders will be the ones listening most of the time. At least the smart ones are. I used to be a banker, and a trader."

Maybe. I was tired of this game. "What am I doing here, Major?"

"Do you think you could fit in with this crowd?"

"You mean can I get a fake tan and pull swaps out of my ass? You'd have to explain why I would want to."

After an elaborate exchange of good-evenings, the maître d' led us to a table at Chez Martine. It was still early in the evening and the place was not crowded. The walls were striped in yellow and white, and the leather banquettes along the right wall were reddish brown. The paintings on the walls were modern with bright colors. Major Hensel looked at the table, between two others that were occupied by couples, and said, "We'd like to sit in the back room, please."

The maître d' tilted his head to one side and shook it and closed his eyes for a moment as if the Major had asked if they served tacos. We stood there between those two tables for about a week while the Major and the Frenchman went back and forth in calm, quiet voices. Finally, the maître d' turned up his hands and shrugged his shoulders. A classic gesture: Take it or leave it. I thought the maître d' held the strong hand and I was interested to see whether the Major would choose retreat or surrender. But Major Hensel spoke in French, one short sentence, and stared right into the eyes of the startled maître d'. Time froze. Then the maître d' nodded and ushered us to the back room.

"I love French restaurants. They serve so much more than food and wine," the Major said after we were settled.

"What did you say to him?"

"I said that if any of the other guests overheard our conversation, their lives would be in danger."

Coming from someone with muscles or a rough presence, it might have been taken for an aggressive, nasty, call-the-police kind of threat. But this pudgy man with glasses and a quiet voice made the arrogant headman want to cooperate. The punch was well timed and well placed.

The table was full of glasses and silverware and small plates and large plates. If I had wanted to put my elbows on the table, I would have had to move some of that stuff to the floor.

"How is Will Panos?"

"He'll be fine. He's spending a little time in Havre. He can deal with the locals while recuperating."

"He'll like that. He has an eye for the widow."

The Major squinted as he tried to picture the match. "He's a very methodical person. I give him a good chance. The ammunition in Montana and in Wisconsin was M118 Long Range. The FBI should be able to determine where it was purchased."

"Or stolen," I said. The M118 was most often military sniper ordnance. The waiter hovered between rooms until he caught the Major's eye and was beckoned forth. He had been warned by the maître d'. The Major ordered wine and appetizers, and fish for himself. "Do you like lamb?" he asked.

"Sure."

He ordered lamb for me. "It'll be better than whatever you ate at Frank Godwin's place," he said.

"Dan used to take me to a French place, Bistro Arletty, when I was ten years old. There were business associates who needed to know that Dan was a family man. He taught me how to handle it. 'Act like you're considering buying the place, but you need to be convinced,' he said."

Major Hensel told me a story about how he once invested in a restaurant and came to hate eating there because he knew too much about the behind-scenes operation. He missed the pleasure of the surprise.

One waiter approached cautiously with appetizers, and another to dance the wine tango with Major Hensel. When the waiters went away, the Major said, "The FBI has no license plates, no witnesses seeing someone fleeing the scene, other than you, of course." He was the only senior officer I ever met who could say that without accusation in his voice. "Someone hit one grave on Frank's list. Ran into the local police. There was a firefight. One policeman was killed." He paused. He knew my question. "The coffin did not get opened and I have not taken steps yet, so I don't know if there is money or a body inside. They also hit one on your fake list. Dug up with shovels. Left the body beside the coffin."

"I wonder which list he gave up first."

The Major looked at me sharply, then said, "They would have killed him whether he gave them your list, the real list, or no list. He was a loose end."

"How did they know we had identified Godwin?"

"Only three of us had that information: me, Will, and you," the Major said without sounding defensive.

"Maybe they're just smart."

"Do you want the rest of the graves on the list dug up?"

"Be best to guard them. I'd like to know if anyone else tries to dig them up," I said.

"But you don't think they will." I shrugged. I didn't know. "What's your next move?"

"I lost a man. I'm going to find who shot him."

"You can do that. The FBI will let you work with them."

He made it sound as if I had requested a demotion. I stared at him while he turned all his attention to his food.

Bearing a full pack, wearing combat boots, toting my rifle, I stepped into quicksand during basic training, lured there by the sergeant. I wriggled and writhed and fought and made things worse while the rest of the platoon cheered and taunted me. I was in up to my hips by the time the jeers made me stop moving. That stopped the sinking. I seemed to be suspended on a submerged platform and I looked with satisfaction to the sergeant. But the lesson was not over. The sergeant ordered the platoon to move out. All he said to me before marching away was "Don't let go of your weapon."

Don't fight, don't argue, you'll sink deeper. Taste the appetizer. I had not told Major Hensel about looking into the eyes of the killer, about his challenge to me, and now I could not tell him because he would take that as an answer and send me back to the FBI agents.

The main course was served.

The Major seemed to be able to time my thoughts. "You don't want to work with the FBI, but, if you're searching for the shooter, the FBI will follow you at the very least. And they'll get involved in the money. Things will get more complicated. Don't you like your lamb?"

I had pushed it away and now I felt like a petulant child pouting for chicken fingers. Was he subtle enough to have manipulated me into that? I cut a piece and put it on his plate.

"Basam Karkukli. Ever hear of him?" He did not wait for my answer. "He calls himself the King of Kurdistan."

"Does anyone believe him?"

"I've interviewed a dozen of the plotters. No one had the full picture, but here's what I pieced together. As you know, the graves contained seed money, enough to get the revolution started in Iraqi Kurdistan. Taking over the oil fields would finance the rest. A few mentioned that they understood the plan called for Karkukli to be installed on the throne and have him lead a cooperative government. No one met him. And no one knows whose plan it was."

"Sounds like Karkukli's plan," I said, offering a simpleton's solution because I wanted this discussion to be over so I could return my attention to the Mask Man staring down at me.

"He's been around, mostly in Europe, dining on the name and the supposed title. Fortunately for him, the Iranians tried to assassinate him about fifteen years ago in Berlin. That bestowed international cachet and gave him entrée to the deposed royalty circuit."

His cadence had the careful measurement I had heard only when being let down in a way that somebody else imagined was easy.

Don't squirm. Don't struggle. Breathe. I sipped my wine. You only sink if you try not to. And there was Dan, delighted, sitting next to me in one of his best suits, saying, *"Why would you struggle or resist? You're about to get an offer."* He spoke the last word as if it were the key to nirvana.

"He's holding court now at an estate in Houston. Had a parade of former officers come through, but now the traffic has shifted to oilmen. He's telling them his takeover is imminent and if they want the oil concession, they have to start paying now."

He waited. I waited. A few thousand questions scrolled in front of me. I chose one. "Whose plan is it?"

He ignored that. "I had someone on it. He died. Ran his car into a tree. I think someone helped him do that, but we can't prove it. He was working from the outside. Watching. Listening. I don't know how they found him out. If you decide to do this, you would have to take a different approach."

"Who was he?"

He told me the dead soldier's name. But I never knew him. He was Army, a major.

For a moment, I longed to be a Marine in a war zone again, a world with clear comprehensible commands like "search and destroy," "engage the enemy," "take and hold." But I knew I didn't mean it. I was now a confirmed citizen of the fog, more spy than soldier; the clarity would confuse me. I would mistrust it. And that would probably get me killed. I asked the dreaded question, knowing the answer would hardly help.

"What is the mission?"

The Major smiled to let me know I chose the right question. "He's a puppet who thinks he's a king. He was a puppet when McColl was alive and planning to put him on the throne, and he's still a puppet. I don't care who ends up controlling the oil. They have to sell it to someone. I don't care if Iraq and Turkey and Iran team up against the Kurds or go to war with each other. It's more than all that. It's more than the money. I want the puppet master. I want the guy who put this plot together." He waited and his expression hardened in a way I had never seen. His right hand tightened on his knife. The waiter paused at the partition and turned away quickly. "If he's military, we'll deal with him. If he's civilian, we'll turn him over. Find him, get something on him. I'm pretty sure that along the way, you'll find the shooters, too."

"What are the rules of engagement?"

"Consider yourself as operating in a war zone. I want him alive. If possible. I want you alive more."

We stared at each other for a while. I could not summon the same passion for the mysterious puppet master. My thoughts were on the Mask Man. Our paths were going to cross. Wartime rules of engagement suited me very well.

"If you don't want to find him, just say so," the Major said. "Someone else will. You can chase the shooters and maybe you'll find them, but that won't mean you solved anything and it won't mean you closed this out the way I think you want to. Maybe the way you need to."

He put the knife down and picked up his fork and ate a piece of his fish, then put the fork down. Finished.

He did not speak again until after desert and coffee had been served. "They're getting desperate. I can sense it. The countdown began when they opened that first grave, the one Dan looted. Without the cash, they'll lose their recruits. This is the time. Find the guy pulling the strings." He signaled for the check.

I reached across and tasted his dessert, something like pudding. "So what are the suits for?"

"*I'll explain,*" said Dan.

8

The first press release said I had left Argos Capital to start my own fund with two hundred million in initial capital. My area of expertise was energy. The release also mentioned my MBA from Columbia. Two articles from energy industry blogs came up that mentioned the degree. One hinted that my biggest backers were Russian. The other mentioned my recent visit to China. Three years later, I closed the fund, having returned an annual average of 18 percent to the investors, and began another fund, a limited partnership specializing in energy investments. One blogger mentioned my undergraduate degree, also from Columbia, in geology. He interviewed me last year and one of the things I told him was "My philosophy is to look for energy efficiency at the source, and at the production stages, to give us leeway as market prices fluctuate." I thought the quote could have used some opaque terms like "aggregation covenants" or "asymmetric volatility," "diffusion process," and "autocorrelation." Major Hensel said he avoided that kind of stuff because someone might ask me to explain what I meant. The important quote was "It is

time for new horizons, new approaches, new partners." And I declined to name the partners so everyone would assume it was the
Russians or the Chinese.

I had a company credit card and I could write a check for two
million dollars on the spot and it would clear.

The plane to Houston was delayed, which suited me fine. I
could have read up on the financial details of oil exploration deals
or on the latest geological detection methods or the extraction
technology, but time was better spent understanding my alter ego,
Robert Hewitt. Did he work through college? Was he always thinking about getting rich or did it come as a result of his interest in
science? Did he have manners? Did he rise when a woman got up
from the table or was he like the slobs at the bar the Major took me
to? Where did his family vacation? He needed a hobby, someplace
he was wasting his riches, a subject on which he could hold forth
when someone became too inquisitive. Posing as a Muslim was
easy compared with this. I sat in the bar to map out a plan. Nothing
felt comfortable.

Somehow Dan made it through security. *"These things can take
a while. Meeting the King, getting in on the bidding game, transferring
money, pinpointing his weaknesses. You'll have to make him betray his
benefactor."*

"Unless he is already doing that."

*"That's worse. You'd have to get in on it. You want to stand out. As
it is, you're going to be perceived as a minor player, someone bidding
the prices up against the big boys. If you were in this for the money, that
would be fine. Someone could be convinced to buy you off. There is
another way, though."*

"I'm listening." It was as if he were relaxing by my side, reeling

me in slowly because he owned time now, and always knew how to stretch it and knead it.

"You're on the wrong side of the transaction. Too much competition. The other buyers can crowd you out. Remember, you don't have to own what you're selling."

I almost spit my drink out. There was the motto on the gates at the entrance to Danland.

"Compete with the King. That'll grab his attention and the attention of the guy you're really after. If he actually exists."

"I'm set up to be a buyer. The background, the Web stories."

"Better. You already bought. Now you're looking for partners. You'll be offered some delicious bribes."

"Can't take bribes."

"You don't want to. You want the word to be that you're the most serious guy in the great state of Texas."

Dan had given me a good idea. But I was not done with him. *"I'm not doing this for you,"* I said.

"Don't see why you should."

"I killed the people who killed you."

"That you did. You did that for yourself, right? I was dead."

"Whoever I'm going after now did not know who you were, or that you existed."

It was best to duck after directing that kind of cruelty at Dan. He knew how to transform it to his advantage, though not to get you to say you were sorry. How could that benefit him? He would target the vulnerability you had revealed and rub salve in the wound until you believed he just might be your savior.

"There's nothing wrong with taking orders," he said.

Salve in the wound. I did not say thank you. The mission was clearly defined: Find the puppet master; deliver him, if possible. Following orders was just part of life as a Marine no matter where you were.

Dan said, *"It's the fog at the beginning that makes you wonder. Just point yourself in the right direction."*

He was right. Finding Dan, killing McColl and his men, tying them to General Remington, finding the money—all that was a personal mission. It was a compulsion. Nothing could stop me carrying it on to the end. It didn't matter if I was good enough. This time I was not sure what I was getting into. I was not compelled. I was ordered. I was not sure I was good enough.

I checked with Major Hensel about the Kurdish rebels, the PKK, sometimes called Kongra-Gel. "They're led by a man named Diyar, we think. He might be real. He might be mythical. No one around here knows. Officially, we wouldn't be having any contact with them."

"If I worked for the government, you mean."

Dan used a lawyer named Jaman when we lived in Phoenix. I think his first name was John, and now I wonder if his real name might have been John J. Mann and my ears just turned it into Jaman, but either way, he was a dirty guy who was always exploring his nose or his ears or his crotch and I had to be careful not to sit across from him because he would load up on food before he started talking and some of it was always flying out. Dan said he was unpolished but smart and good-natured. He stared at Dan, followed his every gesture, would move his hands the way Dan did, hold his head the way Dan did, but he could not hold the pose; soon his hand would sneak, like some uncontrollable pet, down to his crotch and nudge it affectionately in one direction or another.

Jaman wrote contracts for Dan, and letters demanding payment and promising payment. Sometimes Dan would let him negotiate for a few minutes, then interrupt and appear to give in to the other party over Jaman's objections. Jaman always had his legal secretary, Betsy, by his side; she brought the laptop and typed everything. Betsy was pretty, though she, too, was unpolished. The heart tattoo on her smooth, milky thigh was seared into my eyeballs from intense hours of staring. Jaman would catch me longing and smile and point to his chest with pride and say something like "Someday you'll get your own. This one is mine." Then the same finger would be drawn, as if by invisible magnets, to his nose or ear.

Betsy was Dan's, too, of course. I could hear them from almost anywhere in the small house where we were living. I could never understand how Jaman did not know about Dan and Betsy. How could he think she would not prefer Dan? How could he think Dan would not seduce her? How could Jaman read my thoughts so easily and not have a clue about Dan's? More than once I heard Betsy ask Dan when he thought Jaman would "pull the trigger" or "pull up his pants." Once she said she was sure he had bought a ring. And Dan always reassured her that Jaman was on the verge of proposing.

One day, Dan handed me an envelope and told me to deliver it to Jaman's office, which was not far away. It was number 303, with no name on the door. I went into the waiting room and I could hear the argument going on in the inner office.

Jaman said, "No, I don't blame him. I blame you."

Betsy yelled, "You said you were gonna marry me. You promised."

"I'll never marry you. You're a slut. Put that away."

"I let you paw me for years for what? You pig . . ."

That went on for a little while. I could not move, could not bear the thought of missing one mean comment, one insult. And just as Jaman said, "Oh, get out of here," and "How do I open this damn computer?" the shot was fired. He groaned. I was still standing there when the door opened. Jaman was slumped at his desk with one hand on the laptop. Betsy held the gun.

"Tell him he'll have to find someone else to service him," she said, so calmly that it made me think she knew I was out there all along.

I ran. I was about one flight down the stairs when I heard another shot. At home, I reported to Dan. He shook his head, then came close and gently took the envelope from me. "You brought those back. Good boy." Then he drove me to the apartment where one of his girlfriends lived and I did not see him for over six months.

I never found out who received that second shot and that was the only time I had ever been in an attorney's office until I walked into the law offices of Kelekian and White of Houston, Texas. They did have their names on the door. The air was cold in the office and so was the atmosphere. Outside, through the tinted windows, the sun struggled to shine and the city looked dimmed and dusty like an alien, harsh, and desolate colony on a nasty planet, a place of danger and disease to be avoided.

It was no surprise that Darrell White was in the final stages of a really big case, his firm's biggest in years, which he really could not talk about, so he could only give me a few minutes. He was a big man in his fifties, developing a gut but still handsome, with a lot of brown hair carefully shaped into a point resembling the prow of a ship. His jacket hung on a valet stand in the corner. A holster, empty, hung next to the jacket. I guessed the gun was in a desk drawer. The sleeves of his white shirt were rolled up, but his tie was firmly in place. The office was roomy and neat and the view expansive. Pictures of Darrell White with tennis players, golfers, ballerinas, and hockey players decorated the walls. Maybe one of the pictures was of the King of Kurdistan; Darrell White specialized in immigration and had helped the King's entourage get visas.

"Recognize anyone?" he said.

"You're the big guy, right?"

"Some of those ballerinas were tiny as matchsticks. But I love watching them dance. Love it. Now you said oil business, the financial side, yes? Usually, we have a lot of success helping financial people get work visas because no one understands what they do, so they must be essential. The only problem comes when it's a really attractive woman, then no one believes she could be essential for her brains. You're not importing a girlfriend, are you? You don't look the type." He had the gift of being able to seem to give his full attention, which was probably a valuable skill when dealing with all his stars and artists.

"Not a girlfriend. Business associates. From Iraq. They're not financial types. They're representing my new partners. You've handled visas for Iraqis?"

"Of course. I've helped bring an Iraqi soccer team over here for training and a series of games. A cricket team, too. Actors. Not a lot of financial people, but I don't see why that would be a problem. Who are your guys? Why are they essential to your business?"

"Well, y'see, we negotiated some oil rights and these men represent, as I said, our partners and they have to . . . the people we're going to do business with here in the States are going to want to meet them. That's why they're essential." I hemmed and hawed enough for a deaf man to tell I was avoiding the truth.

"They don't need work visas to do a meet-and-greet. I can get them two-week tourist visas for that," he said with a forced friendliness, as if it were going to be a favor.

"That'd be great. That'd do just fine."

"But first, before I can do that, you have to stop bullshitting around and tell me who they are." He smiled with his lips closed and his eyes narrowed. It was his "I'm on to you" look.

I waited a few moments, as if I were getting up the nerve to tell the truth. "We secured oil rights—"

"You already told me that."

"We're working on securing oil rights from the regional Kurdish government in the case of independence and we already have them from the PKK, also known as the Kurdistan Workers' Party, also known as Kongra-Gel. Unfortunately, they are also known as terrorists in some places."

He did not show surprise or any acknowledgment that he had ever heard of Kurdistan. I pulled out my checkbook and a pen.

"I can give you a retainer right now." I wrote a check and tore it off and slid it across the desk. The check was for ten thousand dollars. If he accepted it, I had wasted my time because it would mean he did not give a damn about Kurdish oil rights and did not know anyone who did care. I wanted to know if he was going to alert the King to my presence and my claims. "I don't know if you have many oil business contacts, but if you do, I might like to get to know some of them. We're going to be lining up drilling operations, have our ducks in a row for when the time comes."

"What time is that?" He said it like he was inquiring about a dinner invitation.

"We feel we have a good chance that either the Regional Government or the PKK will be able to move forward as the definitive authority in the area soon. In the next couple of years. Do you know anything about Kurdistan? Fascinating place. Energetic people, great environment to do business."

The check remained on the desk between us. He took his eyes off me to look at it and again he smiled. He shook his head. "Politics always makes the world difficult, doesn't it? That means this is going to require some delicate maneuvering. Quite time consuming. If it can be accomplished at all. I can't make any guarantees," he said.

"What would it take?"

"This is a tough one, and you want introductions as well. About ten times that."

That sounded high to me, but it made me happy. It meant he wanted to see if I was for real before he started alerting the King. I tore up the first check and wrote one for one hundred thousand dollars and stood up and told him I was staying at the St. Regis. He stood up and shook my hand and said he knew some "folks" at the State Department and would get on it as soon as I got him the names and copies of the passports. "And, if it's okay with you, I'll ask around about who might like to get some of your business."

"That would be just fine," I said.

Will Panos said he wished he was in Houston with me, but I did not believe him because when I asked how he was doing with the widow, he said, "Kristen is her name. We're having dinner tonight. At her house."

"Bring flowers."

"Flowers. Okay. Something for her daughter?"

"Too soon. You'll make the kid suspicious, if she's worth anything," I said. "How are you doing on identifying the body in the grave?"

"No progress. We can't exactly put him on exhibit. DNA will come back, but what do we compare it with? The FBI has been around. They want to talk about you."

"See if you can get anything out of them about the shooter. Where the bullets came from, anything on the car. Anything. Try to keep the focus on that and off the grave and what we were looking for."

"And off you." He waited for me to make a comment. I waited. "Are you there?" he said.

"Hint that you know where I am. Maybe they'll offer you information in exchange. In any case, let them know I'm in Houston. You think I'm on leave."

"You want them?"

"And don't tell the Major, please." It was Will's turn to be silent. I said, "Flowers, Will."

With the windows open and the air-conditioning off, the hotel suite began to feel muggy and comfortable. I slowly shaped the moist blanket of air, lifting it, pressing it back into place, angling through, disturbing the dense air less and less until the knotty tension that had been thickening for days flowed out and was absorbed into the soupy mix. Finished with the tai chi, I sat in full lotus.

When I began yoga and meditation, the instructor told me to find a peaceful spot. Lately I had tried envisioning a desert mountaintop, sitting like a guru in a cartoon on the edge of a cloud alone before the striped sky, the quiet of a cave, the murmuring of a stream, an ever-changing woman morphing slyly before my closed eyes, and more. But the farmhouse, my original peaceful place, the place I thought was a fantasy but turned out to be a memory, the place where I learned my real name and found Dan's money, kept pushing the other spots aside and they did not have the muscle to push back. I knew this was all wrong, but meditation is not about fighting and so the vision I would bring up each time was no longer a refuge of peaceful contemplation. Instead, it was a constantly developing puzzle that could never be solved, a set of clues to a mystery that remained hidden. I found rooms that never existed. People popped in and out. Some I knew. It was neither a dream nor a nightmare. It was an immersion in a maze, a ride through a riddle.

First I glided into the basement and the doors shut behind me. Slowly my eyes adjusted to the light just enough to make me think I saw dim shapes huddled in the far reaches, near rooms I had forgotten to visit or explore for too long; they lurked like sea creatures in nooks and crannies, but as I pushed forward toward them, they receded and I only faced deeper darkness at each turn, along with the suspicion, dripping and cold, that something nasty was filling the space behind me. I did not have the guts to turn around. The doorbell rang. I shifted to a spot where I could peek through a crack to see black shoes on the porch. I held still while listening for more. The bell rang again. I could not find a way to see more. My vision was stuck. Then a knock and someone calling, "Mr. Hewitt."

I opened my eyes and hopped up. Room service had arrived. When I finished with that, I called downstairs and asked the concierge to arrange a Maserati for me. She called back a few minutes later and said the Maserati would not be available until the next day, but I could have a Ferrari right away. She hesitated, then said, "It's red. Is that okay?"

All I wanted was something that would attract attention and be easy to follow. I left the room but had to go back before I reached the elevator. I grabbed a sugar packet from the room-service tray and left.

I drove out toward Texas City, where the tankers came in past Galveston Island. I could smell it before I saw it: oil, exhaust, and dead fish, a combination I had rarely experienced. Soon the tanks and smokestacks of the refineries lurked like bullies guarding their home turf. Cranes, dozens of them, hung out to the right, a rival gang, cool, lanky, heads hung, like transformers waiting to be called to action. I parked as close to the port as I could get and put up the top, but left the car unlocked. I stashed the rental paperwork in the glove box, then sprinkled a little sugar on top of the corners. If anyone checked, I'd know.

Along the dock road, I found a low wall to sit on, where I could watch the slow routine of the bay. Two cargo ships stacked with sealed containers were docked. A crane unloaded one of them gracefully and easily. Farther out, an oil tanker hooked up with a smaller ship, a lighter. I snapped a photo with my phone. A helicopter came out of the north, banked, and turned east over the bay. I decided I wanted to do that, too.

The pilot was a former Marine and the proud owner of an MD 520 series helicopter, not too new but very clean, which he chartered, mostly to oil people like I was pretending to be. He had been a Flying Tiger, HMH-361, and he flew the big Super Stallion choppers during the Iraq invasion. Marine was not in my bio, so I told him my father had been a Marine chopper pilot who then flew a traffic copter in Arizona, and I used to go up with him all the time.

When we got up I asked to circle the harbor first. The dark sedan was parked behind the helicopter shed. Two men in suits had gotten out. One was trying to use his phone, though the noise must have made it difficult. The rest of the ride would serve to solidify my identity as an oilman and make the followers worry that I might be going somewhere significant or meeting someone important. Maybe that would make them move faster. I asked to fly over some offshore platforms. The pilot said that was his most requested trip. He stopped talking and I did, too, and before long, the orange and gray dots grew into misshapen ships, forever moored. They grew in clusters that reminded me of the apartment complexes outside Phoenix that would erupt beyond the previous limits of urban life. At first they were brave outposts, but the seeds blew and others grew nearby, and soon after that no one could tell the area had been unpopulated just the other day. The platforms were multiplying in the same way.

During my first tour in Afghanistan, Tom Rickun was wounded in the foot and shoulder and I carried him behind cover, where the medics could help him out. Tom was near the end of his tour, but after he got home, he always wrote to me, mostly about how he wanted to be a writer and tell everybody what he had seen in Afghanistan. He got a job writing marketing brochures for a real estate development company, and because they liked him so much and thought of him as a man of imagination and cleverness, they assigned him the task of compiling potential names for the various new developments. At first it was a pleasant distraction. He kept a digital voice recorder and would riff in the car, spouting out combinations that sounded good. He would edit those and hand over the lists. The boss called him into the office and praised him. It was the most attention and praise he had ever received for anything. They used about a dozen of the names he submitted: Normandy Hill, Avalon Heights, Sagebrush Terrace, Cornwall Crest, Canterbury Ridge are some I remember. The praise brought on something like writer's block; he could do no work on his stories. All his time went into concocting pleasant sounding communities.

Everything began to sound wrong to him, names like Anglesey

Acres and Catalpa Circle, yet the company still liked his work and used the names. Next came contempt, which introduced book and movie names like Manderley, Tara, Twelve Oaks, and Brideshead: each one praised, accepted, used. He would get drunk and become obsessed with moving away from English and French references. The company had to break new ground he insisted: Bremen Sands, Brno Mews, and Stuttgart Court were rejected. He could do no writing other than letters to me, he said, and he feared the direction he was heading. He wanted to name a development near Las Vegas Korengal Valley, another, near Orlando, Peshawar Place.

I wrote a long letter to him detailing a failed rescue mission my unit had undertaken and asked him to write it up as a short story. Instead, he wrote back saying that he would refrain from war locations, but he hated the bosses and was determined to embarrass them with French and German words and phrases like Fernsehapparat Vistas and Malypense Meadows, the job be damned. He asked me how to say "If you lived here you would be home now" in Pashto and in Dari. The real estate collapse drove the company into bankruptcy before they could fire him. I have not heard from him since I've been back, but I think oil platforms might have snagged his talents. They had names like Mad Dog, Cajun Express, and Pride of About Every Place I've ever heard of.

The pilot asked if I wanted to fly over the Louisiana Loop. He would have to refuel there but would discount the time. A huge tanker fed its load into a small dot, just a pimple in the gulf, connected to a pipeline that ran all the way into Louisiana. We banked and dived toward the tanker. No alarm screamed, no jets scrambled, no bodies scattered. One man on deck looked up and waved. The pilot shrugged; he was thinking the same thing I was. The pipeline led to a booster station, a white complex built on swamp-land, and then to a white storage facility. We buzzed them both. While refueling in Morgan City, the pilot said, "I dive and buzz them, hoping someone will wake up and tell me to stop. Just show some awareness."

Anyone taking that ride would have thought the same thing: How vulnerable and naïve we were. The pilot suddenly got talkative. He had theories: "We're like the husband who is a compulsive womanizer but never realizes how much other guys are out to screw his wife or daughter. Of course we have plans, good plans, to destroy oil platforms all over the world. I'm sure we even have plans to destroy North Sea platforms belonging to our closest allies. But we leave ours wide open. It's like we don't want to admit that others think the way we do."

His customers must have been a receptive lot for that rap; it was well rehearsed. But I spent the return trip changing my mind. It might be worthwhile to have some last-ditch defense set up, but the real work would be at the inception, at the point where the bombs are constructed, tested, transported. At the point of training. We had too many targets to protect; forts and castles could not serve our needs. Our strategy was right. We just needed the energy to implement it and the guts to trust it. The pilot had concluded the U.S. government was not sufficiently paranoid, while also accusing it of bad behavior and worse intentions. I have no problem with the accusations; they apply to everyone and every government. But his paranoia was flawed because he doubted the depth of everyone else's paranoia, especially the government's. Besides, the whole philandering husband thing did not hold up. He assumed the wives and daughters were passive participants: another strike against the quality of his paranoia. His plan consisted of chastity belts for infrastructure.

The car was still where I left it. I opened the glove box carefully and ran my finger along the back edge of the rental agreement and then licked it. My finger was not sweet.

10

The approach came on the second night. A blonde appeared beside me at the bar. She ordered a dirty martini and said, "Twinkly, isn't it?"

The man on the other side of her said, "That's why I come here." The blonde ignored him and looked at me. I said nothing. The man on the other side said, "I own those four buildings over there. See that red light?"

She said, "No." But she kept looking at me.

This was my second night of riding up more than forty stories to have drinks in the Wildcatter Club, where the members could gaze out at Houston and feel those twinkling lights filling their pockets. I had never before ridden in an elevator just to get a drink. The bar was full and the dining room was getting there. Last night had been quieter, older.

"You don't like twinkly? Then you came to the wrong place," she said.

"Your ring is twinkly. I like that." The tan, the nose, the hair, the breasts: The ring was the only thing about her that had a chance of being real. Even her Texas accent sounded wrong. She was petite and her blue eyes were large, made to appear larger by lashes peeled back like petals in a flower. She reminded me of a ten-year-old boy's idea of an ideal woman. A doll come to life. But the bold shamelessness and ease with which she carried herself made me like her.

"Are you a grouch?"

"Maybe I'm a jewel thief," I said.

"Wouldn't that be exciting. Are you drinking alone? I don't like to see a man like you drinking alone. Makes me think there's something wrong with me."

"I'm drinking alone," said the guy next to her. He turned to his buddy next to him and said, "Aren't I?"

"Always," said the buddy. They clicked their glasses and drank.

"I love my friends over there, but they're much more interesting when a man is present. Keeps them sharp, I think. Come this way," she said to me. She got up and I picked up her drink before she could.

"Allow me," I said.

She smiled at me, then turned to the guy on the other side and said, "See the difference?"

Her name was Daisy. A second blonde, wider and older, was Marlene. Maya was younger than the other two. Somewhere under thirty. Her mouth was wide and so were her eyes, which were brown, giving her a slightly Asian appearance. Her skin was very smooth, though she seemed to be wearing little makeup. She watched me carefully without self-consciousness.

They sat in leather chairs around a small cocktail table in the corner of the room farthest from the windows and the elevators. A bowl of bar mix sat untouched on the table. Daisy riffed for a few minutes on the jewel thief theme as a way of getting me to protest and explain what I really did. Then Marlene took over and asked how I had been spending my time in Houston. I told them about my helicopter ride.

"We're like skirt-chasing husbands, never thinking that our wives and daughters might be targets for other guys while we're out looking for other's . . . platforms," I said with special attention to Marlene and Daisy, who were wearing rings. They chuckled and nodded. "We need chastity belts for our infrastructure."

Daisy said, "You're right. You're so right. I never thought of it like that. I knew I shouldn't let you drink alone."

I wondered if I should try to fix her up with the helicopter pilot, since her husband seemed to be occupied elsewhere.

"I wonder where Gerry is," said Marlene while staring at the twinkling lights.

"That's a first," said Daisy. Marlene did not smile.

The silence lasted about thirty seconds and might have gone on longer, but a maître d' appeared and announced that their dinner table was ready. Marlene guzzled the rest of her drink and handed the glass to the maître d', who seemed to understand. Daisy asked me to join them for dinner, but it was time to find out which one of them wanted to see me alone. My guess was Maya because I hoped it was her.

I said, "I'll be in town for a few days and I hope I can have a rain check."

"Maya, dear, you coming?"

"Would you mind if I skipped dinner tonight?"

It was the first time she spoke after hello. Her accent was British but slightly off, as if English were not her first language.

"Well, then, you two, maybe we'll see you when we're done. I know I'm gonna see you again, Robert. I just know it. Bye," said Daisy.

"There's Gerry," said Marlene. "Bye."

Maya did not move. I sat down. We watched Marlene squeeze across the room to a short, thick man in his sixties. She pecked him on the cheek and he seemed surprised.

"Another drink?"

"Not right now, thank you," Maya said.

"Dinner?"

"I'm not hungry." She stared at me, calmly and without wavering. I could not tell if she was reading me or if she wanted me to try, and fail, to read her.

"It doesn't have to be about food," I said.

We rode down in the elevator with the guy from the bar and his buddy. The guy studied Maya. Before we got off, he said, "What's your secret, pal?"

Maya said, "Chastity belts and infrastructure. He's an expert." And she winked at him.

The doors opened and we walked out ahead of the men.

The valet parkers were busy, mostly with arrivals. A guy who looked like he could be Middle Eastern sat in a black Lincoln in the no parking zone. He started the car when he saw us, but Maya gave him the slightest shake of her head, and he turned the car off.

Farther down the street, behind the Lincoln, near the corner, a black SUV idled. Maya glanced at it quickly, and even more quickly her mouth tightened and her eyes narrowed.

We got into my car and I drove a few blocks before I said, "Is there any place you'd like to go? I've only eaten at my hotel and that club so far."

"I never want to eat again at the club and I'm not ready to go to your hotel," she said. She gave me directions and pretty soon we were on a highway heading northwest, out of town.

"Don't worry about the car following us. It's his job," she said. She didn't mention the black SUV, which was also following.

We kept the top down. The air was warm and less moist, fresher than it had been since I arrived. As we left the city, forests lined the road in long clumps and scented the air with pine. We did not talk. Maya tied her hair into a ponytail. She leaned the seat back and put the window down and let her hand foil the wind.

The road was unlit. Headlights scanned across us like search beams, without rhythm, as if trying to catch us off guard. I did my best to keep my smile hidden inside. A few times I gave in and glanced at Maya when the lights swept across us, and even though she did not look directly at me, I knew she registered my interest. I did not care if we drove like that until the tank was empty.

I could taste my recklessness and I liked the way it tasted. The follower could have been an assassin and Maya could have been leading me to my grave, pre-dug in the dirt and sand among the pines. The SUV could have been the backup team. The farther we drove into the dark night, the more I enjoyed the mix of anticipation and tension. Her silence increased the pleasure, making me wonder more about her. Did she fear her voice would betray her plan for my ambush? Did she sense my conflicting emotions and so keep her silence to allow them to flourish? Her beauty was tantalizing, her silence intriguing. The allure was like a drug. I fought it, surrendered to it, savored it.

This streak in me, my desire to toy with temptation, bothered me and I determined that if it did not kill me this time, I would address it before next time. And I knew that one day, that kind of lie would lead me into trouble I could not get out of. I have always been partial to indulgence because it is such an especially insidious and honest parasite. It leads you exactly where it says it will: violence or romance, greed or sacrifice.

A memory, as grisly as this night was beautiful, attacked me and would not relent. Trying to block it out just gave it strength, so I capitulated, in order to get rid of it. At an outpost in Helmand Province, two privates, Ernie and Eric, muscle guys with bad mustaches and shaved heads, would spend hours going on about what they would like to do to the enemy the next time they got the chance. Gruesome stuff, of course, but everyone has nasty thoughts about the people who have been trying to kill them. Decapitation and disembowelment were persistent themes. One was Alvarez, the other was Alfredson, but they acted like twin brothers. We all heard the chatter and it was so extreme that we assumed the chatter was just steam.

After living through a particularly intense barrage of shelling, we set out for the village where we thought the mortars and rockets were stored. Every structure had to be searched. Ernie and Eric worked as a team. I was outside, only a few buildings away, when I heard the shots. First order of business was to make everyone who wasn't in a Marine uniform hit the ground. The shots stopped, and for about ten seconds, there was silence. Then voices started from inside the house the shots came from. One guy, Ernie, repeated a version of "What the fuck are you doing?" about a hundred times.

And Eric said in a voice that was eerily calm, "Whaddaya mean? I told ya what I was gonna do. We talked about it, man. I told you."

Another guy and I tried the door. It was locked.

Ernie yelled at us, "Back off." And a second later he was yelling at Eric to stop whatever he was doing. I could hear the horror in his voice. He screamed, "Put it down! Stop it." He sounded like a terrified kid begging his older brother to stop wrecking his stuff. Two shots followed.

The scene was frozen: Afghans on the ground like customers caught in a bank holdup and the Marines standing among them scared as thieves, nobody moving and the only sound was the wind. The bolt drew back on the door. I raised my weapon and stepped back. Ernie came out. He closed the door behind him before looking all around. He settled on me and stared at my weapon, then into my eyes. He shook his head the slightest bit, then walked away. He didn't look like a bad-ass Marine anymore. He looked like an old guy, a tired, scared old guy.

Inside, we found Eric's body and his victims, two parents and a child. At least he never got to work on the child.

Ernie took me aside that afternoon at the outpost. "I have to get out of here," he said. "If anyone gave me any crap today when I came out of that house, I'd have shot him. You, too. I have to get out of here."

I found the captain and told him. He started talking about an investigation. I laughed.

"Ernie did the investigation, held the trial, executed the sentence. Everybody, even Eric, is happy with the result. You should give Ernie a medal, but if you don't, he won't mind. Just send him home. He saw inside all our heads. He can't be around us anymore."

I was pretty sure I would not be chopping off anyone's head no matter how charming Maya became, and I knew I was just seduc-

ing myself. The awful memory served as a helpful wound, a pain
that kept me from succumbing to the drug.

Maya directed me to turn toward Stagecoach, then onto a
smaller road. A few hundred yards along, we went around a curve,
and Maya said, "Here."

Billy's Roadhouse was hidden among the pines, a one-story
shingled building with a painted sign over the door illuminated by
a single bulb. The parking lot was gravel. The mat in front of the
door read: CONGRATULATIONS.

Before we went in, Maya's shadow pulled into the lot. "Should
we ask him to join us?" I asked.

"He won't trust you. He'll think you mean to do me harm and
you're trying to get him drunk, or to drug him."

I waited a moment for the black SUV, but it did not pull in or go
past. That meant it had pulled off just around the curve.

No one sat at the long bar. One couple occupied a table on the
left side of the room and another balanced them at the other side.
The light was low enough that I could not make out anyone's features. A Gram Parsons song was playing on the speakers: the one
about sweeping out the ashes in the morning. The bartender looked
up but did not move.

We stood there a moment, letting our eyes adjust. "This place a
favorite of yours?" I asked.

"Never been here, in fact. I read about it once. I've been looking
for the right occasion to try it."

On our right a hostess appeared and said, "Hi, y'all. How're
doin' t'night? Good to see ya." It was just a standard Texas greet-
ing, but I watched Maya for any sign that she and the hostess had
met before. I caught nothing.

We were led past a long row of booths, each with a high partition shielding the occupants from view, to the last one in the row. A large window made up much of the wall at the end of the row. I did not want my back to the window and did not want my back to the room and did not want to make a fuss about it. I chose to have my back to the room because the window would show a reflection of anyone coming toward us from the entrance.

Maya ordered wine and I ordered a beer. The hostess lit a candle for us and left.

"Most oilmen I've met like to brag," Maya said.

"Would you like me to brag?"

"Very much." She said it with perfect mock sincerity and rested her chin in her hands as if to hang on my every word.

"Okay . . . After years of near starvation, extreme deprivation of all modern, earthly delights and pleasures, sacrifice unknown to others of my generation, I determined that a remote patch of land covered a vast sea of oil. With only a shovel and a pick, I dug the well. With a saw and hammer, I built the derrick. I fought off claim jumpers, thieves, con artists, and the alluring, seductive women they sent to deprive me of my fortune, and in the end I prevailed, and now with my ocean of oil and endless fields of dollars, I'm the richest man in . . . in this booth."

"You're lying."

"How can you tell?"

"The rich men I've met would not brag about dirty hands. You didn't tell me how many cars you owned, or houses, yachts, movie stars you met."

"I have no reason to buy anything. I have no woman to buy it for."

"That's not bragging. That's flirting."

"Isn't that why we're here?"

She looked at me the same way she had at the club, just an expressionless stare. She said, "I wanted to come to the club tonight so I could meet you."

The flickering candlelight accentuated the angles of her face and the surrounding darkness acted as a whisper: I leaned in to be sure I saw her expression. I wanted to erase the darkness, eliminate anything that kept me from seeing her perfectly.

I asked, "Why is that?"

"We might be able to help each other."

The waitress brought our drinks. I had not caught her reflection in the window. "Y'all ready?" We both shook our heads with the same slow cadence. The waitress shrugged and went away.

The spell was strong. Too strong. I could leave the party now, or stay too long. The buzz I was feeling had spread thoroughly, drowning out my thoughts. If I abandoned my self-indulgence at that moment, I could still believe it was a just a pleasurable ploy to expose Maya, or to trick her into revealing herself. It would have been fine to go on for a while if I could keep my distance. I couldn't.

I still did not know who she was.

I thought I saw movement outside. Maya saw me staring at the window and turned to check it out for herself.

"Just leaves rustling, I think," I said. "But maybe you're expecting someone out there." She didn't answer, so I went on. "You can start with who is in the black SUV, or with who you are. I don't care where you start, but understand, we're going to get to it all." I was harsh. But it did not throw her off.

"Forgive me. You came along so willingly that I assumed you knew who I was. My name is Maya Karkukli. My father is Basam Karkukli. He is the rightful heir to the throne of the Kingdom of Kurdistan. I was informed that you were purchasing oil rights to the Kurdish fields in Iraq from parties whom we consider to be rivals. I wanted to meet you so that we could discuss this situation and possibly find some common ground. I did not want to begin in a business setting because I wanted first to assess what kind of man you are. I wanted to see if you are up to the challenges involved in this sort of business."

"How am I doing?"

"Quite well."

"Now then, tell me why we're out here at the Cheating Heart Café in downtown Lonesome Pines."

She laughed and I could feel the buzz zip through me again. I fought it.

"I thought privacy would be essential," she said.

"Try again."

She sipped her wine to buy time. She looked at the menu. I moved the candle closer to her in case she was actually reading. She moved the candle back and slid the menu aside. The flame flickered in her dark eyes.

"You're giving money to the Kurdish rebels. They will never unite anything. All they do is cause problems and anger the Turks and scare the Iranians, making them all hate Kurds even more. And the Regional Government is just a bunch of corrupt bureaucrats. Your money will line their pockets. Nothing else."

"I line their pockets so I can line mine."

"That will never happen. If they do ever gain control of their portion of Kurdistan, they'll ignore you and betray you for a higher bidder."

The cool veneer had melted. She seemed to mean it all, but that did not explain why she did not tell it in town. She would have to be a very confident woman to think she was going to seduce me into investing millions in her father with just one night of mood lighting, no matter how beautiful she was. This didn't have the feel of a con. If it were, she would have waited for me to tell my business, drawn it out of me with a shower of attention and ardent fascination, and she would have concealed her relationship with the King, only offering to arrange an introduction after my dreams had become hers. Variations would follow, but the start-up was a set piece, like a chess opening.

"Did your father ask you to contact me?"

"He doesn't know. He doesn't know about you."

"Why me? There are plenty of oilmen, oil companies, oil funds around."

"We're talking to many of them."

"They all get taken for a ride in the woods?"

"You sound jealous."

"Who is in the black SUV?"

That brought silence. Then she said, "I have to go now." She slid out of the booth. I threw money on the table and followed her outside.

The Lincoln started up and this time she nodded. It pulled up to the front door. Maya turned to me.

"Come to meet my father. Noon tomorrow. You'll see what kind of man he is. You'll want to be his partner." She gave me an address. The chauffeur got out of the car and started around to our side. He was short and stocky, about fifty, with saggy, blue bags under his eyes, and a nose that looked like a swollen thumb. He looked like a guy who had to get back to the crypt before dawn.

"Come with me," I said.

Maya shook her head. "Tomorrow."

The driver opened the door for her. She ignored it. She put her hand on my arm and moved close and brushed her lips on my cheek. She looked at me for a moment, then got into the car. Blue Bags slammed the door and stared at me, but not in the "I'm about to kiss you" sort of way. I strolled toward my car, thinking about seeing her again at noon and laughing at myself for feeling like a teenager who just discovered that the whole world doesn't hate him.

I sat there thinking about that combination of exotic beauty and mysterious reserve and why I was willing to pretend, for now, that it added up to shrewd intelligence and commitment to a cause. Maya could turn out to be nothing more than a True Believer, a faith zombie. From the woods in front of me a troop of Mayas emerged, placid smiles fixed like bayonets to assault my skepticism and so real that I almost turned around to see if they were closing in from behind, too. But I knew I was safe because faith is a psychosomatic disease, infecting volunteers only. The SUV did not appear after five minutes, so I left.

11

recognized the perfume when I entered my hotel suite. Daisy bounced up from the couch before the door was closed.

"There you are. How'd you do? Certainly spent enough time. I ordered a movie on your TV. Hope you don't mind paying for it."

"Happy to."

"Don't worry, it's not porn."

"That's a big relief," I said, and I walked past her to check the bedroom for other uninvited guests. It was empty.

The dress and the heels were gone, replaced with shorts, tank top, and sandals. The wig was gone. Her hair was dirty blond, short. The jewelry was not replaced. All that remained of Daisy was the personality and the implants.

"So, did she invite you to meet her father? I bet she did. I bet you're in." She flopped down on the couch and kicked off her sandals. "You didn't even leave anything on the door to see if anyone came in when you were gone. Y'know, something like a hair or a matchstick. The maid let me in."

There was a knock on the door. Daisy hopped up. "I ordered room service, too. I didn't know when you would get here and I'm starving." She moved past me toward the door, but I grabbed her arm and held it while I looked through the peephole.

"You open it," I said.

"I like a strong grip in a man. Lets me know he means it." She opened the door and the waiter carried in a tray. "He'll sign," she said. And I did. The waiter left. Daisy started picking at the salad. "The food at the club is so bad. Those people have all that money and don't even know what's good."

"You're very charming, Daisy, but I'm tired now. Not in the mood for company. Maybe we can schedule something on another day. Take the salad with you."

I was about to open the door for her exit when she said, "Major Hensel sent me. To help you. And I did help you."

"I don't know a Major Hensel," I said.

"Want me to call him?"

"Do you have a phone?"

"'Course, I do. Let me grab my purse."

"Wait there. I'll get it." I grabbed her purse and brought it to her. "There, now you can call anyone you want, as soon as you leave."

I opened the door and guided her out.

I was picking at the salad when my phone rang. Major Hensel said, "Daisy works for SHADE."

I told him about my progress. He listened, then he asked if there was anything else I wanted. There was, but I said no.

"Okay, then, she's in the stairwell. You still have her sandals. Make use of her if you can."

"I'll try to think of something."

Daisy was peeking out from the stairwell. "Can I wash my feet in your tub?" she asked. "That stairwell is dirty. And don't eat that salad. I'm hungry."

While Daisy washed her feet, she told me what she had gleaned about the King and Maya. It was not much. Most of it came from Marlene's husband and two other oilmen Daisy had chatted up. The King was courting investors who were offering gifts, cash gifts, graciously accepted by the King, but the bids were kept low because of the political uncertainty. The sense was that the bribes were more important than the bid. The King was cash hungry. Marlene's husband, Gerry, was licking his chops because his offer was structured to give the King a big chunk of the gross revenue, and most of the rest for Gerry's company, very little to the people of Kurdistan.

I let her talk, asking as few questions as I could because I was not ready to reveal my plans to her. Daisy did not require encouragement to keep the chatter going. We moved back to the living room so she could finish her salad.

"How did you meet Major Hensel?"

"I babysat his children," I said.

"He has kids?"

"Three. How did you meet him?"

"I don't know you well enough to say." She paused and stared at me. "You're lying. He has no kids. Give me something to do." She got up and pushed the cart into the hallway. "I put on that wig and those heels and I'm another person. I feel like I can do anything."

She seemed like the same person to me, but that was fine. "I want to know who owns the house Maya and her father live in. If they're renting, who is paying the bills. There's an attorney, Darrell White, who might have all those answers."

"Thank you. You won't be sorry. Thank you." She came close to me and went up on her toes, and I bent down and turned my cheek so she could plant her kiss there. She looked at me to see if that was the way I wanted things to be. I nodded. She shrugged and put on her sandals.

I said, "Don't come back here. Assume you're being watched. Assume I am being watched."

"Give me your phone number."

"No. Call the Major if you need to reach me. Give him whatever information you get."

She squinted at me and shook her head. "You are a grump."

The clock beside the bed read 4:12. My phone read 4:09. I left the light off while I pulled on jeans. Through the peephole, I saw two men in suits. They knocked again. Harder this time.

I was hoping for a kinder, more civil introduction: tea in the garden and talk of yachts on the Adriatic. But at least they knocked first and bothered to lie, claiming to be hotel security. I paused only long enough to remind myself to be indignant and scared. The first two moved in quickly and took hold of me. Two others followed them in. A tall Middle Eastern man turned on the lights. I squinted to show how uncomfortable and disoriented I was and I did not struggle too much. I gave them a quick list of the questions they expected: What is this, how dare you, who are you?

The Middle Eastern man stood in front of me, looking me over with distaste. The fourth man was solid and wide with a big square head and calm, careful eyes, a centurion on duty, seeing as much as he could, believing as little as he should. He walked past me into the bedroom.

The Middle Eastern man spoke: "If you assure me of your co-operation, these men will release you."

"Yeah. Sure. I'm not running away, if that's what you mean."

The two suits let me go. "I am Zoran. I am factotum to His Excellency, Basam Karkukli, King of all Kurdistan."

I started to laugh, knowing it would irritate him. "The King sent you? If this is about the kiss on the cheek from Maya . . ."

Zoran swallowed his anger. He had bases to cover. "His Majesty asked me to convey to you his gratitude for your cooperation with this most unusual request. I assure you that he would not disturb you unless the matter were of the greatest urgency."

"I said I'd be there at noon. There's no need for this. Please leave now." The two suits flanked the door. Zoran stared at me as if he had not heard a word. I picked up the phone.

The centurion appeared in front of me. He did not shake his head, but his expression made it clear: I would be better off if we did not get to that stage. I put down the phone. The centurion was holding my phone and wallet. Something passed between him and Zoran.

"This is Mr. Gill. You will get dressed now, please," Zoran said.

"I want to know one thing: Did the King come into your room and roust you and make you roust these guys, or were you all sitting around in your suits and the King ordered you to come over here?"

A vein seemed to come to life in Zoran's forehead. It might have been there before, but I had not noticed it. His ears went back and his eyes sharpened. I wished I knew which chord I had struck.

"In serving His Majesty, I serve a great cause. Perhaps you feel the same way about your masters." He stared at me to let me know he had more answers if I wanted to continue. "You will get dressed now, please." He brushed past me and went into the bedroom.

I considered further resistance, but Gill's eyes met mine and this time his head moved slightly from side to side. I followed Zoran. He was checking out my closet.

"No blue jeans. Wear a suit."

He turned away while I got dressed, but I watched him. Zoran had muscles under his suit. His shoulders were hunched up and he bent forward slightly. The skin on his face was as tight as his personality, with pockmarks on his cheeks. His eyelashes were noticeably long, and the eyes were sunk deep in their sockets, shaded and hidden by his brow. He had camel eyes.

The house was big as a resort and quiet as a church on Monday. The first drops of dawn splashed on pillars, porticoes, wings. Big iron gates at the entrance rose toward the center with sharp spikes on top to deter all but the bravest pole-vaulters. We drove past hedges and flower beds and a couple of enormous oak trees. The roof looked like it had about seven levels to it, some sloped steeply, some mildly. It was hard to shake the feeling that some forgotten prisoner was watching from one of the many gabled windows. It wasn't a castle, not a palace, but bigger than a mansion, certainly fit for a king without a country.

Zoran stopped me before we went in and said, "In all matters regarding dealings with the King or his family you will take instruction from me. The first time you meet the King, you will bow. You will address him as Your Excellency. He may or may not allow you to address him as Mr. Karkukli. You do not sit until you are invited to do so. Do you understand?"

"I do."

"It is an order." He did not smile.

The throne was a high-back chair upholstered in green silk. It looked like it would be uncomfortable, but His Excellency managed to sit straight up and relaxed at the same time. Out back, beyond gardens, was the pool, and past that the dim outline of a fenced-in tennis court was just catching the morning glow.

Gill stood off to my right. Zoran announced me, placed me in front of the King, then moved to a spot beside him. The King did not exactly smile, but his lips curled up a bit in what he must have practiced as his pleasant look. Zoran nodded to me.

I moved forward, extended my hand, and said, "Nice to meet you Mr. Karkukli."

The King craned around to look at Zoran. Zoran was busy making the vein bulge under his tight skin. His dark eyes showed some white. I waited. He hissed. "Bow to His Excellency."

Gill stayed as still and solid as a rock. The King resumed his relaxed posture and pleasant expression: Someone had used the wrong fork, but the gaffe had been corrected.

"Oh, you want me to bow," I said directly to the King. "I'll bow . . . You first."

That took care of the pleasant look. Zoran stepped toward me, but his main concern was apologizing to the King. The King did not acknowledge him. He wasn't insulted, or outraged. His lips parted and he looked like a guy who had been through this before and knew it was coming again. I did not take my eyes off him to look toward the centurion, but if he moved, I would see it.

The King spoke to Zoran in another language. It came fast and it surprised me. It wasn't Dari, but many of the words were close;

some were Arabic. I had to remind myself to keep a straight face, not let on that I understood. But I did understand the King: Worry about this later; question him now. The King returned his attention to me.

Zoran took over.

"You met with His Excellency's daughter, Maya, last night." It wasn't a question, so I waited. "We know this. You will tell us about this encounter."

"Can I have some coffee?"

"You went to a roadhouse. Was it a place of your choosing?"

The King was gazing past me as if he were an actor on a stage.

"Hers. I like it black."

"Did Maya appear to be nervous or on edge?"

"Not especially," I said. "But we just met. Maybe that was her version of nervous. Where is she?"

"What time did you leave her?"

"You know all these answers. Where's the loyal chauffeur? Where's Maya?"

That answer seemed to irritate him more than the others. "You are working with our enemies. We know this. You are allied against us. I assure you we will use all possible means to get to the truth."

This guy was not an artful interrogator. He let me know that he had all the information he needed and that my reason for being there involved something else. The vein in his forehead looked like it was going to burst long before he came out with what was on his mind. Though the furnishings were typical modern American hotel lobby, the atmosphere in the room was foreign: the stiff formality, the deliberate pauses, the reek of suspicion. I looked around for a chair. "I'm going to bring that chair over here. Okay?"

"Stay where you are."

I looked over at Gill: a statue. The King was in another place. The sunlight stabbing into the room seemed to fascinate him.

Zoran went on. "You know where Maya is. That is why we brought you here. I warn you for the last time. Tell us all you know."

"I know that Maya asked me to come here at noon today to meet the King. I know you brought me here quite a bit earlier. I know you haven't asked me to sit down or offered me coffee. I know that the vein in your forehead looks like it's going to pop. And here's what I don't know: what you want or why I'm here. Oh, and I know I've had enough of this and I'm leaving."

I walked toward the door, expecting Gill to stop me, or two of the suits to grab me when I passed into the hall. Instead, the King spoke. "I will assume your refusal to bow stems from a matter of principle, Mr. Hewitt, and is not a personal affront."

I stopped and turned to him. "I don't know you well enough for a personal affront. Not yet, anyway."

The King stood up. He put his left hand on his midsection to smooth his coat and, with his right, gestured with a casual wave for Zoran to stand back. Zoran managed to snarl in my direction before complying. The King was short, heavy chested, and thick at the waist. His movements were careful and smooth. Wavy salt and pepper hair made him resemble the soon to be foiled continental lothario in a black and white movie. He looked tired. His eyebrows flickered slightly before he spoke.

"Bring Mr. Hewitt a chair. And coffee."

Zoran took a moment to scowl in my direction, but he did a lousy job of it. He threw out some orders in the other language and clapped his hands. A moment later, a servant came in and moved a chair near the King's chair for me to sit on.

I walked over. Before the King sat down, I offered my hand. He looked it over the way people look over the lobsters in a tank: something they have no intention of touching. But he overcame his aversion and shook. Zoran's disgust with that was real. I sat down quickly, before he could pull the chair away. I waited like a patient pupil for the King to make the first move.

"I have many enemies, Mr. Hewitt. In fact, I believe you are acquainted with some of them. And because of your acquaintance with these parties, I am put in a difficult situation. I need your help but must first believe I can trust your discretion."

I wanted to laugh. I could have taken my phone back from Gill and dialed *The New York Times* and told them to listen up, and the King was still going to pretend to trust my discretion. "I have no idea if you can trust my discretion or not. Something has happened to Maya and you don't want people to know. Let's start there."

"Maya said you are an interesting man, Mr. Hewitt." The line sounded rehearsed. Everything he said sounded that way, all with the aim of simulating sincerity. But he was not a good enough actor to pull it off.

"Call me Robert."

"Maya called after she left you last night. She had great hope that we would be able to find common ground. I hope so, too. I regret the difficult start we have had. But I warn you that I regard betrayal as the worst possible crime. The only unforgivable crime." He turned away from me and looked out toward the pool and returned to his calm, elegant voice. "Maya did not return home at all last night. Just over three hours ago, at approximately two A.M., we received a phone call telling us that she has been kidnapped. I am hopeful that you could shed some light on this." He was very calm for a guy with a kidnapped daughter.

The black SUV hung from the ceiling, revving, its exhaust filling the room. One of us was going to mention it someday. The King was in no rush. I looked up. "Who was in the black SUV?" I said.

Coffee was served. A servant placed a small table next to me and another next to the King. He was served first. He sipped a bit after the servant left, while he calculated his reply.

"Well, well, Robert, Maya was right about you, wasn't she? Wasn't she, Zoran? I must say you are sharp. In fact, that was what I was about to ask you. You see, we know about it. They were following me earlier in the week and then last night Arun, that's Maya's chauffeur, reported that he saw them. And, of course, that's when you appeared as well. You can understand Arun's suspicions."

"And Zoran's," I said. "How about yours?"

The King flicked his left eyebrow up and down. It might have been a tic, but I thought it was intentional. Showing off? I resisted the temptation to imitate him. "You're in no position, Mr. Hewitt, to banter with me."

"Sure I am, King. I can banter until you call the police. And then I can leave. But, if you don't want to call them yet, that's fine with me; I haven't finished my coffee." Nothing in my manner or tone could re-chisel Gill's features. Zoran was easy. If it weren't for the soft dawn light invading the room, I was sure I could have seen the smoke pouring out of his ears.

They were slow about getting to the point. I did not want to do all the heavy lifting but the vague, meaningless threats were getting to me. Impatience nudged me, though I had plenty of time. I put my cup down and said, "How much did they ask for?"

"That, Mr. Hewitt, is confidential information."

I stood up. "I'll leave now. I don't know anything more than what I've told you and you don't want to tell me anything more." I turned to Gill. "I'd like to have my phone and wallet back."

At last his eyes moved. To the King.

The King said, "Return Mr. Hewitt's belongings to him."

Gill reached into the side pocket of his jacket and held out the phone and wallet. I went over to take them from him because I had caught on that he was not likely to move first.

"Now, Mr. Hewitt, you are free to go. Zoran will arrange a ride to your hotel. But I ask you to stay. I find myself in a difficult position, Mr. Hewitt, in two ways. The first caused by the abductors of my daughter. The second is, well . . . frankly, it is not my habit to ask for help."

Help. I understood that language. Help meant money.

Maybe he knew who kidnapped Maya, maybe he was in on it, maybe he was innocent of that part, but he was going to use it to con me out of money. That was certain. That was the first priority. He was fit to be a king, after all. That he was doing exactly as I wanted him to only made it seem worse.

Dan, to his credit, was not poking me in the ribs and saying, *"See, I wasn't nearly that bad."* Instead, he said, *"He scares me."*

"I didn't know you could be scared, even when you were alive."

"He scares me. I know you won't leave, but I would."

"I can't leave because I'm a greedy, cocky, overconfident business whiz who is slavering to take advantage of their misfortune. And I have to stay and be patient enough to let them make the first offer."

"I think he's dangerous."

"You think he's the puppet master?"

"I think it bothers him that he's not in charge. He suspects he's a fraud. That's what scares me."

I should have tried harder to understand what Dan was seeing. Instead, I looked at the King and said, "How can I help?"

13

The magic words earned me a guided tour of the grounds by His Majesty himself. Zoran and Gill were left behind. A path lined with rosebushes led to the swimming pool, which had one of those automatic cleaners floating in a corner. A large pool house was fronted by a wide patio and flanked by beds of flowers. When we got to the tennis court, the King soon lost interest in talking about the grounds. "Do you play?" he asked.

The only time I ever touched a tennis racquet was when I stole one, brand-new, from a sporting goods store just to prove I could do it. I threw it into the dumpster behind the store. "Yes," I said.

"We must play then, sometime when this matter is cleared up."

"I look forward to it," I said.

"My people, Mr. Hewitt—"

"Please call me Robert."

"Robert, my people are an ancient people. We have been without our own country, the ability to control our destiny, for too long. We yearn for freedom and unity. I know you are sympathetic or else you would not have allied with the Kongra-Gel. We are spread across four countries, and in each one we have been murdered and oppressed. All this is well documented. Yet we persevere. I know that my dream, my goal of uniting all the Kurdish people in their own nation, is regarded as foolishness by most people. I know this. But my life is dedicated to this quest. This burden has been placed on me and I must live up to it. I must and I will. Imagine not only your father's faith and hope for you, but his father and fifty generations of fathers. It is only under the ancient crown that our people can ever be united and free. Only under our ancient crown can we regain our glory and achieve our destiny. I am a patriot first and last. A patriot beyond borders."

He stopped, satisfied with himself. I kept quiet as we walked back toward the pool house. I once had a teacher named Miss Bagnolia. Miss Bagnolia wore black the whole time I was in her class because someone in her family had died. She thought she would solve me by making me repeat, "Every day in every way, I am getting better and better." At first I thought it was a lie I was practicing to convince others what a great teacher she was. After about a month, it dawned on me that I was supposed to convince myself. The King's speech was passionate and passionately delivered, but more for his benefit than mine, as if he needed to repeat it to remind himself that the pain was real.

At the pool house, the King opened a laptop and played a video for me that laid out the whole case for Kurdish nationalism from thousands of years back. There was a Median Empire and they fought the Assyrians and eventually lost. The real Aryans were Kurds, and they are the original rulers of this vast territory that now is divided into Iran, Iraq, Syria, and Turkey. The video showed an ancient tomb cut in the rock face and supported by carved pillars that had been eaten by time. "Thought to be," "Might be," "Regarded as": Those phrases dominated. Names repeated, adding to the confusion. If it were history, I would have paid attention, but it felt like Sunday school. I couldn't know what really happened. I would never know. No one ever could. They would believe instead of knowing. I could not believe.

My eyes glazed over and I thought about the King and what he was selling. What is patriotism to a king? Egomania. The loyalty, the passion, the fervor were to the King, to himself. All the insane vows and deceptions that go with zealous patriotism are put through the turbocharger of self-interest. This king seemed soft. I tried to keep Dan's warning in mind. Softness can be used as a weapon, too, when combined with egomania. I could not picture this guy as the puppet master. He did not have the focus. The passion felt canned, salted, gooey. The man who put this conspiracy together would own intensity. This King owned wistfulness.

Servants were setting a table on the patio. The King held my arm. "My situation is complicated, Robert. I cannot access the necessary funds, a million dollars, for Maya's freedom in a timely manner. And I doubt whoever has done this will be willing to listen to reason." He wiggled the eyebrow again. This time I was closer and wanted to put my thumb on it to make it stop.

"I don't know who we're talking about, or why they kidnapped Maya. But I never heard of reasonable kidnappers. They're going to want cash and fast. The police have experience with this kind of thing."

"We are guests in this country. I don't trust the police to be discreet, or to understand the complexities of our situation. You can see the difficulty of my position. On the one hand, my daughter's life is at stake. On the other lies the fate of my people. I cannot betray either. But if I had help, if some friend helped, my gratitude would be boundless. That friend would be honored in the Kurdish nation. I promise you that."

"How much can you put in?"

I suppose once you have convinced people you're a king, even if you don't have a throne or a country to rule, you have handled the toughest task, and convincing people to cooperate in other ways is relatively easy. People will put up money just to be near you, figuring they can peddle influence elsewhere. Until you have a country to run, you're not expected to put up your share. The King shook his head and looked at me as if I were a thief who wouldn't take credit cards.

"To obtain cash immediately would mean disrupting most delicate plans and operations."

"So you'd need the full amount."

"You understand. I knew you would."

"What form would your gratitude take?"

"Ah, Robert, you're negotiating. I should have known."

I could not offer to turn over a million dollars without something valuable in return, and I could not demand too much because I was supposed to be wise enough to know that he couldn't sell out his nation, imaginary as it might be. A million does not buy much in the oil business. One small block of oil rights costs many multiples of a million.

"You're going to have plenty of companies bidding on the rights. Different blocks are going be attractive to different bidders. And you're going to have investors who want to get in on any pipeline construction arrangements."

"What do you have in mind, Robert?"

"How are you organizing all that?"

"I don't understand."

I shrugged. "Do you use the pool much?"

"Please, Robert, my daughter's life hangs in the balance. Speak your thoughts."

"I could organize the auction for you. Take my cut from that. We'd be partners. Say, two percent."

He stomped his feet, walked away, came back, pulled me close, accused me of disrespecting his throne and his country, being a Turkish agent, a Syrian thief, an Iranian spy, and about everything else he thought he could get away with and still have the deal go through.

When he was done, I said, "One and a half for the first one hundred million. Two percent after that."

He shook his head, looked to the sky as if for advice, or at least to pretend he was thinking about it. "Maya was right about you. We have a deal."

He was sure he had me conned and that the negotiating was over and I let him think that for a while. Breakfast was waiting on the patio. Zoran stood a few feet from the table and barred my way for a moment so the King could sit first. A servant poured coffee for the King, and then for me. The servant poured cream over a gooey looking pastry and sprinkled it with sugar as carefully as one would fill a syringe. He served it to the King. I had eggs and toast on my plate. The King dug in as soon as the servant finished his work. After savoring a few bites, he stopped long enough to say, "It's called kahi. I like so many things Western, but I insist on kahi for breakfast whenever I am able."

When he finished the pastry, he downed the rest of his coffee and said, "Well, the banks should be open momentarily. I'll have Zoran arrange a ride for you."

"I have a few questions before we get started."

"But this is hardly the time."

"Not about our arrangement. Tell me about the chauffeur."

"Arun is completely trustworthy. He has been with me since I was in school. He's devoted to Maya."

I asked about threats and his contact with the enemies he mentioned. There had always been threats but nothing new and particular. He would not put a name on any enemies. The call came in on his cell phone, from Maya's phone.

"Did you answer the call?"

"Zoran screens my calls."

"But this call came at two A.M. Were you concerned that Maya was not home yet? Did she often stay out that late? What did Arun say about the black SUV? Was Arun suspicious of me?" I bunched the questions fast to see if he would get flustered. He didn't.

"You act as though you have done this before. Not like an investor in oil."

"I'll deliver the money myself. I'll need your cell phone so when they call, I can make arrangements with them."

"But you agreed to give me the money."

"I agreed to put up the ransom for Maya. That's what I'm going to do."

He looked all around. I thought he wanted Gill or Zoran, but a servant came out and poured the coffee that was inches from the King's hand. "That is not what I understood, Robert. Zoran and Mr. Gill must handle this. Mr. Gill has a team of security people.

Most competent. You yourself saw this at your hotel. For Maya's sake. I insist."

I held my tongue and let him move at his own slow speed to the only conclusion. He smiled at me. I smiled back. The eyebrow went up to show that he had made an excellent case and it was my turn to give in. I poured my own coffee. The soft swoosh of the fan held the beat for the chirping, invisible birds. Again, the King looked toward the trees beyond the tennis court. I did not know him well enough to tell whether he was dreaming, whining, or calculating. I expected another brief plea to see things his way, but he turned to me sharply, suddenly. He seemed startled by his thoughts. For a guy who appeared to have rehearsed most of his act in front of a mirror, it was a naked and puzzling moment. I thought he made me for a fake. But he said, "I'll let you handle it your way. What's the first step?"

The suddenness worried me and so did the omission of threats and warnings about the consequences of failure. I did not understand what it meant. I couldn't have. And I'm not sure, looking back, if I had understood what made the King react as he did, I would have changed anything. "I'll need Maya's cell phone number and Arun's."

The King slipped his arm through mine as we walked to the house. He had the style and elegance to pull it off. "Zoran and Mr. Gill will cooperate fully and give you any assistance you require. Those will be my orders."

"I'd rather leave them out of it."

"If you insist. You will deal directly with me."

He delivered the bad news to Zoran and Gill in the throne room. Zoran scowled. Gill might have been breathing. And immediately the King undercut it all by telling Zoran to write down the phone numbers I had asked for.

Zoran spoke to the King in that other language. The seething tone made the message clear, though I could understand enough of the words: Don't trust this American. Zoran warned the King that I might figure things out. The King said something that sounded like it meant "Who is your brain?" Zoran lowered his eyes.

I did not wait to see if this argument was going to continue. "I'll go get the money now. I should take your cell phone with me so if they call, I can make the arrangements."

Zoran did not like that. The King did not like that. "It's not enough that I trust you, Robert. You must trust me as well, wouldn't you agree?" I did not agree, and after more unpleasantness that I was not supposed to understand, they gave me the phone and one of their cars.

14

Robert Hewitt, cocky investor, got cold feet at the very last minute and nervously allowed Gill and his men to handle the exchange, which took place in Bayou Park at the end opposite the sculptures. Robert Hewitt then hid, leaning against a tree where he could watch the transaction without being seen.

Matching goons marched forward holding Maya. She looked like the prize in some fraternity dress-up ritual. Arun, the chauffeur, was not there. All my attention focused on the kidnappers in the hope that I would recognize one set of brown eyes. He had loomed over me, so I assumed he was tall. Nita had said he was shorter than me. It didn't matter; I was too far away to make out the color of their eyes.

The choreography broke down when the kidnappers opened the briefcase and counted the money. I put only two hundred thousand dollars inside but forgot to mention that to Gill.

Guns came out. A thin female jogger cruised alongside the confrontation, her earphones keeping her oblivious to the threats.

The two sides froze: mannequins misplaced. She glanced their way, had to see the guns, but she never broke stride. The moment she passed, the kidnappers were pulling Maya away, and Gill was craning around to scan the park for me. But I was on my way back to my car so I could follow the kidnappers.

The Ferrari was parked in the bank parking lot where I had picked up the money. The borrowed town car was parked at my hotel. I was driving a blue Honda. The kidnappers drove their black SUV southwest out of the city. They were in no hurry and thick traffic provided ample cover for me. I had the rest of the million dollars with me.

Five minutes into the ride, the King's phone rang. No number showed on the caller ID. I did not answer. A minute later, another anonymous call came in. The first message was from Zoran, the second from the kidnappers. According to the Rules of Dan, the more severe the threats, the more room there is for negotiation. Zoran threatened a lot and even accused me of malfeasance. The kidnapper, who had a Boston accent, simply said he would call back in one hour. Both sides needed me: one for the money, one for Maya. But I decided to stay silent for a few hours to give them the opportunity to realize how important I was to them.

On the outskirts of Sugar Land, the SUV turned down a private road. A small wooden sign identified either the road or the property as Runnymeade. I could not follow without being spotted. Three times I drove past the entrance to Runnymeade. It never changed. I did not want to go down that road without some idea of what I might be facing. The phone rang again. I ignored it again.

I called Major Hensel and asked for Daisy's number. The Major asked if I needed help with anything. I thought I better ask for something or he would be suspicious, so I asked for background on Mr. Gill. The Major said he would get back to me soon.

Daisy did not bother with hello. "I don't have any information yet, but I'm going on a date with Darrell White in a little while, so expect success," Daisy said.

"Can you have him meet you at your house?"

"Apartment. Yes, of course, he'll want to come here."

I arrived first. Daisy was decked out in full mufti, heels to wig. "You look beautiful, Daisy. I'm sure he'll fall madly in love." I gave her instructions: Let me in when I knock, pretend you don't know me, play along.

"I won't let you down," Daisy said.

"If it goes right, you can still have your date."

Darrel White drove up in a dark blue Bentley and left it in the loading zone right in front of the building. He wore a beige sport coat and brown pants and it looked like he had paid special attention to making sure the prow on top of his head was aerodynamic. I gave him five minutes, then took the elevator up to Daisy's apartment on the fifth floor. I knocked and said, "Delivery." When Daisy opened the door, I moved in fast, grabbing her arm. "Hello, Darrell," I said.

He reached inside his coat for the gun in his holster. He was slow. I slugged him in the gut and it felt like my fist went all the way through to his spine. He fell backward on his butt, then toppled flat on his back. I jumped forward and reached under his jacket and pulled the gun, a Colt .38 revolver. I pointed it toward Daisy and ordered her to get Darrell a glass of water.

I doused him with the water and said, "C'mon, big guy, sit up and we'll have a quick talk. I believe I still have you on retainer." He coughed a bit and propped himself up and felt for his gun. I poked him in the ear with it. "Who pays for the King's rent?"

"How would I know? What are you doing?"

I mussed his hair. It made him look younger. I asked again and received the same answer. I said, "Darrell, I can start kicking you in the head or you can start talking." He shrugged, so I kicked him in the head. He moaned and fell on his side. "The next one takes out teeth."

Daisy yelled, "Leave him alone. Get out of here."

I took her arm and tossed her roughly to the couch. She overplayed it, of course, and almost went through the wall. "Stay there or I'll kick your boyfriend harder."

The King's phone rang.

"Hear that, Darrell? That's the King calling, or the people who kidnapped the King's daughter. If I answer it, I'm going to tell them I'm here with you. I'm guessing you'd prefer more kicks in the head from me. Should I answer it?"

I held the phone out and turned the ringer up. I could see Darrell's shrewd lawyer look returning to his face, measuring my resolve. I answered the call and put the phone on speaker so Darrell could hear the low, vicious voice: "We've had enough of this. The girl is going to die. And so are you . . ." Darrell tried to hide the panic, but it was too strong. He shook his head vehemently and waved his hands like a referee signaling the play should stop.

I hung up. I kicked Darrell in the head once more to remind him that it was time to speak up. Daisy yelled, "No!" and rushed off the couch.

"Get him some more water," I said. Darrell drank the water

and I let him stagger over to the couch and ordered Daisy to sit next to him. She sat close to him, soothing him. Daisy was a very convincing actress.

"A guy showed up with cash for the rent. I passed it along. Three months in advance. That's all I know."

He knew a lot more. His expression when he heard the voice on the phone told me that. "What about Runnymeade?"

"What's that?" he said.

"You're disgusting, you know that? Why don't you just get out of my apartment right now? You got what you wanted. Git," said Daisy. She took Darrell's hand in hers.

"They gave you money for another residence, didn't they, Darrell? They paid more for the second one. All cash. How much?"

Darrell seemed to take courage from Daisy's support. He would not budge from his previous position.

"Darrell, think it through. I know where the house is. If you don't cooperate with me, I'm gonna tell them you spilled their secret. You're boxed in. Time to be smart."

Darrell just stared at the floor.

"Miss, what's your name?" I said.

"Daisy."

"Daisy, you're a very beautiful woman. What do you think Darrell should do?"

"Will you leave us alone if he cooperates? Promise?" Daisy spit it out, but it was just the kind of help Darrell needed to move him.

"I promise. Start with the payments. Tell me who made the payments."

"He called himself Mr. Clark."

"He paid for both houses?" Darrell nodded. "You knew who

the one house was for. The second one, Runnymeade, who was that one for?"

"Mister, they gave me enough money that I was not asking too many questions. Just like with you. It was straightforward: Find us two houses, pay the rent, keep the rest for yourself. I knew about the King because I had to do visa work for him. Once I had the payment, I never heard from Mr. Clark again."

"Until just now on the phone," I said. Darrell nodded again. "What kind of security system is there at Runnymeade?"

"None."

"That's a big house not to have a security system, Darrell."

"The landlord had ADT, but these people disconnected it." There was not much more to get from Darrell except the landlord's name, which he gave freely, some big-time basketball player who was traded. Darrell's story made sense except for one part. "Why are you so afraid of them?"

"Because I'm not as stupid as you."

"You tell him," Daisy said.

15

Pre-Marines and on the road, it happened that I grew tired of parks and hostels and unlocked cars for sleeping. Sometimes I would pick a house and watch it from about six A.M. until the adults left for work, and if there were no kids, I would break in and eat, set the alarm clock, and fall asleep. Most home alarm company signs were just beware-of-dog signs in disguise; if there was a home alarm system, it wasn't hooked up. I tried hard to get security companies to give me the codes: I was a son home from college and couldn't reach my parents, a new renter being cheated by the owners, a repairman on the job, a repairman who left his tools behind. Nothing worked. Another homeless kid, Vic, had a different approach. Vic was working as a busboy at a steakhouse near the marina in San Diego and he overheard people talking about a monthlong trip they were taking to Europe. He found the house, broke in. All he took was one extension of the cordless phone. That afternoon he stood in the yard and canceled the alarm service. The security companies think if you call from the home number, you're legit. Though they'll usually start the service from any number. It was a good plan, but Vic was paranoid and greedy.

Vic worried that someone else was going to try to usurp his new turf, so he bought a new keypad for the alarm system, put in his own code, then called a new security company and signed on with them, using the family's credit card, of course. His paranoia was justified, but being right did not help him. Within a week, there was a break-in, some other guys from the steakhouse. Cops came. The robbers ran away, Vic got hauled away.

I guessed right one time on a house that had the security sign but no alarm. A single woman lived there. Fifties, short dark hair. She left for work every morning about seven thirty. I went in the back door, ate cereal, cleaned up, then went to sleep in a guest room. I was always out before five. On the sixth day, I woke up at about noon and there she was, staring at me.

"Please don't call the police," I said. I got up slowly and straightened the bed covers, trying not to look at her.

"I thought it might be my husband. Hoped, anyway. I saw the Cheerios. They were almost gone one day and full the next."

"I replaced them."

"And you changed the alarm clock. I use this one sometimes because it makes me get out of bed to turn it off. Otherwise I go back to sleep. He left three years ago. I don't even know if he's alive." The tears started. She was blocking the doorway and I wanted very much to get through it, but the sobbing got worse and she was not going to move.

I hugged her. She just stood there. Arms limp. Eventually she said, "Thank you. That's enough."

"I'm very sorry," I said and I edged around her so I had a way out. "You should turn on that alarm. It's all rigged up. Probably worth the money. Not everyone will replace the Cheerios."

"I turned it off after he left. After a few months. He could never remember the code and I didn't want him to come back and not be able to get in."

"He'd probably just call you and complain, say, 'Why the hell's the alarm on?'"

"You talk like you know him."

Everybody knows him, but I did not want to say that. I could tell she was going to offer to let me come back, so I got out of there fast as I could without running.

Websites gave me an overview of the Runnymeade property, and the virtual house tour was still up on the listing realtor's site. Eight bedrooms, a ballroom, and a basketball court, indoors, to help the goons ward off boredom between kidnappings. I called ADT, claiming to be the landlord, and told them to reactivate the alarm system at nine P.M. I planned to be inside the house by then.

The mist reached critical mass and became a soft, light rain. The headlight beams scattered their power in the drops. Two young couples, teenagers, got out of a white BMW and came inside and took the booth next to mine at the Delta Diner. The girls were pretty, a little heavy, wearing shorts and sandals. The guys wore jeans. One had a small tattoo on his wrist. They had been to the movies, something scary, and they were still feeling the excitement. A girl said, "Why would she go back to the lagoons? I would never go to lagoons. Why do they even have lagoons anyway?"

A boy answered, "She heard the voices. She felt guilty. She thought she could help her friend."

The girl said, "There's always something in a lagoon that's going to hurt you. A creature or something."

Another boy said, "Not if you get out fast, or outsmart it."

The girl said, "Right. You know you're gonna slip or trip or get sucked into the muck. Why do they even have lagoons anyway? Can't they just be filled in?"

The other girl said, "I could see going, but not alone."

A girl and a boy said together, "Right."

The King's phone rang; Zoran calling. When his tirade died down I said, "I'm just waiting for them to contact me. I'm going to arrange to give them the rest of the money and then Maya will be freed." I said it loud enough for the teens to hear and they must have, because their talking stopped. Zoran went on a bit, but I would not tell him where I was or what the plan was, only that I was waiting for the other side to call.

The other side called fifteen minutes later. This time I spoke more quietly. I let them dictate the terms of the meeting. When they said they were not bringing Maya along, that she would be released later, I protested a bit for show. I was hoping they would pick a spot miles away, but they chose a restaurant just a mile from the diner. One hour.

As I was leaving, I heard one of the girls say, "Maybe we should call the police." I turned back and glared to give her a thrill.

The gate at Runnymeade opened and two black SUVs barreled through the mist. Their windows were dark, so I could not see how many men were in each one. I had plenty of time to slip through the gate before it closed. It was 8:50.

Two guesthouses stood to the right of the big house. I cut behind them, hoping I could avoid any motion-detecting lights near the front entrance. All the structures were made of light, chalky looking stone, with sharply slanted roofs. The main house spread out away from the guesthouses, then curled back, forming a J. Plenty of downstairs lights were on. The only upstairs light was at the far end of the house before the curl. At the end of the J, I found an unlocked door and I entered a small room furnished with wicker and cushions, a sun room.

I stepped across the room and waited for a full two minutes, just listening. The staircase was straight ahead. The lights were on in the hallway to my left and I thought I could hear a TV somewhere down that way. They had brought six goons to the failed exchange in the park. I was hoping six went out to meet me this time. I figured no more than four stayed behind at the house. I wanted to deal with as many of them as I could first, before I found Maya.

The hallway was so long it needed a moving walkway. I passed two doors on the right and two on the left. All were closed and I left them that way. Large action photos of the basketball player who owned the house lined the walls. His feet never touched the floor, so the pictures gave the impression he was skipping along on air.

The TV grew louder as I got closer. Its light flickered against the walls as the scenes shifted. Someone shouted on-screen and a man laughed in the room ahead of me. I stopped and leaned tight to the wall. I peeked in. An enormous television was playing some historical action movie.

A man's voice said, "Do come in, Mr. Hewitt. No need for caution anymore. Actually, there wasn't any need for caution at all. We've been watching you all along."

I checked behind me: Two goons in suits materialized down

the hall. I might have been able to take them and get away. But I did not want to get away yet.

I entered a large den. The man doing the speaking stood behind a love seat, made of beige fabric, which was perpendicular to the television. Maya was sitting on the love seat. This man was not the Mr. Clark I heard on the phone. This man had a singsong Welsh accent. He was tall and big: big chest, big belly growing out under the chest. His head was shaved. His cheeks were flabby. That combination made him look like a gigantic, overgrown baby. A baby who played rough; he wore a patch over his left eye. At first I thought he was holding a gun, but he jabbed his right hand toward the enormous TV and paused the movie that was on-screen.

The goons behind me closed in and positioned me in front of the love seat, in front of Maya. Her expression was indecipherable. I was looking for panic, pleading, pain, hope. But I must have been looking for the wrong things. I could not break through.

The bald man sat down next to Maya and crossed one leg over the other. He spread his arms across the back of the love seat and smiled as if to taunt me.

"I was watching Stanley Baker. Well, I was watching Stanley Baker and you alternately. Know him?"

"No." I looked at the TV. A thin-faced, dour looking leading man in a red British Army uniform, top button undone, was staring out into the distance at grassy hills. His dark hair was mussed up. He held his rifle casually in his left hand.

"Great actor. This is *Zulu*, one of his best roles. When I was a boy, I saw every Stanley Baker film. Mostly on TV by then. Sometimes sneaking into theaters. I wanted to be Stanley Baker. Joined the armed forces. But life isn't like the movies, is it? No, it is not. In the movies, the hero doesn't lose his eye. The hero's wounds always heal quickly on film. But I still enjoy a Stanley Baker film whenever I have the time."

I looked at the screen again. The real Stanley Baker looked the opposite of the man on the couch. "I can see the resemblance," I said.

He didn't smile. "Now about you, Mr. Hewitt. The alarm trick is a good one, though a bit unusual for someone with your résumé. Don't suppose you spent too much of your youth breaking into houses, did you? Not with that résumé. Here's a test. When you break into a house equipped with an alarm system, do you prefer to find an open or a closed circuit system?"

"When you kidnap women, do you prefer they struggle or do you prefer they pretend to like it?"

Maya's eyes flickered and her mouth tightened.

Stanley Baker said, "I enjoy a good lie, Mr. Hewitt, as much as the next man. A lie well told is a powerful tool, but like any tool, it must be used at the appropriate time to be most effective. I know who I am. I am comfortable with it. Comfortable enough to accept all the different aspects of my—"

"Oh, c'mon. It's a simple answer and no one cares what you say anyway. I was just asking to be polite."

He nodded and a fist landed hard in my lower back. Before I finished grunting and trying to straighten up, Stanley Baker resumed his speech about being who he is, virtues and all, like it or not. He droned on, entertaining only himself, holding all of us hostage. The goons must have heard it a thousand times. They were the kind of hostages who pretended to like it. Maybe by now, they convinced themselves they did like it. At last, Stanley Baker finished by saying, "So, of course, I prefer them to be afraid because that's the honest response. And honesty is essential for knowing who someone is."

I thought both responses were honest but decided not to press the point. Maya fell somewhere in between, detached, in the wings, waiting for her moment.

He went on. "Now, open circuit or closed?"

"I don't know."

Stanley Baker said, "Sure you do. You know the answer. I'll prove it." He nodded.

A goon hit me in the kidney again.

"That, by the way, is Mr. Clark, with whom you spoke on the phone."

I could not see the advantage in stretching this out. "An open circuit. I prefer to find an open circuit. I would, if I broke in anywhere."

"And why is that?"

I heard movement behind me. Two goons entered from the side nearest the front entrance. I figured they were the ones I saw leaving in the SUVs. That put eight of them in the room, plus Stanley Baker. I wasn't going to fight my way out.

"When you trip the alarm, the circuit closes, but you just have to snip the wire to reopen it," I said.

"You're right. You're absolutely right. I knew you knew. I just don't know how you knew, but I'll get to that in due time. All in due time. Those were great days, the days of breaking into houses. Responsible only for myself. Free. A free agent in the world of minor crime. Minor crimes and major dreams. I could dream of one day being like Stanley Baker. Ever see him in *The Criminal*? You must,

you really must. I used to ponder this question: Do we define ourselves by those crimes, or by the dreams? Well, we know the answer, don't we, you and I. I encourage all the boys to ponder that as
they proceed with their lives. Don't let the little crimes define you,
I say. I know you agree, or you wouldn't be head of an investment
firm. Oh well, just for future reference, I told the security company
to call me directly before turning the system on. Now, I see you
didn't bring the money."

"You could have started with that. I forgot the money," I said.

"No matter. I thought you might. We went to your car and
helped ourselves."

He nodded toward one of the goons behind me. I turned. The
goon held up my briefcase. But the briefcase is not what held me.
The goon's eyes seemed to be smiling at me, eyes I had seen before.
And he fit the description: shorter than me, thicker, dark complexion. The moment passed quickly and I tried to convince myself it
was wishful thinking. If it was Mask Man, then my cover was
blown. My cover was not blown, so it must not be him.

I turned back to Stanley Baker and said, "Does that mean you'll
let Maya go now?"

He was waiting for that. He slid his arm down around Maya's
shoulder. He didn't draw her close and she didn't move. "I have a lot
of questions to ask you, Mr. Hewitt," he said. "And it will take some
time. So I'm going to allow you one question, any question, which
I will answer as truthfully as I can. You have my word."

His fat baby face wobbled a bit. His lips reminded me of Play-
Doh after it rolled in your palms. Even the color looked like Play-
Doh. Maya gazed right at me. Did she want me to rescue her?
Should I have been looking for mockery, victory, contempt? She

had not turned to Stanley Baker once. I looked around the room, pretending to need time to decide on a question. I just wanted another look at the goon who might be Mask Man. I could not read him, either.

"Don't be shy now. Anything you want."

I looked once more at the real Stanley Baker, frozen in his heroic, painless pose on-screen. I understood him. He was precise and specific. I don't want to kill them; I will kill as many as I can: I am tired of this; I need more of this: I want to run away; I will never leave.

"All right. One question. When you read my résumé, did you use a monocle?"

"No." He said it flatly as if he were disappointed at missing the opportunity to tell the truth. "Now," he said. Goons held my arms. Another stepped in and rolled up my sleeve. I stared at Maya. Did she flinch or did she shrug as the needle went into my arm?

Questions flew at me, buzzed around, circled back, changed colors, held hands with each other, and squeezed. I answered each one willingly, for the first time in my life. The drug closed the circuit in me, pushing out more words than ever before. I was hungry for questions, more questions, because I wanted to talk and they gave me direction. Otherwise I might have talked about the taste of dust in Afghanistan, or killing people in caves, or the way Amy Petersen could go cross-eyed in fifth grade.

"Who backs your fund? Who pays you? Who is your boss? Who do you work with? Are you a Chinese agent? A Russian agent? How did you meet Maya?" Maya was there. Her tears were so close to me, I could feel them dripping into my eyes and taste them sliding off my lip. Stanley Baker pumped and the well gushed.

All of it about Robert Hewitt's life. None of it felt like lies. It was a story, the true story of a fake character. I didn't know any lies about Robert Hewitt. If they asked me about Rollie Waters, I would have had to lie and might have said too much and might have been caught. But they stuck to the résumé built by Major Hensel, who knew how to build one. I forced myself never to turn away and look at the Goon Who Might Be Mask Man. The thoughts that went with him had to be kept inside. I spewed out stories I had never imagined: the professor at Columbia who introduced me to the Chinese deputy U.N. ambassador at a private dinner in Harlem; camping in northern Syria while searching for Kongra-Gel leaders; turning away an investor I didn't trust in spite of his deep pockets. And then came the stories I had lived as Robert Hewitt: seeing Maya across the club, a dark beauty turning the corner of the room into the center of the room, riding in silence to the roadhouse beside her. I stopped there, worried that Stanley Baker would notice that I preferred silence. The King, Zoran, the money.

Stanley Baker was disgusted. He rose and shouted at the goons. I was still talking when the blow fell on the back of my head. Still conscious, I rolled onto my back.

The Goon Who Might Be Mask Man stared down at me, and there could be no doubt. I recognized him even without the mask.

16

The anvil attached to my neck could not be moved. Light darted at my eyes, so I closed them. My ears woke up sometime later. I'm sure it took only a few minutes for me to understand that the sound of a drill boring through the anvil was an alarm. A burglar alarm. An imaginary crane attached to my head helped me get up. The real Stanley Baker was still staring out at the enemy on the TV, rifle in hand, hair messed up. I found the remote and turned him off.

Voices shouted over the alarm, coming from the front door area. I went the other direction and up the stairs. The alarm stopped while I was searching the second bedroom. Outside, beside a police car, a security company car, and a Lexus sedan, a cop was speaking with two women in business suits. The security company man came out of the house and started talking. The cop seemed to be bored. He drove away. The security company man got one of the women to sign something and he left.

All the bedrooms were pristine, made up, including the master, which I assumed Stanley Baker had occupied. I couldn't find anything personal. Even the wastebaskets were empty.

The women in business suits were looking through the kitchen cupboards when I walked in.

"Good morning. You must be the realtors."

The taller one jumped. The shorter one, holding a clipboard and a pencil, shrieked. "What are you? Who are you?" the taller one said.

"Sorry. I guess I overslept."

"The house was supposed to be empty."

"Did Darrell tell you that?" I smiled and shook my head to indicate I thought ol' Darrell was a rascal. I went on and told them I stayed behind to make sure everything was left in order and they could find me in the guesthouses if they needed me. They promised to give my best to Darrell.

The first guesthouse I entered had a living room with another huge TV, a small kitchen, and a bathroom on the ground floor. Everything was neat and clean. Upstairs, there were two bedrooms, each with two twin beds. You could bounce a coin off them. The drawers were empty. There was nothing under either bed.

I didn't have to search the second bedroom. On the pillow on the bed closest to the door, spread out so I could not miss it, lay a knit hat that unfolded to become a mask. I had seen one before. I had one.

My head hurt for another reason: I couldn't understand Stanley Baker. He should have been wining and dining me, begging for a small part of what I had to give, instead of staging a fake kidnapping to grab the short money. I was an oil investor and he was in the business of scaring money out of oil investors. Maybe the coup was imminent and he felt he didn't have the time to squeeze me for more money. He would just settle for the quick pocket change.

Did Stanley Baker regard Maya as an honest hostage or not a hostage at all? Deciding Maya was complicit felt like an extension of jealousy. She didn't seem to be afraid: She should have been afraid. I had to allow the possibility that she held her expression so tight and veiled to hide her emotions from Stanley Baker, not just me.

Daisy didn't answer her phone. Major Hensel had not heard from her either. I entered my hotel room and realized that I hoped to find her there. She wasn't there, though, and she still didn't answer the phone. I called Darrell White's office and told them I was waiting for him at our breakfast meeting. They said he hadn't come in yet but they would leave a message on his cell phone. I took that to mean he wasn't picking up his phone either.

I took the elevator to the seventh floor of Daisy's building and walked down to the fifth. I didn't see anyone. I don't know if anyone saw me. I knocked on Daisy's door. No answer. Music played, too softly to make out what it was. I turned the knob and entered.

The music was coming from the bedroom: Barry White singing one of those late-night lovers' ballads. Two wineglasses and an empty bottle and another half-full bottle sat on the coffee table. Darrell's jacket hung neatly from the back of a dining chair. Daisy's sandals were next to the couch. The door to the bedroom was closed. Maybe they had a great night and were sleeping it off. I was going in anyway.

Darrel was a naked whale facedown. The bullet hole in the back of his head was caked with black coagulated blood, making it look more like a recently active volcano than a blow spout. Another bullet hole opened through his spine. Daisy was underneath him, also naked. Her arms were bent at the wrong angles and her legs were spread out wide as they would go. I went close. Her wig was askew. I bent close and saw that she was breathing.

Daisy gasped and her body jerked as I rolled Darrell off her. His chest was black and blue. Daisy was lucky the bullet had not gone all the way through him.

"My arm."

I lifted him off her arm but kept him on the edge of the bed. Daisy closed her eyes to deal with the pain. I pulled the sheet up to cover her. She gasped again. "Daisy, do you think you can walk?"

She shook her head, eyes still closed. "Leg feels broken. Arms broken." She sobbed briefly and caught it. I went into the bathroom. Daisy had a good collection of pills. The Percocet was expired, but it would have to do. I got a glass of water and helped her take three of the pills.

"I never took more than two before," she said. "Can you turn that off?" I turned off the music, then I made her take two more pills. I found a robe and managed to get her into it. She looked at Darrell's body, listing now at the edge of the bed, the whole time. "He was an all right guy. Kinda nice."

She was tiny, perfectly formed, and tough as she acted. I picked her up like a groom carrying a bride over the threshold. Her arms hung limp. I hoped the drug was kicking in but did not ask. As we left the bedroom, Daisy opened her eyes and looked back at Darrell's body. Her usually wide eyes squinted; I saw more fear than pain. "What about him?"

"I'll come back and take care of it."

"No."

I closed the bedroom door behind us. "I need your key."

"No." Louder this time.

I didn't understand it. I didn't think the pain was making her delirious. I spoke as calmly as I could. "I have to take you to the hospital. And I have to lock the door behind us."

"No."

"You don't want an ambulance, do you?"

She shook her head. "My keys are in my purse."

In the car, I said, "What's your real name? We'll use that at the hospital. There's going to be a police report on this. We don't want them going over to the apartment to investigate. At least not until I get the body out of there."

Daisy started to cry. We were near the hospital, but I slowed down and took a wrong turn and pulled over. I couldn't find a tissue, so I used my sleeve to wipe her eyes. She swallowed hard and faked a smile, an attempt to be Upbeat Daisy. It failed and she started talking in a flat, low voice.

"I can't use my real name. And if they go into that apartment, they'll find my fingerprints and they'll be sure I killed Darrell no matter what I say or how broken my bones are."

I was willing to let her stop there. Maybe someday I would hear the whole story over a drink. "Okay," I said. "You'll go in as Daisy. I'll make them think I did this. They'll be looking for me instead of going to the apartment." I started the car.

Daisy said, "No. Wait." I waited. "I killed a man, a colonel. We were having an affair. I was in the brig. I did it. No one will believe I didn't kill Darrell. Major Hensel saved me. I was on trial. He can't save me this time."

"That's why you didn't yell for help." It wasn't a question and she didn't answer. The Major got her off because he was able to explain to the Army that they didn't want to tell all the female troops that officers could beat and rape them and they had to take it. Maybe the Major explained to the Army that it did not want officers to think they could get away with it either. In that moment, watching Daisy embracing the pain and fighting her future, a familiar shiver of doubt shook me: Would I be as tough as she was? Major Hensel had a good eye. Daisy drifted off. I started the car and pulled out.

Before we went into the hospital, I asked, "Did you see the shooter?"

"He wore a mask."

I straightened her wig for her. She kissed me on the cheek. "You're okay when you're not a grump," she said.

"Tell them you just met me. It all happened at my apartment, somewhere across town."

The triage nurse was as suspicious of me as she should have been and I let that brew. I told her I was a neighbor and heard Daisy yelling and how many Percocet were in her. After a minute of acting like I was going to wait, I went toward the men's room and kept on through the hospital corridor and out a service door.

When I was sixteen, a sporting goods store in Big Bear hired me to stock shelves and clean up when I was living at Loretta's shelter for runaways. I had stayed with Loretta longer than anyone and we had grown close, closer than I had ever been with anyone. She wasn't like a mother to me, and not just a friend. I don't know what Loretta is to me; she's my safe zone. The store was a big place that carried everything from bicycles to bocce balls. I was grateful for the easy work and clear rules. Of course, I was interested in the system and how they caught the employees when they stole. Everything was tagged and would trip an alarm if it went through the sensors without being scanned. My supervisor, Rhys, was about ten years older than me, a skinny guy with zits. At closing time during my second week, Rhys offered me a ride back to Loretta's place. He walked out holding two boxes of shoes, basketball shoes. I was pretty sure he didn't pay for them, but I didn't say anything. He gave me a lift a couple of days a week, and every time, he took something from the store: clothes, fishing tackle, a tent. He never tried to hide it. Twice we saw the owner in the parking lot. Rhys waved.

One day I gave in. "How come you're not afraid of getting caught?"

Rhys said, "The trick is to act like nothing's wrong. They don't expect anyone who is stealing to wave and say good night. When the stuff arrives at the loading dock, I put it aside so it's never scanned in and never tagged. They'll never catch me."

That was one of the first times I understood there could be value in being Dan's son. If I were doing the stealing, the guy getting the ride home would have been carrying the stolen goods. Rhys was right about everyone's expectations and the benefit of boldness, but I knew somebody with such rudimentary understanding of stealing was going to get caught, so I stopped accepting the rides home. He got caught a few weeks later and tried to implicate me. The store owner came to Loretta. Loretta made him donate five tents and five camping stoves as penance for daring to accuse me.

I had no one to carry out Darrell's body for me and could think of no good way to hide it. Boldness was going to have to do. I parked

131

at the grocery store two blocks from Daisy's building and took a shopping cart up to her apartment. Darrell weighed at least two hundred and fifty pounds. There was no need to be gentle, and I had handled a few dead bodies, but this time I realized how much clothing helps. Darrell was as uncooperative in death as he had been in life. I pushed the cart next to the bed and managed to dump part of him in at a time. His ass barely fit and his legs hung over the end. I searched around Daisy's closet for a hat that would stay on my head and found a wide-brimmed straw job with cloth flowers attached. It had a chin strap.

Covering the body with a sheet would shift everyone's eyes to me, so Darrell was going for a ride in the buff. I pushed the cart out of the building and down the street as if I was taking my baby for a walk. At one point, I ran my fingers through his hair to fix the prow. A secluded spot between dumpsters at a construction site looked like a good spot to leave him. The police could deal with getting him out of the cart. I walked away, still wearing the hat.

17

The big gate at the King's house opened and I drove the Honda up to the house. Two goons were waiting for me. As soon as I closed the car door, they stepped beside me and held my arms.

"Guys. Not necessary," I said. I was tired of goons. They did not let go. I stopped walking. "Please. I don't want to be manhandled. I don't want to fight. I don't want to hear a long list of lies. I just want to go inside and find out what the hell happened to my million dollars. Is that unreasonable?"

They were silent for a moment, unsure how to respond. Then the goon on my left said, "Yeah. That's not gonna happen." And they started to pull me.

Gill appeared at the door. He almost shook his head. They let go.

Zoran waited in the living room, still simmering. The vein in his forehead wiggled like a worm struggling to escape. All he could come up with was "How dare you come back here?"

"Calm it down," I said. "You might evaporate. I'd like to see the King. Now."

Zoran's camel eyes lowered as if locking in the memory of this moment for later retribution. Instead of spitting at me, he turned abruptly and walked out of the room. I was left alone with Gill, and the furniture and the lighting fixtures and the walls. Gill surprised me by speaking before the walls got around to it.

"Turn around."

I was prepared for a fight.

Gill said, "You left me holding the bag in the park. I didn't like that."

"Next time I do it, don't let the other side run away with the money."

I put my hands on the back of a chair, ready to make that the first weapon. It was a good solid chair, which was going to shatter like balsa when it came in contact with Gill. But I didn't need the chair.

Gill said, "Next time?" And his mouth curled slightly, lips closed. His eyes seemed to sharpen as he did it: He looked slightly mad. Roid rage came to mind. But the smile was too heavy for him. He let go and the eyes reverted to their flat challenging intensity.

Zoran reentered. "This way," he sniffed. He led me through the garden, past the gazebo, pool house, and pool. Behind the green screen at the tennis court, a short figure all in white stood in one spot. In spite of the inaction, the sound of tennis balls bouncing and being hit came in a slow, regular beat. Zoran followed me inside.

The King stood across the court, in tennis whites, playing

against a ball machine. He did not stop, so I stepped over to the machine and turned it off. The King held up his racket to stop Zoran from turning it back on. A servant, whom I had not noticed, waited in the far corner with a towel that he delivered to the King. At last, the King came around the net.

"Robert, I'm relieved to see that you are okay."

"Why? Didn't you get your share of the money? Looking for more?"

"Please, let me explain. Come . . ."

It was back to the gazebo for tea and pastries. I waited for the King to have a few bites. Zoran stood at his side.

"You were most generous yesterday, Robert, in offering to ransom Maya," the King said as he finished licking his lips of the sugar. "I believe I owe you an explanation, and perhaps it will answer some of the questions you must have. Maya's kidnapping was genuine. But the kidnapper was not unknown to me. Nevertheless, my concern for her safety was genuine."

He stopped. He sipped his tea. He had shown one card in his hand and thought I was going to fold.

"What about now? Are you still concerned? He still has her."

"I have spoken with her."

I knew I could frighten it out of him, but Gill was around for moments like those. The smugness that came from withholding information, the keeping of royal secrets, was probably a big portion of the kingly feeling. Insults would not crack that barricade. But, if the secrets were known, a weak man like the King might want to commiserate.

"King, I know this is the guy who is backing you. Backing your bid to take over. He's got a basket full of American officers and maybe a few Brits, too, on his payroll. You believe he can make it happen, so you don't want to piss him off."

The King looked to Zoran, who was shaking his head to show he had not revealed any of this to me.

"I was there last night, King. It isn't hard to figure it out. You feel like a prisoner a bit, too, I bet."

"Very much, Robert. Very much." He was excited. He wanted to share the story of his bondage with someone who would not judge it shameful. Gill came into the gazebo. I feared his presence might inhibit the King, but I forgot that it hardly mattered what servants heard.

"He is Maya's ex-husband. At first, as with many partnerships, our goals were congruent. More recently it has become clear to me that I am to be a figurehead. Maya has been encouraging me to break from him. But he has the finances. I trusted this man with the money advanced me by the oil companies. In turn, he has placed me here in Houston and made me into his salesman, soliciting more contributions from the oil companies, all of which has gone to him. I have very little of my own. It was a bargain I made believing he would be able to install me on the throne of my forefathers so I might fulfill my destiny, and the unification of Kurdistan could begin."

I wasn't in the mood for another video, so I stopped the unification train before it picked up too much steam. "What's his name?" I said.

The King fluttered his eyebrows and counted his fingers and searched the clear sky for rain clouds. That one was staying in the royal vault.

"Without a name it's just a good story, but not all that convincing." I knew Zoran wasn't going to cooperate, so I turned to Gill. "How about you? You're not afraid, are you?"

"Afraid of . . . ?"

"This guy. The devil behind the throne."

"No. Not afraid of him," Gill said as if the thought never occurred to him before.

"Then what's his name?"

"John Bannion. Johnny."

I turned back to the King. He looked like he was considering diving under his chair to avoid the lightning Johnny Bannion was sure to hurl. Eventually, he realized that was not going to happen right away so he puffed up his chest and tried a little flattery to blind me. "Maya has been looking for help for some time. She thought you might be the person. You have the money and the confidence. And the connections. She was very hopeful and I agreed. Unfortunately, John somehow understood our intent to ally with you. He wanted to demonstrate his control, so he has taken Maya with him. She will be safe as long as I cooperate."

"Where's the chauffeur?"

"With Maya."

I shook my head. "I didn't see him and no one referred to him."

Zoran looked worried. The King smiled, "Arun will stay near Maya."

"Somebody in this room tipped Bannion that I was coming."

"That's impossible. I assure you we all wanted you to succeed. We did not betray you." He spread out his arms, palms up. I expected him to pull up his sleeves, too.

"Somebody here did betray me."

"Robert, please."

"I'll make it easier for you. I called the security company and asked them to turn on the alarm. They called Darrell White because I was calling from a number they didn't know and they wanted to confirm the order. Darrell White couldn't get in touch with Bannion, but he knew I was on the loose. He called here. And somebody here called Bannion. He knew I was coming. That's the way it was and there's no other way."

I had already decided who did it. Zoran's hump grew rounder, and when he licked his lips, I thought I glimpsed a tongue that could stretch across the room. The King spoke in his native language, asking Zoran if he did it. Zoran replied that they were lucky there wasn't a shoot-out; Maya could have been killed. The King said something I wasn't sure of, but it sounded like he was agreeing.

"No one here did that, Robert," he said.

"How is Bannion financing his coup? My million won't go very far."

"As I explained, the oil companies. Just as you have allied with the Kongra-Gel."

It did not matter to me if he knew about the money in the graves or not. I wanted another bit of information.

"Maybe it's okay with you, King, if Maya stays with Bannion, but I paid a million dollars to get her out and I want my money's worth."

"Please, Robert, for Maya's sake, I urge you to reconsider."

Shaming the King was tempting, but too easy. He was hostage to Bannion whether Maya was free or not. He was hostage because it was easier and safer and it was a sure way to keep the dream intact, far from the danger of becoming a reality. I knew he would not answer me, but I gave him dibs.

"Where is she?"

"You are entering into matters beyond your understanding."

"Well, King, if I only dealt with things I understood, I'd be a hermit." I turned to Gill. "Where is she?"

Gill moved his eyes to the King and then to Zoran and then back to me. With all that activity, I knew he was excited. He said, "I'll go with you."

The King said, "Mr. Gill, I forbid it."

Zoran came forward fluttering his camel eyes in lieu of spluttering out a lot of angry sounds. He and the King stared at Gill, waiting for a response to the command, but that just meant they had delved into matters they did not understand. I let the silence run a little because I remembered the King moved slowly in moments like this. When I thought he had all he could take, I got up and moved close to Zoran and spoke to him in Dari, which I knew he would understand. The message was this: If you warn them this time, I'll kill you.

Zoran jolted upright and his long eyelashes brushed his eyebrows.

I turned to Gill. "Ready?"

I packed, showered, and lay on the couch for a nap. A cop-knock woke me. I counted out the seconds until the notes repeated. At eight, the knock came again. Though I have never been able to articulate the characteristics that distinguish a cop-knock from others, I enjoy holding on to the belief, fantasy or not, that I can tell when a cop touches my door. This time I was cheating: I had been expecting the FBI for a while.

Agent Hanrihan looked as if he had been beamed in from

Chicago; he wore the same blue blazer and beige pants and striped tie. His hair fell over his forehead in just the same way. Agent Sampson had changed into a blue skirt and a beige sleeveless blouse. I sat them down in the living room and made a show of closing the bedroom door before joining them. I asked if they wanted me to order up coffee. They declined. I ordered coffee for three anyway.

Sampson took the lead this time. She was calm, encouraging, confidential; we were teammates, comrades; she had forgotten Hanrihan's aggressive hostility and I should, too. She showed me a scrap of paper with a name and the name of a graveyard in Kentucky, handwritten, all in capitals, in pencil. Hanrihan kept eyeing the bedroom door like a cat that heard scratching on the other side. The effort it took to play backup was making him sweat.

"We found this at Frank Godwin's apartment. The grave was raided. Do you know anything about this?" Sampson said.

"Why would I?"

"You knew Frank."

"I don't know anything about that slip of paper or who attacked the grave. Based on conversations with Frank and others, I identified the grave in Havre as one that might have the wrong remains in it. I went to see him again to ask some more questions." I sounded like a lying call-center clerk trying to placate an angry customer.

Sampson took time to do some thinking. Hanrihan had already finished all his thinking for the day. "Why are you here, then?" He sneered as he said it: a sniveling prosecutor thinking he has trapped a witness. I was in no rush to answer. Hanrihan's eyes drifted to the bedroom door. A different kind of knock sounded. I opened the door for room service and told the waiter to put the tray on the coffee table.

Hanrihan stood. "Who's in there?" he said.

"That's not your business."

The waiter held the pen out for me to sign the check. His head held still, but his wide eyes were moving between the agents and me. He wanted no part of this. Sampson shook her head slowly as if to warn Hanrihan. He ignored her.

"I'm going to see for myself."

"Bill, leave it alone," said Sampson.

"Sir, could you sign, please," said the waiter.

Hanrihan stepped toward the bedroom and I stepped in front of him.

"I could make you hit me and be rid of you forever. But I won't do it. Because I want you around."

"You do?"

"Yeah. Because you're so stupid."

Hanrihan's back was to Agent Sampson or he would have seen her shrug and nod in agreement. The waiter put the pen down next to the check and moved quickly for the door. Hanrihan smirked and stepped around me and opened the bedroom door. I watched Sampson, expecting her to get up and follow him. She sat back like someone intending to turn on the tube and hang out.

"I don't get it, Lieutenant," she said.

"What's that?"

"I don't get why a smart, aggressive, angry Marine like you isn't in a war zone. Why he's digging up the dead."

"Therapy."

Hanrihan reappeared. "Where are you going? His bags are packed. That's why he didn't want me to go in there."

"He closed the door so you would go in there," Sampson said.

Hanrihan blinked away that ray of light. "Where are you going?" He said it slowly to make it sound threatening.

"Where are you from?" I said in the same way.

Most cops would ignore that, stick to the business of getting an answer to their question. Hanrihan jolted his head back like a rooster. Maybe he didn't like where he came from.

Sampson spoke up. "What would you do, Lieutenant, if you wanted to know who killed Frank Godwin?"

"I do want to know."

"Then help us out. How would you proceed?"

It was a good trap. I didn't know how much she knew. If I led them too far astray, she would know to focus on me.

"First I would tell surfer Sid to stop guzzling the salt water and leave me alone. Then I would get to work identifying the body that came out of the grave in Havre."

Hanrihan kept guarding the bedroom door. I wanted to ask him to take my bags down to the lobby.

"We're working on that," Sampson said. "But I don't see what it gets us. Thing is, as soon as the shooting stopped, you rushed to see Godwin. You could have called. You could have waited a day. But you thought someone else might get to him first."

"Anything else?"

"Not until you answer that."

"Find out whose body it was. Then we'll have something to discuss."

I didn't have to provoke Hanrihan. He was on a timer. The

threats started and the insults. Sampson saw right away that there would not be any progress, so she got him out of there, and when I set out for the airport to meet Gill, they followed me, letting me know it from the start. I used the time to check in with Major Hensel. I told him only one lie: I did not yet know the puppet master's name.

18

ill took the car keys. "I'll drive," he said. I did not know if he wanted to show he knew his way around, or if he wanted to stress that he did not trust me.

The flight to Baghdad and the waiting for flights added up to more than thirty hours, and over the course of those long trudging hours, Gill began to open up. He did not reveal details about where to find Bannion or what their relationship was. Instead, he showed feelings and voiced opinions. The subtext was that he was more than mere muscle; he had brains and energy. Preconceptions had constrained his potential. His frame was a cage.

"I'm much more than a bodyguard to the King."

"What kind of stuff did you do for him?" I tried to sound like I didn't care.

"They're foreigners. They don't know the first thing about how to navigate the U.S. All those servants have to be brought over. The King is a company."

Lesser men reaped rewards while he stood guard, but that was going to change. The King was exempt based on his lineage. "Some things can't be changed," Gill explained. "I understand that." He seemed to be bragging about that insight. Bannion was either a worthy rival or an example of the kind of man Gill would soon surpass; the assessment bounced around. But Gill was just as worthy. He was brawn and brains. Maybe the flights and the waiting wore on me. We were halfway across the ocean by the time I realized he was pitching me. I was a wealthy potential backer.

It was clear from the way he handled things upon landing that he knew Baghdad well. We skirted the town and headed north toward Erbil. I did not sleep. The baking desert air and the clear undiluted sunlight evaporated the Houston mist from my system. I felt easy, alert, sharp, and relaxed, at home in the desert I had never seen.

A small convoy of military trucks came toward us on their way to Baghdad. Gill was careful not to show interest.

I asked, "Do you have a plan?"

"Why don't you just sit back and wait until you're told what to do." Landing in Iraq had stirred up his arrogance. We might have reached Finland before he revealed any information.

"What's your gripe with Bannion?" I said.

"How did you contact the PKK? That's a neat trick."

I shrugged. I was sure he knew where to find Bannion and that was all I wanted from him. And I was sure I would have to try something other than occasional quips to get anything out of him.

"Tell him you plan to storm the castle," said Dan.

"Tried that. I have no plan."

"That's the best plan. Opens you up to possibilities. I was fishing down in Baja once. With Greta. Remember Greta?"

"Greta, yes. She wanted me gone." I did remember Greta and I remembered the story that was coming, but a good Dan story was

new each time I heard it. I could measure my progress in the world by how many facets I had never noticed before.

"Greta was a one-man kind of woman. We were out on a charter with three guys from Cleveland and one of them didn't know that about her. He started throwing his money around, showing off for Greta. He paid for the charter and demanded we join them the following day for more. Champagne on board.

"I had no plan, but I knew something would pop up once the picture developed a bit. The big shot, Mr. Cleveland, revealed that he was in the auto parts business. That was good news because I knew where there was a chop shop nearby. The plan took shape from there. I told him I was in a similar business and that was one of the reasons for my trip down to Baja. Greta seemed a little surprised to hear that, but she kept quiet.

"I left Greta to entertain Mr. Cleveland and his entourage while I went out and found a kid to steal two of the newest cars he could find and deliver them to the chop shop. The kid claimed the going rate was five hundred dollars each, and I let him overcharge me. It wasn't the right time to shop around. I bought the chop shop owner a couple of beers while his guys took the cars apart. The next day, I escorted Mr. Cleveland down to see the operation and to get a sense of the high quality stuff he could pass off as new back home.

"Though the prices for the parts were low low low, I bargained hard. Demanded fifty thousand dollars to buy in and an initial fifty-thousand-dollar order paid in advance. And, when the chop shop guy came in, I made a point of lying to him about the amounts I was demanding so Mr. Cleveland would think I was cheating my partner. Early next morning, Mr. Cleveland was at the chop shop making a deal with the owner to cut me out of the deal. He transferred the money and paid cash, of course, to get a discount. The chop shop owner split with me and I split for Phoenix."

"Almost a clean getaway," I said. "What about Greta?"

"Almost clean. Two days back home and the final phase of the plan was stalled. That's when I needed your help."

"I never heard this part."

"I took away your bicycle on some trumped-up charge. You helped by throwing a fit. That night before getting into bed, Greta got to the point. She was a one-man sort of woman and she didn't like fishing and she didn't like Mexico and she didn't like it that I had a business down there. I acted as sad as I knew how and offered to pay for the ticket to Cleveland."

"Because you knew she already had it in hand."

I had no Greta, and Gill was nothing like Mr. Cleveland. Maybe the PKK was my chop shop. Dan's style did not include direct lessons, which too closely resembled lectures. Dan's mission was to delight, not teach. Even in death, even as a ghost, even as an unwelcome intruder, a lingering wound, a blight, a raw nerve, Dan's aim was to charm, always to charm so that the listener would be oiled and eager to be included in the next adventure. I was going to have to work on getting Gill to open up. He wouldn't start conversations, but maybe he liked to interrupt.

"I know people in government," I said. "Some people not in government who might be aware of Bannion and might be persuaded to get involved. The government people can pressure him. We could get them to work with Baghdad to revoke his visas and the visas of his goons." I went on, making it up, and the worse and less convincing it got, the better it was.

After a few miles, Gill pursed his lips and winced and cut me off. "You have money. That's what people want from you. People here. Don't think about persuading. I'll do that. You think about spending. And no more tricks." And then he switched tones to sentimental. "More than two years since I've been here. I miss it. I like being around the Kurds. Erbil is going to be a great city. Where do you usually stay?"

Major Hensel had counseled me on the hotel issue. "At the International, not far from the Citadel."

We approached Kirkuk but stayed on the ring road and never entered the city. Traffic slowed. Two armored vehicles and many military jeeps lined the southbound shoulder: an Iraqi Security Forces checkpoint. By the time I finished scrutinizing that, we reached a matching situation on our side of the road. But we faced different uniforms: Peshmergas, the Kurdish Regional Guard Brigade.

"This is the line," Gill said. "They won't call it a border. But it's a border."

Kirkuk had oil. The Kurds claimed it, Baghdad held it. I watched the action at the Iraqi checkpoint across the road as we crept forward. Most cars were waved through quickly. Closed trucks were ordered off to the side for further inspection, but I didn't see anything too severe. Weary contempt and tense boredom hung like capes on the soldiers on both sides. They had to look, but they dreaded seeing anything. To leave the realm of routine could mean injury or death. It looked like every checkpoint I had ever passed through. The ISF soldiers paid most of their attention to the Kurdish forces. Suspicion clogged the flow. The Peshmergas asked us where and why, in English. Gill told them Erbil and business.

I had to assume I was more prisoner than partner, assume that

Gill was now or had been a Bannion goon. I began to regret showing off my Dari in front of Gill at the King's house because he would figure I had Arabic, too. Until I knew better, I would assume Gill had Arabic, too.

High desert flowers grew in defiant patches. Mountains vague as low storm clouds loomed far ahead like bruises on the horizon. Then the cranes, skeletons, more numerous than at the port of Houston, popped up. Erbil.

A jumble of languages beyond Arabic and English filled the hotel lobby. Russian, French, Spanish, German, Hindi, something that I guessed was Swedish. Goons like Gill, oilmen like me, Kurds like Zoran and the King swirled like bubbles in beer. There were women. None like Maya.

Robert Hewitt, esteemed guest returning, was greeted with heartfelt apologies and extra drinks and services offered as compensation for lack of available suites. Major Hensel's foresight at work. We accepted two rooms. Gill took the one on the eighth floor. I took one on the tenth. He did not like the arrangement. We were oilman and bodyguard disputing in the lobby, eliciting knowing shrugs from anyone with the time to notice. I carried my own bag. Two goonlike creatures skulked in close conference in the corner opposite the elevators. Their eyes grew wide and their ears went back like excited teenagers spotting a sports star. They recognized Gill.

Gill and I agreed to meet in the lobby in two hours and Gill would show me Bannion's headquarters. I washed up, stripped down, and sat in half lotus, steps in removing the grime of the journey and the tension of being always on guard in Gill's company.

On this day, it was night at the farmhouse in my vision. Just a curved sliver of moon balanced on an invisible shelf off to the right. The swing sat still and the curtain hung straight and limp. I wanted to stay outside and let it all fall into place. But I kept moving closer and closer and I was through the window with ease before I could stop.

Voices drew me toward the dining room. I peeked in. Candles were lit on the table and the mantel and the windowsills, and in the window on the far side, I saw my reflection. The main voice sounded like Dan's, but I could not see him. "He wanted to be like Stanley Baker," it said. Someone chuckled. The voice went low. A woman said, "I want you to meet him. Come tomorrow at noon."

The kitchen was dark and clean, unused, the way I remembered, and outside the low hump hills were just a shade darker than the sky. I watched them for a while, searching for movement but could not see any. Then I was in front again and out the door, and there was a welcome mat I had never noticed before and a single bare bulb. The upper floor would not appear. I knew I was in the wrong place but let the vision stay as it was. I looked through the window, through the sheer curtain. Dan was entertaining a dark-haired young woman at the dining room table. But I could not see her face.

I decided to stop trying.

Major Hensel called. "A man was found dead in the trunk of a Lincoln town car parked at your hotel. Would you know anything about that?"

He described Arun. I told him my fingerprints would be all over the car. "How was he killed?"

"Don't know yet. There were no bullet or knife wounds. What about Darrell White?"

"I didn't kill him, either."

"Is there anyone else you didn't kill? Anyone I should know about?"

"Not yet." I told him I was closing in on the puppet master. He asked me to keep in touch.

The two goons who recognized Gill lounged self-consciously on leather chairs at the outer edge of the lobby bar. I watched them from the mezzanine for a minute before descending the staircase. They tried not to stare at me as I walked past them and took a seat behind them. I ordered tea. Every minute or so, one of them found a reason to swivel and sneak a glance at me.

Gill got off the elevator, stepped away, and scanned the area. He marched toward me, passing close to the goons, never glancing at them. The goons did not come over for an autograph. Instead, they dug money from their pockets, slapped it on the table, and rushed for the exit.

They followed us.

19

We walked south, away from the Citadel and city center. After a couple of turns, we were in a residential district of small, well-kept homes behind stone walls and iron gates. Gill never looked behind, but he said, "Can you lose one of them?" I said I could. "Okay. The indoor mall near the Citadel, third floor, one hour."

He turned at the next corner and I went straight. I crossed a wide boulevard clogged with traffic and saw a hotel about one hundred yards ahead. I went inside so I could find out what kind of follower this guy was: Did he want to know who I met with, or was he satisfied to know my destination?

Speaking Arabic, I asked the front desk clerk for a guest: Diyar. The clerk looked around to see if anyone was watching him. "That is the last name?" he asked cautiously.

"No last name," I said.

He excused himself and went into a back room. An older guy with a better suit came out and asked if he could help me. He spent some time pretending to check the computer and pretending it was slow. Eventually, a thin guy in his fifties came up behind me. He wore a tight black T-shirt with glittery lettering saying L.A. LAK-ERS underneath a cheap brown pinstripe sport coat. His hair was a hopeful comb-over. Someone must have borrowed his pencil mustache.

He wanted to converse in English. "Excuse me, sir. Could you identify yourself, please?" I told him who I was. "I am with the Asayish. We are a police force here." He did not offer to show an ID or a badge. We sat next to each other in uncomfortable chairs in the small lobby. He had failed the courses in menacing and bullying at secret police school. "You can call me Eddie," he said. "You inquired about a man called Diyar. May I ask why?"

"A friend asked me to."

"Your friend wanted to find Diyar here?" He raised both eyebrows and turned his head halfway to express his skepticism.

"I'm thinking now that perhaps he was playing a joke on me. Who is this Diyar?"

Eddie could not discuss that, but he seemed to believe my explanation. I complimented his English. He had lived in northern New Jersey, working at a dry cleaner. He liked New Jersey but longed to live in Los Angeles. He pulled back his coat to display his T-shirt fully. The cleaner lost his business. Eddie's younger brother worked in Erbil in the Regional Government and hooked Eddie up with the Asayish. The work was easy and he met such interesting people.

The follower entered. He stopped when he saw us.

"Is that your friend?"

"Yes."

"He is not your friend. You must not ask for Diyar anymore."

The follower walked out. Eddie and I chatted for a few minutes more. He gave me a business card. "Maybe you'll need some introductions in Erbil."

I found a taxi and asked the driver to take me to any big hotel other than the International. He was delighted to be able to make the choice.

Traffic lurched and the driver gabbed nonstop in Arabic. He guessed I was Italian and I let him think that. He turned to politics and the current situation in Erbil, where the two opposing political parties controlled their own security forces. It reminded him of ancient Rome when armies were loyal to their generals rather than the state. The refrain blamed the Americans for pulling out, the verses included the need to secure control of Kirkuk and its inclusion in the glorious Kurdish future, the corruption of the Baghdad government, the extremism of the rebels, the absolute need for reform in Erbil. His cousin was in the Asayish, the security forces, a combined FBI, CIA, and police swat squad that operated in Kurdish regions and in the Kurdish sections of Kirkuk. One moment his cousin was a scoundrel on the take and a bully, the next moment he was a brave patriot.

At a stoplight, I glanced across a small park and saw a large tree with arms, legs, and ears: Gill. Two Iraqis wearing sport coats stood in front of a bench and faced him. They were shaking their heads and gesticulating to prove their resolve. Gill's right hand flashed up and slapped one of the men on the cheek. It hurt. The man staggered a bit and plopped down on the bench like a scolded child. The other man pulled a pistol.

The light changed and the driver started. "Wait," I said in a gruff whisper, as if Gill might hear me, as if it might disturb the pantomime. The driver hit the brakes.

Gill put out his right hand, palm up. His shoulders tensed, as spooky a movement as a big cat crouching. The man with the gun looked to his partner. Then he handed over the gun. Gill had won. A car behind us honked. My driver started. I turned to watch. Gill raised the gun and smashed it across the man's face.

The driver had not stopped his screed. He got around to the diabolical Iranians and, of course, the real devils, the original land-lords of hell, the ones ruining all life on the planet from their tiny strip of desert between Syria and Egypt.

"Where can I buy a gun?" I asked.

Another cousin sold guns that worked, surplus American weapons only. Before we reached the hotel, the driver told me we were being followed. I told him that was okay.

At the hotel, I thanked him and asked if I could find a taxi near the service entrance. He understood. Security was tight there and I would have to walk to the end of the parking lot, where he would wait. I paid him in dollars and gave him an extra twenty-dollar bill. His mouth fell open and his eyes got wide with embarrassment. "I didn't know you're American," he said.

"I'm Israeli."

He gulped, like a man facing a bear. I waved off his excuses and told him I was grateful for his honesty. I tore a hundred-dollar bill and gave him half of it to make sure he showed up on the other side of the hotel.

The follower followed. I passed through the lobby into the restau-rant, almost empty, into the kitchen where it was prep time. Nobody questioned me. A linen delivery was coming in at the loading dock as I went out. Two security men looked me over but did not rise from their chairs. My taxi pulled up before I reached the end of the lot.

From the back of the taxi, I watched the follower, frozen among the rows of dusty sedans with the realization that he had no good options. He dashed back toward the service entrance. That brought the security men out of their seats to block his way.

The cabbie dropped me in the city center. The walkways were filled with tourists strolling along with merchants and shoppers and men doing business, and those hoping to find business. Men strolled arm in arm. Some women wore burkas, but many did not. A few let their hair flow. Fountains splashed into shallow pools connected by bridges.

The Citadel sits like an ancient uncle, venerated and avoided, at the head of the table. It's a man-made, almost round mound about one hundred feet high surrounded by stone walls, mostly crumbling, some restored. If you gaze at it for more than a few seconds, someone will inform you that it is more than six thousand years old and has been continuously inhabited. Pretending you don't understand them doesn't help because they change languages and try again. I approached the southern gate. Merchants selling rugs, Kurdish flags, mementos, colorful paintings of great Kurds and other scenes that meant something to Kurds, and more rugs and more flags, formed a gauntlet. I passed through without too much interference.

The Citadel looked like a good place to avoid running into Gill. I had no good reason to meet him on time, if at all, and plenty of good reasons not to. Learning some of the ways he went about finding me would help me lose him later. Maybe if he got riled up, he would open up about who he was and what he wanted.

The road curled upward between the ancient stone walls that held back the more ancient stone hillside. Once I passed the lone antiques shop, no one was around: a ghost town. Near the top, I paused to look back at the city, muffled though still close, and the moonscape stretching far to the east, and Iran. Close around me was a warren of stone rooms, long abandoned, a step above cave dwellings. I plunged deeper into the maze.

The quiet was absolute. The walls rose high enough that the town was no longer visible and I could only use the sun as a guidepost. It was still more than thirty degrees above the horizon. A flagpole stood near the center of the mound, marking a police outpost. I slowed down yards away. A fat cop slept on a bench in the shade of an awning.

I turned up an alley and then into another one, just wandering and considering the possibilities of what I might face.

The voice said, "Hey, Rollie."

No one was in front of me or behind. I thought it was an illusion or that I had spoken out loud. But I recognized the voice. I looked into the nearby rooms, but the slanting shade drew soft curtains of darkness across the entrances. I waited. A boot, then another, showed at the edge of the room behind me. Two arms. The boots moved forward and the face emerged into the light.

Mask Man.

He removed his sunglasses and, as if remembering his original intention, turned up both palms to show he held no weapon. "I thought we should talk before things heat up," he said. I wanted him to put the sunglasses back on to hide the manic look behind his eyes. His attempt at sincerity exaggerated his strangeness.

"Start with who you are."

"I thought you knew." He said it apologetically the way a friend reveals a party he forgot to invite you to.

"I know you're the guy in the mask who killed Frank Godwin and you're one of Bannion's goons."

He was puzzled by what I said, and his expression puzzled me, too. I was right and I was wrong. I did know him from somewhere else, somewhere before Wisconsin and Houston.

"Well, yeah, y'know I had to kill Frank, or Bannion never would have kept me on. That's what I want to talk to you about. I think we should be partners. I've been studying you and how you operate and I've learned a lot and I think we'd make a perfect team."

"What's your name?"

Again, he was surprised that I had to ask. "Victor . . . Victor Kosinski." He put out his hand and I shook it. He smiled. He was a figure from a nightmare who appears randomly, referring to events that hung just beyond my memory. I fought the impulse to place him so I could focus on what he was saying there on that eternally crumbling hill. "Bannion has the money. At least most of it. I don't even know how much. He keeps it in his vault here. I can't get it alone. You can't, either. But together . . ."

Victor Kosinski had the zany enthusiasm that television ads and amateurs associated with salesmanship: salesmanship done the opposite of the way Dan did it, salesmanship that came from self-help books about positive thinking, books that explain that you can have anything you want by simply wanting it a lot.

I knew this guy.

"Bannion is planning something, something big. It's gonna happen soon, tomorrow night, maybe before that. I don't know what. Only his inner group knows."

"You're not part of the inner group?"

"I'm pretty new. I'm like you anyway, y'know, never really part of the inner group." He paused to let that insult sink in. "There are seven core guys who have been with him a long time. We'll probably have to kill them all. But that won't be a problem. I figure there's at least seventy-five million in there. What do you think?"

I thought: I should kill him right here. Small, shaking, birdlike Loretta would have done it if she could and never looked back. Dan would have found a way to get out of town. Victor Kosinski was Myron the Maniac, and I was transfixed, fascinated to find out I was his role model. I should have killed him, but I had to know more.

"Seventy-five million sounds about right to me," I said.

"Can you crack a safe? Otherwise we'll have to use C-4. I can get plenty, but it makes a mess."

"Some safes."

"I knew I did the right thing in Wisconsin. Not killing you, I mean."

I did not feel like thanking him. A million questions floated in front of me, but the answers wouldn't come from asking. He had the advantage in this "I know-you know-I know-you know" continuum and would keep it until I closed the loop by figuring out where he fit into my past.

He had no plan other than to wait for the action, meet at Bannion's compound, and take advantage of the chaos. We would have the advantage of surprise; no one would anticipate our partnership. He did have information that I believed: The King was coming into Erbil that night, and Bannion was going to have me picked up and brought to him sometime soon.

"He wants to be in business with you, too," Victor said, and he found that funny.

"Fifty-fifty?" I said.

"Sure."

His intensity was repellent and captivating at once. He was an ostentatious TV preacher, a crazed junkie ranting at the bus stop. I could not help staring, looking for the key, listening for that clue that would help me understand.

I made a guess: "What about Gill?"

"Oh, don't worry about Gill. He thinks I'm going in with him. But I'd much rather be partners with you." His eyes were backlit by an evangelical madness, bright even in this bright sunlight. "And you'll get the girl out of this, too. Unless you want to give her to me. This is going to be great."

Trying to match Victor's mixture of enthusiasm and insanity was futile. That recipe can't be faked. I had tried numerous times through the years of juvie hall, street life, and Marines, but the falseness always made me self-conscious, always felt transparent. I knew I was a few degrees this side of sane and suspected that it showed up as weakness. The solution was to agree quietly, as if I had deep, silent currents sweeping me to the edge of the waterfall. We could argue later about who got to ride in the barrel.

"I came for the money. I think you know that," I said.

He smiled and nodded. "You leave first. I'll wait here."

And I remembered where I had heard that before.

The poppy fields were still green, before the flowering, when I arrived in Farah Province at the end of my first tour. We found him sitting alongside the road from Bala Buluk to the capitol on my first patrol. He was thin, scrawny, with long hair and a beard: a hippie hitchhiker who got dropped off at the wrong exit. He was high from sampling the local product. "I don't mind needles, not afraid of needles," he said. "But won't touch one around here. The Taliban soak them in curdled pig's blood. You have to be smart. Outthink them."

We loaded him into our vehicle. He looked me up and down for about thirty seconds. "Simmons . . . Sam Simmons," he said, with an emphasis on "Sam" making him sound like a drugged-out James Bond. He also sounded like a liar.

Someone asked if he was with the nutrition and farming NGO in the southern part of the province. The way Sam Simmons bent his head gave me the impression that he never heard of that NGO, but he said he was with them, or supposed to be. He claimed he had been robbed. "They took everything. Everything but my clothes, which they probably didn't want because they're in good shape." They took his ID, too. "Who cares," he said. "It's not like you need a driver's license around here."

"You need a passport around here," said Major Richardson from behind his makeshift desk at our base.

But Sam Simmons convinced Richardson to allow him to travel to the village where the Worldwide Sustainable Farming Information Network was teaching the people how to eat. I did not see Sam Simmons again for a few months, though I heard many references to him, which fell into two categories: Sam Simmons is welcome all over the district already; all the female NGOs have a yen for Sam Simmons. And Sam Simmons is strange.

To explain what happened there and the decision I made, I have to describe the situation and the other people besides Sam Simmons who were involved. Simmons and the others had been put out of my mind for many years. I don't regret that. Thinking about it would not have helped anything, and probably would have hurt because I sensed I got it wrong, and worrying about it would have made me question myself other times when I had to make quick decisions.

I had been reassigned to poppy eradication as punishment. It took no time at all to understand that the only thing I would be eradicating was time, which was the specialty of our CO, Major Richardson. He was a scholar who knew that Alexander the Great had been in the district before him and had gotten out. Major Richardson devised a plan to walk in Alexander's footsteps that involved busyness without results. He did not put it that way to me, but after many hours, mostly after dark, listening to him explain his interpretation of history, I came away with an understanding of his approach: Results would stop time, mark an end to a project; a halt in time was the opposite of an absence; in a halt, time might build up; a halt could lead to extra time. That would mean a failed mission.

A fight with another Marine began my journey to Farah. I was a corporal, soon to be busted down to private, stationed north of Kandahar. Lance Sylvester was a lifer from Nevada, a master sergeant, last into every fight but big on playing the big-time warrior. He was all about the gear and the look. We didn't like each other. Early one morning, our platoon engaged the enemy on a hillside, catching them off guard. Three enemy fighters were killed. Sylvester was the casualty assistance officer, so he was in charge of the bodies. Regulations forbid the taking of personal effects and no one expected to find anything valuable on those corpses. Even their guns were usually lousy. Everyone knew Sylvester pocketed the rare worthwhile find. He shipped the stuff home or sold it to guys in other units. This time he found a knife in a scabbard. I didn't see it, but I heard about it. So did our CO. Sylvester was called in, and when he came out I was summoned. My gear was searched and the knife was found. It looked like something from the Middle Ages, a crude version of a fancy dagger in a carved and polished wooden scabbard. Sylvester had been tipped about the CO's interest and had planted it on me.

I was busted back to private. I stewed for a day, contemplating ways to retaliate. Sabotage would not provide satisfaction and everyone would know I did it. I decided the best course of action was to deal Sylvester a good beating. First I had to accuse him in front of others of planting the dagger. I added a number of other nasty things, most of which were accurate. He was bigger than me, older, and outranked me. He had to respond. He tried to hit me. Once that door was open, the rest was easy. I broke his nose right away. That flustered him.

That's how I got transferred to the poppy fields of Farah Province, where the farmers were concerned only with making enough money to feed their enormous families. That meant co-operating with whichever side allowed them to grow poppies and sell the opium. Flexibility gave the farmers control of their fate. The U.S. and Taliban each had reasons to want to stop poppy cultivation, but the U.S. wanted the farmers to love them, and the Taliban wanted the money from the opium trade, so they both made this one tiny exception to their really, truly, absolutely serious principles, the ones they were willing to sacrifice every-thing for.

Lieutenant Howard Spera could see that our mission made no sense, but he was not wise enough to keep that insight to himself. On my first night in the area, he explained to me, "We want the Taliban to leave the area, but they will never leave as long as there is opium being sold because they like and need the money it brings them. To get rid of the Taliban, we have to get rid of the poppy fields. And if we get rid of the poppy fields, the people will all join with the Taliban."

"So what is our mission?"

"We will educate the farmers about other crops to plant, pay subsidies for each poppy field they destroy without harvesting the opium, and protect them from the Taliban."

"Will that work?"

"Officially or really?"

So I became an inmate in the time-eradication program, riding from village to village to meet with the elders and farmers to discuss their lives and hand over money and advice. The villages consisted of one-story mud brick houses and dusty streets that always made me feel like I had been dropped into a cowboy movie. The sun, the silence, and the dust blended into an ominous concoction smelling of ambush and showdown. A lizard scurrying out of the shadows was enough to make us halt and rescan the doorways and rooftops. Shortly after I arrived, an NGO and a Marine were killed in one of the larger villages. Major Richardson conducted meetings at which he explained that the next time there was an ambush in one of the villages, he would set fire to all the poppy fields. That was the last ambush in a village during my stay in Farah.

Lieutenant Spera was a thin guy from Macon, Georgia, with sandy hair and glasses. He had attended Georgia Tech and married a waitress from one of the local beer halls the week after graduation. She was four years older than him. His parents hated her. "The idea of her is what they hate. Not her." He was the type who thought there was a difference between the two.

Like a lot of naïve people, Spera was brave. He practically begged the villagers for information about the enemy, and upon receiving any he led us out to follow up. That meant he led us into ambushes because the people who gave him the information either reported the conversation to the Taliban or were instructed by the Taliban to drop the information in the first place. Spera was well trained and clever, and an ambush without surprise is not too effective. Spera was a good teacher. Major Richardson did not like him.

"You're putting the men in jeopardy," he said.

"They're Marines. They signed up to be in jeopardy. They're trained for jeopardy. Besides, it's the Taliban putting them in jeopardy."

"Our mission is to pacify the area. You're causing conflict."

Lieutenant Spera asked to be transferred.

Richardson said, "I can't afford to lose you. You're the best fighting man I have."

Lieutenant Spera related all this to me out in Ahmed Wali Benizad's poppy field, where we watched Ahmed Wali and relatives wade through the poppy stalks, carefully making little cuts in each bulb so the creamy goo could begin to ooze out. He had twelve kids and a mass of other dependents too numerous to count. The only way to stop him from growing poppies would have been for the U.S. and Taliban to team up on the issue. Ahmed Wali wasn't a smart guy, but he knew that wasn't likely to happen. He cultivated us as relentlessly as he cultivated his poppies.

"They're like children in a divorce," I said. "Playing one parent off against another."

Spera did not like hearing that. "We were never married to the Taliban. We were married to the Mujahideen. The Taliban defeated them. So it's like one parent and one stepparent." Spera intended to become a lawyer when he finished straightening out the military.

Ahmed Wali smiled and waved to us. Over the next few days, he and his entourage would be scraping the oozing opium into plastic bags. In his compound, where they could sit, one man would construct baskets from the stalks, fill them with opium, and fold them up like party favors.

We were supposed to go away at that point so we didn't interrupt the process of selling the opium. Lieutenant Spera had other
ideas. He brought me and two other privates with him to spy on the
buyers. We didn't try to hide, just sat in two jeeps far down the
road, watching through binoculars. Two trucks stopped outside
Ahmad Wali's compound. And Sam Simmons climbed down from
the lead truck.

Spera begged Major Richardson for permission to bust Simmons. Richardson dithered. If we busted the buyers, Ahmed Wali
would have a hard time selling his next crop. He would turn to the
Taliban for help. Time would restart. Spera complained to me and
a horrible impulse to help overwhelmed me: I made a suggestion.

"We don't have to bust them. They take the opium across the
border into Iran, right? What if we let the Iranians know they were
coming? The Iranians would do the busting and no one would
blame us."

"And we'll follow them so they can't back off when they see Iranians at the border. They'll be trapped." I did not like that part. It
left an opening for Spera's bravery. Spera loved it and sold it to
Richardson. We hired two Kuchi guides. The Kuchis are a tribe of
nomads who often pass through the borders west and east, Iranian
and Pakistani. The plan was for two platoons to dog the buyers all
the way to the mountains where the Taliban protection would
break away. The Taliban didn't want to go too near Iran, and once
the buyers entered the mountains, they would figure they were safe
by virtue of their superior position.

Spera, another Marine, and I joined the Kuchis ahead of the
buyers. The other Marine was a skinny, book-loving kid who had

made the mistake of telling Spera he grew up in the mountains of Vermont, which made him an experienced mountain man in Spera's eyes. The Kuchis explained that there were two passes the drug runners usually used. Lieutenant Spera wanted to accompany them through the passes to the border. Excitement was blinding him. "This is what I came here for," he said.

I shivered. Dan waited for marks to make comments like that so he would know they were thoroughly cooked. Coming from an officer, it was scary. I pointed out that the border might not be clearly marked and we should not enter Iran, but Spera was beyond listening. He was in love with the adventure.

"The Kuchis know every inch of this territory. They know where the border is."

"The Kuchis don't care where the border is," I said.

The Kuchis nodded, agreeing with both of us.

We parked the jeeps far off the track where the boulders jutted out, forming a shelter that would keep them hidden. The Kuchis led us up toward the border along something resembling a path, which grew steeper and rockier as we went. Before we reached the top, we were able to look back and see the drug runners unpacking the bags of opium from the vehicles and repacking them on camels that had been brought to them. The Kuchis recognized the camel herder: He was one of them. Sam Simmons shook hands with the leader of the Taliban escort and counted out his payment. Someone had to help Simmons mount his camel. The Taliban watched the camel caravan until it reached the point where vehicles could no longer navigate. We watched the Taliban and, far back in the distance, the rest of our squad.

An hour later we reached the crest. If that was the border, it was a great place to sneak into Iran. The Kuchis said they knew where to find people who would alert the border guards.

Again, Lieutenant Spera misunderstood them on purpose. He claimed they said there would be guards at the border. Ten minutes later, the Kuchis told us to wait. They went ahead.

"Let's go back," I said. "We're going to be trapped."

But Spera wanted to be a guy who met with the Iranians and made a deal with them.

"There are no Iranians," I said.

"This is Iran." At least he acknowledged that.

"I mean border guards. The drug runners are being met by their partners or customers. That's who the Kuchis will see first. The contacts on the Iranian side of the border. We're going to be trapped."

He was arguing with me when the first shots dropped all around us. We scrambled behind rocks for cover and began working our way back to the top. I could not see who was firing at us. Might have been drug guys or even Iranian border guards. It might have been the Kuchis, though there were certainly more than two firing. RPGs landed near us. At the top, lying flat, looking back toward Afghanistan, I could see some of the drug runners turning their camels around and others firing blindly up toward us as cover. I could not see Sam Simmons.

Once we were over the crest, the firing from the Iranian side subsided. The firing from the drug runners was inaccurate and they were moving away from us. The original trap was going to work. Our men were taking positions at the bottom of the trail, where they would kill or capture the drug runners. Lieutenant Spera stood up and began firing down at the drug runners though they were too far away to hit.

He was brave and naïve and having fun. An RPG cruised over the crest and hit him square in the back and obliterated him.

The other Marine was splattered with bone, blood, and all the goo of life. He stumbled around while wiping it off his face. Another RPG hit close by, and the Marine jumped away from it. His body stopped bouncing off boulders about thirty feet below.

The Marines below were closing in on the gun runners. No more fire came from the Iranian side. I looked around for Lieutenant Spera's tags but didn't see them, so I edged down the hill to check on the Marine who had fallen.

The Marine lay on a flat, wide ledge. His head was bloody and bent at an awful angle. It looked like the fall had killed him. Sam Simmons held the Marine's sidearm. I watched as Simmons, on one knee, removed the Marine's tags. He didn't notice me. "Put it down," I said. He dropped the tags. He still held the sidearm. "The weapon." He stared at me a while before tossing the gun aside.

"Private Waters, right? How are you? I don't see you all this time and then here you are." He sounded like we ran into each other at a bar. He was still a scrawny guy, but his eyes were clear. I didn't think he was high. He flicked a piece of Lieutenant Spera's flesh off of the Marine's shirt and stood up. Then, as if he were concerned that I thought he was being insensitive, he said, "I didn't kill him. He was already dead." Two large plastic bags of opium tied together lay on a rock behind Sam Simmons. "Damn camels are more trouble than they're worth. I just carried what I could. Ever ride one?"

"Who were you meeting?"

"Oh, those guys had the contacts. I was just the money man on this deal."

He watched me for a moment, then reached down to get the dead man's tags. I raised my rifle. He stopped but came up with the tags in his hand. I climbed down and told him to back away from the body. I knelt down to check for a pulse. There was none. The intervals stretched in the firing below. Nothing came from above us. Whoever had been shooting at us was not coming across the border.

"I've been watching you, Private Waters. You didn't know it, but I saw how you operate. You're very good. I could learn from you."

Flattery? "Shut up."

"The others turned back, but I couldn't. You understand? I couldn't," he said.

Sam Simmons was just a would-be drug dealer, one of millions. I had spent the last few months carefully making sure not to interfere with the poppy business, so I did not feel too sanctimonious about this guy's participation. The honest way to lead him down the mountain would be to put a leash and a bell on him so the U.S. military and the Afghan authorities could have the thrill of human sacrifice. Would bringing him in honor Spera's preposterous idealism? I fought that foolishness while Spera was alive, so it made no sense to hand over Sam Simmons and condone that foolishness now that it had killed Spera. And burning behind all those thoughts, behind the months of nonsensical futility and my ambivalence about life as a Marine, was the instinct to avoid being a cop. I was born with it and experience reinforced the tendency. Every organization and institution I had come in contact with pushed toward making me, and everyone, into enforcement drones, and that bumped hard against my instinct to be contrary. I didn't do a long analysis while standing there on that mountain, pointing my rifle at Sam Simmons, but I could not see the benefit in handing him over. He was probably going to die getting out of there anyway, but he put himself in that position.

"Leave the bags," I said.

"Y'sure?"

"If you pick them up, you're going down the mountain with me."

"Can I take his shirt? It'll help me get out of the country if I'm . . ." He looked at the tags. "Kosinski . . . Victor Kosinski." Just like James Bond.

I nodded and he got to work on the shirt. I saw him shift his eyes to the sidearm, but I shook my head and he made no move. He had to pick more bits and pieces of Lieutenant Spera off the shirt before he put it on.

He slipped the tags over his head and smiled and shrugged. He was a guy who had been having narrow escapes his whole life, and I had just helped reconfirm his belief that he would always escape.

"You go first. I'll wait here," he said. I picked up Kosinski's sidearm and slung the bags of opium over my shoulder and walked past the new Kosinski. "Hey, man . . . Thank you. I really appreciate it. I won't forget it."

I turned back and raised my rifle and glared at him. I hated him at that moment more than I ever hated anyone. More than Dan at his worst. More than any foster parent or pompous colonel. It wasn't until I raised the rifle that I understood how much I disliked having to make this decision. If he had spoken, I would have shot him. But he did not speak, and I walked down the mountain and managed to push him from my mind until that moment on the Citadel in Erbil.

And following the flood of that memory came the realization, a side issue, one I never considered before, that Sam Simmons had probably done that ambush in the village in Farah that killed the NGO and the Marine. The rumor was the NGO had a lot of cash on him.

21

Three old men argued at a stall selling nuts. They were vehement, heated, and one grabbed a handful of pistachios. I thought he was going to throw them, but he let them fall back into the bin. They respected the nuts. At the next stall, teenagers browsed the DVDs and tapes. The marketplace below the Citadel was crowded but orderly: souk meets mall. The smells, the sounds, and the swirling motion kept my head from spinning off. Men and women I had never seen looked familiar, like old friends. A secret past malingered behind the eyes searching mine and avoiding mine. A zombie world of bad decisions traipsed alongside me. But one Victor Kosinski was enough to last me. He had popped up and would pop up again. I did not need to do anything to make that happen.

Two tough guys in short jackets cut me off and hurried to a stall selling packaged food and groceries. They moved with the arrogance and insolence that serves as the international symbol for secret police: in this case, the Asayish. When the proprietor saw them, he kicked something farther under the counter. They were not fooled. One grabbed him while the other pulled out the box of contraband. I moved on, never finding out what it was.

I veered right, along a row of stalls selling scarves and hats. I took a left and followed that to the end of the row, where I found the gun-selling stall belonging to the supposed cousin of my cabbie.

The guns were hung on hooks and laid out on red cloth, an impressive array: Colt 1911s, M9 Berettas, Glocks. The merchant and his son pointed to one after another, held them out so I could handle them. It was the jewelry store experience for mercenaries. I declined them all.

I asked the merchant to open the boxes at the back and show me the SIG Sauers. The merchant's son played dumb, asked me what those were. They conferred in Arabic about how long to hesitate to get the maximum price, then brought out two guns. I chose the SIG Sauer 226 over the 228 because it had two extra rounds in the clip, fifteen. They brought out two boxes of 9mm ammunition.

The merchant and his son started at twelve hundred dollars. I offered three hundred dollars. The merchant moaned, his son threatened. I paid four hundred and fifty.

Cold high-desert air had descended on the city. It felt refreshing despite the smell of diesel. Shades of blue stretched across the sky, darkening steadily, subtly toward the horizon. Green, red, and yellow colored lights made the fountains seem fake, like rippling plastic. I don't know how many cars followed me as I walked toward my hotel, but the driver that stopped beside me was Maya. She put down the window and leaned across. The driver behind her honked his impatience. When he stopped, she said, "I can't offer a fancy convertible like yours. But please get in."

I got in and readjusted the side mirror so I could watch any followers. "I bet you know where there's a roadhouse here, too," I said.

She was wearing a long black skirt and a blue silk long-sleeve blouse. This was not an outfit Muslim elders had in mind when they decreed women should be covered in public. I said, "Your blouse matches the color of the sky just ahead of us."

She laughed. "I didn't take you for one who delivers cheap compliments like that."

"It's not a compliment. I was wondering how you managed the timing."

"I wore the black skirt in case you came along later."

She turned a few times and we left the traffic behind and entered a large park.

"Johnny sent me. I am to charm you. That's what he said. 'Charm him, my dear, because he has fallen under your spell.' That's how he put it."

"Turning on the charm is usually only the first part."

"He wants you to meet with him. He promises your safety."

A Mercedes just like the one we were in turned into the park: charm insurance. She kept driving through to the other end of the park, then turned onto a broad boulevard that led to the Kurdistan Parliament building, a five-story sandstone block pierced at regular intervals by thin window slots. I wanted to get to Bannion's, but more than that, I wanted to know how thick a coating of charm Maya would be willing to spread to get me there.

"I don't want to go to Bannion's," I said.

"Where would you like to go?"

"The airport."

She checked the rearview mirror. "Johnny guarantees your safety."

"If I fly out of here, I guarantee my safety all by myself."

She forced the faint smile, the glimmering tease in her eyes. "I thought you were a man who doesn't give up. A determined man."

"I'm going to declare victory and go home. Mission accomplished. You're no longer a captive."

"You mean you came all this way just for me? I'm flattered."

"Your father made me a very lucrative offer. It's odd, isn't it? He knew you weren't in any danger. Do you think I should try to hold him to it?"

She did not like that remark, either. I was struck by how less exotic she seemed here, removed from the mongrel luster of Houston. Her aura of mystery mystery faded against the hometown background of war and its spoils.

"You think you understand what is going on, but you don't." She didn't have the pleading in her voice that I expected. It was the declaration of a disciple, a True Believer.

"I think I don't understand at all. And I think you're not going to explain it to me."

She had no answer. To explain meant narrowing the story; the details would diminish the wild ecstasy of the dream. Experience and training told her to protect her devotion from a skeptic. I did not think she knew all the twists in Bannion's plot; no one did. I wanted to push her to see how far she would push me. I concentrated on the silence and did not register the growing roar overhead. A shadow lowered across us from the left and passed quickly. The plane touched the runway just a few hundred yards beyond.

I said, "If I don't go to Bannion's, will he take it out on you?"

She pulled to the side of the road and it was as if the veil of vagueness overtook her again. She stared forward, then checked her mirrors while she decided which answer would best serve her purpose, which answer would make me come to Bannion's willingly, without the men who were following having to grab me.

"No, Johnny won't hurt me." She waited for my reaction, then she laughed. "You can't decide if I'm telling the truth or not. It wouldn't matter how I answered. How do you get out of bed in the morning? You can't trust anyone."

"Can I trust you?"

"Don't you think I know what that feels like? Don't you think I had to spend my life wondering about everyone? Every moment? Who the liars are? But I figured out how to handle it."

Instead of dwelling in doubt, she had resorted to pulling down the veil, and that had the effect of making most people give more, pushing for a reaction, a confirmation, even a refutation, until, finally, they gave too much. Her eruption of honesty seemed to fill the drab brown desert with colors.

"You think that if you question everything I say, you'll find the real me, the one you can understand and trust, but the result is just a muddier picture." She smiled, emphasizing the challenge. She was more beautiful in that moment of pugnaciousness than ever before. She laughed again. "The truth is as good as a lie in dealing with you."

I wanted to tell her we were talking about faith, not trust. But I remembered Dan's True Believer rule: Never allow them to draw you into a conversation about their faith unless you are prepared to let them think they have converted you. No argument can ever defeat faith. I said, "We're back to the night we met. You want me to help your father."

Her shoulders dropped and her head tilted with relief. She had moved me back to the holy quest. Victory. The veil descended. "I don't know what Johnny has planned or why he wants to meet you. I only know that I'll feel better if you're there."

She made a U-turn. All the way to Bannion's I tried to reassure myself that I was going there for my purposes, not Maya's. I had loaded up five cylinders for Russian roulette with chivalry, gallantry, righteousness, sincerity and plain old lust. One was going to kill me soon enough if I didn't stop playing. I spent the ride back wondering which would hurt the most.

Dan spoke up on that subject. *"You know the answer."*

"I don't want the answer."

"The only one you're not faking."

A new white van idled in the middle of the courtyard, which was lit like a landing zone. Maya pulled past the gates, which bore a sign reading DS SECURITY SERVICES, and maneuvered around the van. A video cameraman waited for a pretty redheaded woman to fix her hair, near the side door to the office building. A harried man in his forties brought her a scarf and helped arrange it over her hair. He was her producer. She scrutinized the mirror, flicked a few hairs across her forehead, handed over the mirror, and pointed to the cameraman. The soundman nodded to him and he said, "Ready."

"Though this northern section of Iraq is peaceful, we have been advised that the prudent approach is to hire a security escort as we tour the outer-lying cities and towns. Ah, here they are now. . . ."

Four security men marched out of the office, all of them dressed in khakis and black jackets with DS embroidered on the chest. The first three men lined up behind the woman. She put out her arm to invite the last man to join her.

"This is Mike Jensen, who will be leading us as we search for the best authentic, indigenous cuisine and boutique inns of Kurdistan. It looks like I'm the luckiest woman in the entire region. Certainly the safest. Well, the van is loaded and waiting, so, Mike, are we good to go?"

"We're good to go, Zooey," Mike said. It was clear he had rehearsed.

The producer yelled, "Great." Zooey removed her scarf and rushed the cameraman.

"Let me see how it looked."

But the cameraman had swung the camera to follow the security detail. A goon, one of the original Houston goons, had come out of the house behind the offices. The goon froze when he saw the camera catch his exit. Three long strides brought him to Mike Jensen. Jensen listened carefully. He was taking orders. Gently as he could, he took the camera away from the cameraman. The producer protested, but the other security men swarmed and he was kept away.

The goon melted away.

Seconds later, that goon and another were patting me down and removing my gun in the foyer of the back house. Johnny Bannion's cooing singsong cadence bounced from the hallway. "Well, I had said I wanted to meet with you, Mr. Hewitt, and Maya said she would undertake the assignment. She was confident of success and

I can see her confidence was warranted. Did she remember to assure you of your safety?" He put out his hand and the goon put my gun in it.

"I can't remember."

"Thank you, Maya, dear."

It was a dismissal. Her half smile could not hide her hatred for him. He held his Cyclops gaze on her, soaking in the venom until she broke off and moved down the hallway he had just come from. Bannion faced me and forced his fat baby cheeks and doughy lips into a saggy half smile. "You and the boys have never been properly introduced, have you. Neil Bess, Gethin Berry . . ."

He spoke deliberately, wanting me to take note of the names. The goons were dismissed and went outside, where the video camera had been tamed. Bannion turned his gaze along the hallway after the shadow of Maya.

"She used to love me, you know. Truly loved me. Painful knowing it will never come back. Can't stop checking, though, looking for any feeling. Like with a missing limb. What's that called when you prefer to feel the pain instead of just nothing?"

"Hope."

"I think you know exactly what I mean, Mr. Hewitt. We both know what it takes to keep us feeling alive."

"You think we're alike?"

"You're here, Mr. Hewitt. Halfway around the world, armed and outnumbered. I take that as the proof."

He was sincere, or the closest he could come to it. He managed to reverse the purpose of sincerity. He used it to show how transparent and vulnerable I was: I had not duped him, could not dupe him. He handed over my gun. "Only a fool would travel around these parts without a gun, and I don't want to be in business with a fool. Come along."

Twelve of the thirty or so desks were occupied on the second floor of the office building. Industrial gray carpet, weak lighting, and maps pinned to the walls gave the office the feel of a short-term rental. Computer screens were planted everywhere. Cases of Coca-Cola were stacked beside the men's room door. Two large shisha hookahs sat on an unused desk. Houston goons occupied four desks in a supervisory cluster set up facing all the others. Bannion made the goons stand for our introduction. Again, he spoke their names slowly, wanting me to catch them. It seemed the names were some sort of waving flag I was supposed to be looking at while the magic trick was performed with the other hand. But I didn't know what the trick was. As a distraction, the goons were effective: a bunch of guys getting their knives out. That was fine; I expected that much. It was the forks that bothered me.

"We contract for the security of events and locations all over northern Iraq. And for visitors, as you saw outside. The boys supervise and monitor the operations from the borders with Turkey and Syria to Kirkuk, where things are often quite tense. We employ over a thousand guards at any given time dealing with threats and some very real violence."

It was a pat sales speech. The million dollars that passed between us was forgotten. I missed his tone of bullying condescension, replaced now with synthetic confidentiality.

"He cares as much about this part of the operation as I do. This is the 'we make do without you' part of the game. He wants to con you. He wants to be conned," Dan said.

"Where are the employees in charge of making the threats and doing the violence?"

"We located here because people do all that for free. All volunteers."

He led me back down the narrow, dark staircase. The office and what I had seen of the house were short on windows. Victor and another goon were on the way up. Bannion backed them and made another elaborate introduction. I had met all eight from Houston.

"I hope you can stay for dinner, Mr. Hewitt. I have guests who would like to meet you."

"And you guarantee my safety?"

"Would you believe me if I did?"

Between chunks of roast beef, Mr. Garner, sitting across from me, said, "Strange we've never met. I make it my business to meet most of the Americans coming through Erbil."

I recognized him, in spite of a stomach that had expanded to match his entrepreneurial ambitions. He had been a Marine lieutenant general. There was no danger of him recognizing me; he was known for ignoring anyone who couldn't help his career. "My driver today thought I was Italian. Maybe that's the problem."

Dan whispered to me. *"I always enjoyed contempt more as a secret, like knowing what I had done with a man's daughters or wife."*

"Did you ever serve in the armed forces, Mr. Hewitt?" Garner stuffed a potato in his mouth as he spoke.

"No. Did you?"

Before retired General Garner could challenge me to a duel, Bannion spoke up. "Mr. Garner and Mr. Tagliaferro are retired generals and are partners with me in DS Security. All of our employees are ex-military." He turned to the generals and made the best excuse for me he could. "Mr. Hewitt is from the Ivy League. Cornell."

"Columbia."

"Of course."

Maya sat on my right. The invisible veil engulfed her again. I glanced at her periodically to see if she was concentrating on any of the men at the table, but I only saw her looking dutifully at whoever was speaking, even Bannion. Across from her sat a burly Iraqi, introduced as Mr. Hafiz from the Regional Government. Hafiz wore a rug and glasses with thick plastic frames. Two places were still unoccupied. Bannion had decided to start dinner before those guests arrived. Uninvited, Dan flitted around the table.

Tagliaferro said, "How do you feel about foreigners coming in and reaping the benefits of America's hard work and sacrifice?"

Dan sounded excited. *"He wants you to take his money. Did you hear that?"*

"I don't want his money."

"He's begging you to cheat him."

"I'm here for another reason."

"You don't know why you're here, so in the meantime allow him to begin thinking he can cheat the Chinese or the Russians or whoever he is afraid of. This is the value of contempt. This is how you use it. You allow them to cheat you."

"Did we conquer Iraq or liberate it? The Iraqis will make the best deals they can," I said. "Inside those deals will be many other deals. Everyone can get in. The people making the first deal aren't always the ones who make the money. Chinese can buy Exxon stock. Exxon hires executives from many countries. The money flows around the world. Exxon does not pay a huge amount of tax to the U.S. government. Why does it matter whose money develops these oil fields?"

"They can cut off the supply. We have to control the supply," Garner explained.

"Would you rather be defending an oil field or attacking it? Speaking as a general?"

That brought looks around the table. Bannion said, "Are you asking as a philosophical matter or a practical one?"

"Is there a difference?"

I could see him struggling to hold back his gangster arrogance. He rolled his lips against each other, causing his wobbly cheeks to ripple. "I would rather own something than not own it, Mr. Hewitt. Perhaps you would like to explain to us how that's wrong, practically or philosophically."

"I didn't study philosophy. Maybe I'm in over my head here. You're the military people. Former military." This was Dan 101: Back off when challenged; make them pursue.

Hafiz spoke for the first time. "The entity with the strongest force always argues that it is the most practical choice. Philosophically, that might be repulsive."

A goon entered and spoke low to Bannion. We could all hear him say, "HH is arriving." Bannion nodded. He looked at Maya and soaked up another dose of her disdain. "Your father is here."

Bannion and the retired generals rose and I decided I would, too.

The King was not happy to see that dinner had started without him. He curved his lips politely while Bannion oozed fake respect and regrets over having started without the King. Zoran was not happy to see me but tore his scowl from me to glare at each man in turn, making sure the King was receiving the proper dose of respect. The King kissed Maya. He sat down in his place at the head or foot of the table and pushed his plate away. Zoran pushed his away, too.

"I have not been back in Erbil in over ten years," the King said. "I feel as though my dreams have blended with reality." "Collided" would have been more accurate, but it didn't seem like the moment to correct him. The elegance was on full blast. Grand condescension wafted across the table. Bannion raised his glass of beer. "To a triumphant return."

We all drank to that. It felt like a secret dinner of a banished cult. One member to be sacrificed to the greater good. I assumed the King was first in line for the poisoned goblet, but a look around the table brought doubt. I pushed my plate away, too.

The King went on a bit about how invigorating it felt to be back in his glorious homeland. When he mentioned that he could feel his roots being refreshed, I thought he was asking Bannion to provide him with women. Bannion asked if the measures taken to assure the King's anonymity upon arrival were sufficient and well executed. "I'm reminded," he said, "of King Richard the Lionheart sneaking into England on his return from the Crusade."

The King was pleased, but Zoran suspected mockery in Bannion's tone and shot him one of his dirty camel looks he had been wasting on me.

The King took over. "Our first hurdle is the Regional Government. Not the people in it, mind you. Many of them are with us." He nodded toward Hafiz. "They want a separate Kurdistan, a united Kurdistan, a Kurdistan that is free. Those members of the government are our allies. We must combat the concept of a government subservient to Baghdad. Our other problem, the part of the puzzle we have not solved, is the PKK. That's why we want to talk to you, Mr. Hewitt. We want to ally with them. We want to bring them on board. If we do that, we're confident we can accelerate the process. These men, these generals, have done great work preparing us. Johnny has orchestrated it all. They are all great friends of the Kurdish people. We want you to be a great friend as well."

It was like a presentation at a Marine Corps training session: just background noise before the sergeants and the officers who knew how to actually do things took us out and trained us. Zoran batted his long lashes in silent applause. The generals had made careers of nodding and harrumphing along with these kinds of speeches, so they nodded and harrumphed. The King stared at me, working the eyebrow up and down like a signal to stand and salute.

"I don't control the PKK, King."

"They must trust you. You gave them money. You have a relationship with them, don't you?"

"Yes, we have a relationship."

"Then be on the winning side of history, Robert. Bring them on to the winning side."

Everyone, even Maya, watched me, and every expression said, with deep and forthright indifference: Would you prefer to be hung or shot? "You make an excellent case, King," I said. "I'll have a word with my contacts."

"That calls for dessert," declared Bannion.

He didn't clap his hands to make the treats appear, but I expected enormous pieces of pie, representing the pieces of the giant pie the generals and the King were drooling after, to be served. I eyed Garner's fork, figuring how I could steal it. He would eat his pie without it. Instead, a cakelike dessert called gilacgi was served. Everyone managed to hide his disappointment. The King ate it and so did Garner. The rest of us talked about how wonderful it would be if one day Erbil could host the Olympics. Dinner was over. Fariz shook my hand and said, "I shall see you soon, Mr. Hewitt." He did not make me look forward to that event. Tagliaferro looked forward to more of my "outspoken views." Garner wiped his hand on his coat after shaking mine.

Bannion saw them out. The King, Zoran, and Maya remained at the table with me. I had something that had to be said. "Your driver, Arun, was found dead. They found him in the town car I borrowed from you."

Zoran put both hands on the table. At first I thought he was going to bound at me. But he did it to stabilize himself. When he finally was able to turn his eyes on me, the King and Maya followed him.

"I didn't do it." And I didn't know if Zoran believed me. But the King looked like he knew who the killer was. I thought I knew, too.

"I believe you, Robert," the King said. "He was a most devoted servant. A gallant soldier sacrificed to our great cause."

For the first time, Zoran looked at the King with anger. Maya saw it. The King was oblivious. His attention was on his ascension; on the magnanimous gestures he might offer; on the way he swept his hands as he spoke; on the shade of velvet for his new throne.

"I'm sorry, Zoran," I said.

The moment stolen for talking of his most loyal servant was over. The King went on, "Our previous differences will mean little,

Robert, once events unfurl. When we first met, I was struck by something, some . . . vision, that it was you who would help deliver me to my destiny. I said nothing, but I felt it and trusted you. And now, here we are."

Luckily, Bannion returned.

Bannion led me through the living room, down a short hallway to a locked door. He entered a code on a pad and we entered a study. Two ceiling fans turned slowly. The floor was made of large brown tiles. There was a skylight, but no windows. Books lined a far wall. Framed photos were interspersed with the books: Bannion as a young man, pre–eye patch, thick shoulder-length hair parted in the middle; the King; Maya; a boy. Next to the bookcase was a closet with a ventilated grate in the bottom panel. Opposite the wall of books stood an enormous safe, at least five feet high and wide. Bannion held up a bottle of scotch. I nodded and he poured drinks for both of us. No ice. He maneuvered me to a chair facing away from the safe. He faced it.

"I had a friend, a mentor really, a Jew he was, dead now, poor man, but he used to tell me by way of advice, 'A full purse isn't as good as an empty purse is bad.' You know what I said to him? I said—"

"You said, 'You're full of it, you old fool. It's all about the brass ring.'" And it was a pretty good imitation of Johnny Bannion, too.

He chuckled. "You and me, Robert, we could be partners. I like you. I feel like you understand me."

"Does that mean I'm in danger?"

"That's just what I would have said. I sincerely hope that's not the case."

"That's not an answer."

"You're too young to think of a nest egg, but I'm getting there. This villain business becomes taxing. I'm ready to take my old mentor's advice." Like a vain man facing a mirror, his eye kept shifting to the safe.

"Didn't do him much good. Maybe you could spend his nest egg."

"The problem is we're on the brink of something enormous. You think you might make a lot of money in oil investments, but just imagine owning a country. Imagine." He looked past me at the safe as if the county were going to be locked in there.

I recognized this part of the pitch: the dazzling vistas, the future revealed as a shimmering palace as compelling as a mirage. And as real. He did a few minutes on revenue streams and then lamented not having a suitable successor. The goons were, unfortunately, mere goons, not up to the task. He said, "Our backgrounds are quite different, Robert, but we seem to think along like lines. We could be very successful partners."

His delivery was different from Dan's. Thuggish undertones skulked in the pauses, but the pattern hit the marks. He was a clue giver. He was a salesman who hid the product from view. All the talk of the future made me think Bannion did not believe in the future, and he saw no glittering prizes. He had the money he wanted and he wanted it all for himself.

"If I were your partner, I'd wonder why we were in the king business."

"I'm thinking about alliances, Mr. Hewitt. Arrange a meeting with your PKK contacts. Can you do that for us? We all benefit. Tomorrow night. Anywhere they wish. They'll be safe. I'll guarantee their safety."

"And before we begin the road to my possible partnership, there is still the matter of the one million dollars you took from me."

He looked at the safe and smiled and squinted as if the sight flooded him with pleasure. "It's right behind you. Arrange the meeting and I'll bring along the money. How's that?"

He pulled his cell phone from his chest pocket. "Maya, dear, would you be good enough to drive Mr. Hewitt back to his hotel?"

Victor was the goon in charge of the gate. He flinched when the headlights hit him and I was glad to be spared his insinuating grin.

Maya did not speak until the hotel was in sight. "My father has prepared a speech. He believes Johnny when he says he will bring my father to power. It's to happen soon. Tomorrow night, I think."

The only car following us was a marked police car. "How?"

"I don't know. I don't believe it anyway." She sounded like she wanted me to contradict her, tell her it was possible.

When she pulled up to the valet at my hotel, I said, "Would you like to come in for a drink?"

"Downstairs or in your room?"

"In my room."

I expected to see Gill waiting for me in the lobby, but he was not there. I bought drinks at the bar and we carried them upstairs.

Maya sat down on the desk chair and said, "I cannot read Johnny anymore. I could once. I thought I could."

"I can't read you."

She smiled at that. "I was sixteen when I married Johnny. In England. He was famous among the Kurdish exiles for having helped smuggle refugees out after Saddam cracked down. Very dashing. Fancy suits and an eye patch."

"And now you wonder if that's fake."

She almost backed out because her father pushed so hard for the union. She felt like she was being sold. But she loved Johnny. She grew up around intrigue and suddenly it all felt real. Gun runners over to the flat for dinner, telling wild stories of their narrow escapes and lucrative deals, and bankers listening patiently and nodding along like fans at a jazz club counting the beat. Then the Americans started showing up. Officers, even diplomats. And Maya knew it was getting serious because she was excluded from the talks and from the trips. But the King was excluded, too. Bannion trotted him out for show and then shunted him away from the serious conferences. "The nuts and bolts, darling; he wouldn't know one from the other, would he?" Johnny would say when she protested the disrespect her father had to bear.

And Johnny's cruelty became more apparent, or she grew up enough to notice it more. He always had a mean streak, a disparaging sense of humor, but that added to his aura and reinforced her belief that he was a man of action, the man of action, who would be the catalyst to her father's ascension. But as she matured, the cracks became visible and soon the cracks were all she could see. He made trips to Iraq. She stayed in London. Even shut out, she could see that the cronies were mercenaries, the officers were traitors. She heard of murders. Johnny's cynicism drowned her idealism. She left him. But her father did not leave Johnny Bannion. The King was like a gold prospector: A few glittering specks were all that was required to keep him knee-deep in the creek. Bannion had only to fail to return a call, miss a meeting, or let it be known that he was courting others, in order to bring the King to heel. Maya determined to free her father and to destroy Bannion. She wanted my help.

She shifted her focus to what a great leader the King would make, but I had heard it already and cut her off.

"Haven't you left someone out?"

Her eyes clouded and she looked past me. "I told you the truth."

"Part of it, maybe even most of it. But there's your child. Your son." It was a guess. I had seen the photo of a boy. There had to be an heir, someone to take up the banner the King had carried so feebly.

"Did Johnny tell you that?"

"Yes."

"He's at school in Switzerland." She finished her drink and she finished talking about the boy.

"We're right back where we were before," I said. "Maybe Bannion just wants money, and you and your father are playing along. Maybe there's another kidnapping in the works. Just Houston all over again. Maybe you have honorable reasons to do it. Why should I care?"

She stood up and came close to me. I struggled to keep my hands at my side. She reached up with her lips and kissed me. I didn't respond. She turned and stepped back. "I don't know what he's planning."

I'm sure there were a million good reasons not to believe her, but suddenly I could not think of any. She started for the door. I stepped forward quickly and caught her arm and turned her toward me and kissed her. I drew her to the bed. We kissed more. I held her and said, "You weren't going to walk out that door, were you?"

"I was determined to stay." She stepped away from me and turned off the lights.

She was as determined as she claimed. It wasn't love and it was something other than just lust. It was as if we were contesting who was hungriest. I tried, but I don't think I won. In bed, in the dark, in silence, Maya's vagueness shattered. I understood a little about her for the first time: the need to leave the confining compartments and tight curves of intrigue and ambition; the use-it-or-lose-it fear that passion would wither; and the longing to just show off who she was.

While I was getting dressed, I considered playing along, agreeing to help, which really meant agreeing to kill Bannion. That is what she wanted. But she deserved better; at least I told myself she did. "I'm not a killer. I'm not going to kill him for you."

I didn't have to watch her to know she was reassembling her armor. "That's not why I came here." Her voice was direct but faint, not fully in place. The slight smile had formed. I no longer saw myself reflected, and seeing behind the smile no longer felt important. I was immune to the mystery. I just had to deal with the woman.

She got up and stood beside the bed, completely naked.

"Maybe I shouldn't have slept with you until you did it." Her voice was filled with mocking bitterness at the assumption I made. I still believed I had it right.

She moved close past me to reach for her clothes. Her scent hit me and made me want to linger in it. She turned the opaque, enigmatic gaze on me, the one I thought I had moved past.

"You don't have to go back to him."

She laughed and kissed me. "Such nobility. You're as bad as Johnny. I don't know where you're going, but I bet you're going out now. Yes?"

I did not care that she was a liar who would betray me with barely a nod. I wished she had stayed.

I called Major Hensel and identified Bannion as the puppet master. I told him about the meeting with the retired generals. The Major already knew about Garner, but not Tagliaferro. I told him that I kept hearing whispers about big doings set for tomorrow.

"A coup?"

"Bannion is certainly not going to try to put the King in charge. And he can't take on the Peshmergas. I don't see him attempting a takeover. Baghdad would come in and crush him."

"Then what are those generals doing there?"

"I think it's okay to assume Bannion is not leveling with them about his plans. They're looking for paydays. They think he has money from the graves, other graves than the ones we know about, and is going to be using that, and they can grab a share."

"And Bannion doesn't have that money?"

"Not here." The picture of Bannion's fake beatific expression directed toward the safe floated in front of me. I asked the Major about Gill again. He said he had already checked, and found nothing. "Can you check for a soldier or Marine by that name who died in action?" I also told him the names of the seven goons Bannion introduced me to. Hensel said he would put Will Panos on it. I left out Victor Kosinski. I thought we were done.

The Major said, "Get Bannion and get out of there as soon as you can."

"I want to find the money."

"That's an order."

"I can get him anytime."

"I'm not thinking about him. I'm thinking of you."

As soon as I hung up, I called Will Panos. "How's it going with the widow?"

"We'll see," he said.

"We'll see is pretty good. Want me to ask you to go back to Montana on important business?"

"Yes."

"Another time. I gave the Major a list of names. I don't know what the common thread is other than they don't belong to the men using them. And there's another name."

"I know. Gill. The Major already sent it to me."

"Another name. But you can't tell the Major. Give me your word."

"Okay."

"Victor Kosinski. There can't be too many. This one might have been traveling as a Marine. I need to know every time he entered or left the country and where."

"Where he went?"

"Where he entered or left from."

I called Gill's room. He did not pick up. I called the front desk and asked if he left me a message. They told me Mr. Gill had checked out.

Then the gunfire started.

23

grabbed a fat German in the lobby. "The Prime Minister has been shot," he said in perfect English. "It's a revolution." He pushed his way to the elevators. The traffic was bumper to belly. Some wanted to hide in their rooms, some wanted to peek out the windows or shout at hotel employees for information or for help escaping. I wanted to get to Bannion's. Between the bar and the front door, two Kurdish men in their thirties grabbed me by each arm. The one on my right said, "Come with us, Mr. Hewitt."

"Where is that?" They did not answer. I relaxed my arms for a moment, then jammed both elbows down. The Asayish were caught off guard and I slipped free. I pushed away from them and clawed through the mass until I caught a wave that carried me toward the elevators. The cops were falling behind.

The stairs were empty. A valet rushed into the garage kiosk, grabbed a set of keys, and rushed to a Toyota. I grabbed the key to a Mercedes and found the car and drove out. At the top of the garage exit ramp, one of the cops was waiting. I steered toward him and made him jump away.

I did not get far. Cars jammed every inch of pavement. The drivers who stayed inside played their horns without rhythm, a frustrated toneless bleating. Pedestrians flowed toward the colored lights and the Citadel beyond. Everyone moved fast to reach the thick mass where movement slowed. I opened my car door and a man crashed into it. I tried to help him up. He shook me off and moved on. The Asayish kept coming.

The crowd was thick and fluid. The fastest way forward was to ride the current. The cops would not outpace it. Flashing their badges would get them trampled. The bridges sliced the crowd into wide lanes. Fountain mist swirled in pastels. I was pushed toward the left, toward the souk. Gunfire sounded in lonely bunches like neighborhood fireworks set between beers.

Strobed stills of the battle in the stalls of the souk between looters and merchants flashed as I slid past. The Asayish were out of sight. A skinny teenager emerged with a bundle of women's scarves, which dripped from his grip as the crowd jostled him. A man in his sixties, dirty, with a beard and a red-checked ghatra raced to the edge of the souk and stopped to decide where to push into the flow. He held pistols in each hand like a cartoon cowboy. Two shots hit him in the back and he fell flat on his face and the guns clattered on the pavement. A kid bent to get one. But the shooter loomed over him. It was the gun merchant's son.

The crowd flowed on. Only a few stepped on the body, just one wreck in a long-awaited cavalcade. Another, oozing more obvious agony, undoubtedly waited ahead. The proximity to violence sustained the feeling of release, extended it to the point of ecstasy. And the ecstasy foamed in a chain reaction, feeding on itself, surging, overflowing, devouring its own fascination.

A man spoke in Kurmanji, feedback screeched, the man began again, "My fellow Kurds, my people . . ." I recognized the voice: the King. A faint echo bounced around the plaza and fought with the thickness of the cheap sound system and the intermittent feedback. I scrambled and pushed and elbowed toward the Citadel, where the voice seemed to come from.

I could understand most of it and could fill in the rest since it was only a slight variation on every speech the King made.

"Our moment of destiny is upon us. The rights of the Kurdish people of all regions cannot be denied any longer. From Turkey to Iraq to Syria to Iran, we are uniting as one people. Now . . ."

On a bridge, approaching blue and green and red lights, the railing broke. People fell into the shallow pool and bathed more in faint color than water: too minor a catastrophe to earn any wonder. I was swept across. First I saw the huge Kurdish flag hung against the wall of the Citadel. Beneath it stood the King with a microphone in his hand, gripped lightly, the way a crooner would. He was standing uneasily on the top of the cab of a black pickup truck. Goons guarded the truck from the crowd and two stood in the bed with Zoran next to them.

"Peace with our neighbors that we might all prosper. Peace among us. Safety for non-Kurds . . ."

I moved to a spot on the left, in the lee of a column, and stood about two feet off the ground, on its base. For the first time, I realized how much the temperature had dropped. The pickup blocked the gate to the Citadel, causing the crowd to swirl away like smoke blown against a window. The goons were not scaring anyone. The King of all Kurds might have been a street performer for all the attention he received. His speech was background noise, part of the wall of sound essential to prolonging the exhilarating sensation of fear and danger.

"I am ready to assume my rightful throne, my ancient seat, my legacy. Our former glory can be restored only with the restoration of our glorious kingdom . . ."

To the right of the black pickup, on a low cinder-block retaining wall, the red-haired TV star stood tall and faced her cameraman on the ground below. She waited until he signaled, then she tore off her scarf with a dramatic flourish and began talking. The soundman struggled against the jostling to hold the mike close enough to her. She gestured her frustration. The cameraman swung around to catch the King. The redhead was yelling at him, but he had sense enough to document the better performance.

Hundreds of shots tore up the sky. Floodlights beamed from behind me, toward the Citadel. The King was caught in the glare, and as he moved, the microphone cord wrapped around his ankle. He stumbled. Maya stepped out from behind Zoran in the truck bed as if to steady him. He signaled that he was okay and resumed his speech. She stared adoringly. I saw more faces turned toward her than toward him.

Bullhorns announced, in Arabic, that the crowd should disperse. I looked behind, into the spotlights, where Peshmergas in riot gear made their way forward over the bridges. The crowd squeezed toward the Citadel. The cameraman jumped onto the wall next to his star and kept his focus on the King. A line of Peshmergas in the rear fired volleys again into the sky. Flares went up and their bright, cold light drenched the faint colors of the fountain lights. The crowd had nowhere to go. The vortex swelled with frantic energy. Zoran scowled at the crowd. His hands went up, palms out, as if he could push them away. The pickup rocked. The goons jumped down. Maya reached toward her father, still talking, though no sound came through anymore. The plug must have been pulled.

The pickup toppled over. The King went down the way a statue does: erect, stiff. The crowd rushed into the Citadel.

I jumped into the back of the taxi. "Go. Go." I spoke in a desperate whisper. Dark stone two-story buildings lined the quiet street in the old city behind the souk, just about a half mile from all the tumult. Dueling tailor shops faced each other across the road. They both featured headless mannequins sporting dark men's suits. A police cruiser came around the corner two blocks ahead and the headlights hit us. Both of us turned away from the light. I looked behind. The Asayish who had been chasing me appeared down the street. The driver started to put the car in gear. "No," I said. "Wait. Pretend to sleep."

I lay on the floor of the back, facedown, gun underneath me. I waited.

Footsteps. Men catching their breath. They spoke Arabic. "Oh, come on. Come on. Did you see a man running past?"

The driver apologized profusely, admitted to sleeping. "I cannot sleep at home. The children . . ."

The men ran on. After a minute, I asked, "Has the police car come past?"

"He turned around."

I sat up and pulled five one-hundred-dollar bills and tossed them on the seat beside him. "If you can help me find anyone connected to the PKK, I'll give five more of these."

The mirror occupied him more than the road. He turned south through a run-down section, then west into a large park. We were the only vehicle. A black monolithic monument stood guard. A long lake ran on the left, and to the right a fatter one was dotted with fountains. Erbil liked fountains. Headlights hit us. Then others came from behind. The cabbie did not wait to find out who they were. He stopped in the middle of the road and pulled the money from his pocket. I stopped his hand. "Keep it and go."

"Do not tell them, please." He got out and ran.

I ran in the opposite direction. I did not get far.

The hood smelled of gas. Wherever we were smelled of rotting food. Cuffs dug into my wrists. I hung, my feet just barely touching the floor. The tall man's torture chamber must have been occupied. I was stripped down to my underwear and I was cold. My feet were cold.

Fariz was more offensive than the odors or the pain. His cultured voice grated like a steady siren. "Diyar is a terrorist. Your own government calls him a terrorist. Yet you do business with him. How do you justify this? What is your relationship?"

I did not answer through the hood. Someone cuffed me around for a little while, but it could have been much worse. "Can you see my breath? It's cold in here."

The door creaked and slammed and no one answered, though they might have been there. They wanted what I did not have. That was the secret I had to keep. If I convinced them I was useless to them, they would want to get rid of their mistake. I wanted to extend our time together, though I knew I would like it less than they did. Again, Fariz spoke. "Why are you looking for Diyar?"

"You asked me to. I was trying to please you."

Someone hit me in the gut with a stick. The blows were predictable, but each one held a surprise in its timing and location. The cold was worse. I did not want to give in to shivering, which would take over like an alien force once it turned on. Shivering on a mountaintop in Afghanistan came to mind, shivering in Big Bear, shivering in a closet the first time angry men came for Dan; I fought all those memories. It was easy to come up with sweating stories, but they did no good. The sun. I tried to bask in the light that shined on me.

"What are you and Diyar planning?"

"We're planning on finding out about you and Bannion."

"How do you contact Diyar?"

Cold water drenched me. Don't shiver. Where was Dan? I needed him to tell me not to shiver. No, Dan did not give orders or advice. I needed an old story about the time he refused to shiver, no, refused to sweat, no, ignored the charges against him and eventually they disappeared, like this cold. But Dan was busy elsewhere. Tempting the devil. Reliably unreliable whenever you need him to be.

"Diyar is your partner. I heard you say this."

"Bannion is your partner."

"Diyar is a terrorist. You are a terrorist."

I felt the tickle in an armpit and almost gave in to the shivering. The earth exploded and my body split, every inch spread out, fire covered me. Fire filled my lungs and gut. Freezing fire. The fire went out, but I still burned. More cold water and I was sure my skin was smoking and fizzing like a dying campfire.

"Did I ever tell you about my father?"

Fariz laughed. "Tell me about Diyar."

"He's dead. He's having dinner with Diyar."

The tickle again. The blast. My lungs came up my throat. My balls burst. I was in two dimensions, just a flat flash of lightning. More water. More sizzling. A door creaked open. A conference. A shadow moved in front of the light, and I shivered at last.

"Get out of the light," I said. I sounded like an old man trying to read the small print. The figure moved, but the chill stayed. The hood came off. My arms went slack and I fell to the concrete floor. I kept my face to the light, though it blinded me. Someone put me in a chair. Feet shuffled. The door opened and closed.

Gill threw a towel. I was reluctant to rub hard, certain the flesh would peel off. As soon as I was done, I threw the towel at Gill and dove into him. I hit the concrete right after I hit him. There was no difference between the two. He lifted me back into the chair and threw a blanket over me. I took a look around the room. The floor was concrete and so were the walls. Above me was the hook I had been hanging from. Two fans were installed just below the ceiling on either side of the very heavy steel door. They swiveled enough to cover the room. There were no windows. Gill sat in a chair opposite me.

"Tell me where Diyar is and I can get you out of here."

I understood then why Major Hensel could not find him. My bait caught the wrong fish. "You must be at the bottom of the CIA ladder to get a job guarding the King. Probably typecast you because of all the muscle."

He did not answer. He did not move. "Tell me how you contact Diyar and you can leave here. We'll send you home. Anywhere you want. We need Diyar."

We had been set on parallel paths: assigned to the King. Maybe he knew Bannion beforehand from his Special Forces stint in Kirkuk. Maybe there had been Maya infatuation, too. He repeated his demand for Diyar.

"It was you tipping off Bannion from the start. The SUV that first night wasn't following Maya. It was following me. Darrell White was your contact. He alerted you that an oilman with PKK contacts was in town. You're the one who took his call and told Bannion I was coming."

"I told you I did a lot for them."

"Why kill Arun?"

"He attacked me."

I laughed at the picture of that pouchy little old guy attacking Gill. His insecurity was grotesque, festering behind the stolid wall of silence. "What could you be getting from Bannion?" But that was a wasted question, I knew. Bannion had the chests full of fake emeralds and rubies waiting to be loaded onto anyone's ship.

"Where is Diyar?"

"What does 'DS' stand for in DS Security?"

"Who cares? Where is Diyar?"

"What does the CIA get out of this? Why kill the Prime Minister?"

"Diyar. How do you contact Diyar?"

"I would have to know why."

"Are you always bargaining?"

My turn to use the silent stare. I could have told him who I was and asked him to contact Major Hensel, but I told myself that wouldn't work, that he would find out my identity but keep my whereabouts hidden. The truth was that I didn't want him releasing me and pretending we were on the same side. I was never going to be on the same side as Gill. I did not want any orders to the contrary.

He stood and took the blanket from me.

Before he got to the door, I said, "Hey, Gill. You better kill me. You better kill me here. Because if I get out of here, you're dead."

Gill shrugged.

Two men in heavy coats entered; one held a bucket. The other one was Eddie, my pal from New Jersey, even more sheepish now. He met my eyes, asking me not to acknowledge him. I didn't see why I should. His partner poured ice water over me and any big ideas I had. They didn't stay to watch the show. Maybe they had other buckets to empty.

Don't shiver. I could have sat in full lotus and lost myself, but those fans were the enemy, the source of all my problems, and they had to be dealt with before any meditating took place. Standing on the chair and yanking at the fan did nothing. Lifting the chair and smashing the fan worked. The cover flew off. Sparks flew when I smashed the spinning blade. It bent and stopped. The chair was wrecked, too. I stomped on it to separate the two parts. Holding on to the two back legs, I moved over to work on the second fan. The door creaked and opened. I swung the chairback right into Gill. That hurt him. He yelled, but he kept coming. Another man came in behind him.

I measured them for another swing. Gill just stood in the middle of the room, next to his chair, waiting for me to make a move. The second man tried to slip around behind me. Gill yelled at him, "Get out of here." The man hesitated. Gill repeated it in Arabic. The man left. Gill slammed the heavy door with a flick of his wrist.

I circled left, holding the chair fragment by the legs, and jabbing at Gill. He did not reach or lunge. I moved toward the other broken section and stumbled over it on purpose. Gill stepped in to take advantage. I hopped to the right and swung the chair. The edge hit him in the neck. I swung again. He ducked and his fist hammered into the back of my left shoulder. The force drove me into the wall. I swung the chair again. He leaned back to avoid it, but I let go and it clipped him above the ear. I punched him in the middle of his face and felt his nose crunch. He deflected my next punch with his forearm and hit me in the gut and then the jaw. My head slammed against the wall. I stayed there wanting him to try again. If I could make him miss, he would break his hand on the concrete. But he hit me in the gut again and moved in close and grabbed me. I kneed him in the groin, but Gill kept his hold. He was stronger than any man I had ever fought and he was well trained, too. I was finished. He slammed my head against the wall again.

Gunshots woke me.

The shivering started. The chair remnants were gone. I was slumped against the wall. Blood marked the spot above me. Very little of it came off the back of my head onto my finger. I figured it was frozen. The shots were coming from some distant part of the building. I hopped around for about two minutes, but the insides of my head were bumping against the skull. Just as I was about to sit again, the door creaked open. Masked men carrying rifles rushed in.

On the way out, I saw Fariz slumped in a hallway with a bullet hole in his forehead. I did not see Gill. Or Eddie.

25

They clothed me and fed me and gave me aspirin. Giddy from the successful raid, they laughed while watching the TV, which repeatedly played the cameraman's video of the King toppling over. That was followed by a news update featuring a photo of me. The announcer said I was wanted by the Asayish and might be working with the PKK. They turned off the TV and opened a computer and read the stories about me and my investment with the PKK. They got serious.

"Why did you claim to have given money to the PKK?"

"Aren't you the PKK?"

But they had no time for answers; they had questions. "Why did you search for Diyar? Are you an agent of the U.S. government? Do you want more soup? What kind of torture did they use? Do you have any money for us?" And more. I sat in a plush, comfy chair. Four sat in front of me and one behind. We were in the living room of a modest house. I told them I claimed to be in business with the PKK to gain leverage against the big oil companies who were making deals with Baghdad and the regional oil companies. I was trying to get attention.

"You got lots of attention."

"Are you an agent of the American government?"

My silence made the questioner launch into a long anti-American tirade about illegal occupation and ending that occupation prematurely. "Your plot failed. The Prime Minister has not been assassinated. The shooter missed his mark."

He sat back with satisfaction. The others did not seem to share his certainty that the U.S. was behind this.

"Have they caught the shooter?" I asked. They didn't answer. "Is the man they caught one of yours?"

Two of them answered at once, "He did not do it."

"Has he been missing for some days? A week or more?"

Their faces gave the answer.

Bannion's brilliance dazzled me. Magna cum laude from Dan U. He had fed the hounds a taste, then unleashed them. The King was out of the way. The PKK would be taking the official blame for the failed assassination. I still could not figure his goal. But every move made sense. Every move threw someone else off and solidified his own position. I wanted to get hold of him.

The man behind me said, "What is your relationship with John Bannion?"

I watched the faces of the others. The guy behind was the boss. His question almost made me laugh. I was Bannion's fool, his protégé, maybe his executioner.

"You can have the money if it's there," I said. "I want Bannion."

He asked, "Have you been inside the compound?" He was a

thin, handsome man, about thirty-five, with messy, curly hair and light brown, very steady eyes.

They gave me a piece of paper and I drew the layout for them the best I could.

We piled into two trucks and stopped at another house that served as an armory. They loaded up with pistols and rifles. The leader handed me a SIG Sauer that might have been mine. They had grenades and a rocket launcher. I kept waiting for the pat on the back before the knife, but there was no fake friendliness and no shunning. The mood resembled preparation for a combat mission under a good commander: efficient, with minimal emotion or speculation. It did not surprise me that I felt so comfortable with them. The leader pulled me aside before we got back in the trucks.

"You can call me Rajan," he said.

"Robert."

He showed his skepticism. Maybe he was mimicking mine.

"You get Bannion. We get whatever is there."

"I don't guarantee any money."

"I said whatever is there."

"Why are you bringing me along for this?"

"If it goes wrong, I will negotiate to give you up to help the rest of us escape." He smiled, but I don't think he was joking. Maybe he was Diyar. Maybe he was nobody. There was no reason to ask.

The rocket blew out the front gate. No one returned fire and we moved into the courtyard, taking out as many surveillance cameras as we could find with rifle fire. Grenades for the office door and tear gas inside and up the staircase. Grenades into the building on the left. The rest of us went toward the residence at the rear. The door was unlocked. Rajan ordered one of his men to lead the way inside. He took three steps before the fire hit him. We backed out and tossed two grenades. I went in. I almost tripped over one goon groaning in the foyer from the shock of the blast. I smashed his head with the butt of my gun and moved forward. Rajan ordered one man to guard the entrance. Two of the PKK were taking fire as they worked their way upstairs. Two more worked cautiously down the hallway to the left.

Rajan joined me in the living room. I told him to expect at least eight goons. It was possible the house would be stocked with other DS Security men but they would have to be stacked on top of each other. The place was not huge.

A shot came from behind us. We hit the floor and turned. The goon I had hit was on his knees, firing unsteadily. Rajan shot him in the belly. We moved to both sides of the door to the dining room. I picked up a lamp from a side table and tossed it. No reaction. I thought I saw the flicker of a shadow. Rajan was about to go inside, but I signaled to wait. I stepped back from the wall and fired three shots through it. Rajan did the same on his side. Two goons fell. We stepped into the dining room, and Rajan put a bullet in each of their heads. Three down. There were at least two goons upstairs. That left three.

One of the PKK men joined us. The kitchen had two doors. Rajan and his man prepared to go in through the first one. I slipped past the first door and waited next to the second one. Rajan went in first, his man following close by. I stepped in. The goon was crouched behind the center island. I put my gun to the back of his head and ordered him to put down the weapon. He complied. I lifted him.

"Where's Bannion?"

"I don't know."

I hit him across the jaw with the gun. He crashed back into the stove. I shot him in the knee. "Where is he?"

"I don't know, man. We weren't expecting the attack."

We left him with the PKK man, and Rajan and I went to the study. The door was locked. Rajan shot out the keypad, but that did not work. He shot the lock. That did not work. The firing upstairs had stopped. I asked Rajan if he had a grenade. He shook his head and said, "Not for this room."

A goon came into the other end of the hallway. I shot at him and he dived back. I doubted I killed him. We were trapped there. I signaled to Rajan that we would have to retreat up the hallway. We hugged the near wall and crept forward. After three steps the goon showed himself at the end of the hallway again. I shot. He ducked back. We did not hear the click of the door behind us.

A goon, the one named Neil Bess, knife in his right hand, leapt out at Rajan. Rajan managed to duck under the knife and turn toward Bess. But Bess hugged him and was pushing the knife at Rajan's throat. My head swiveled back and forth like a puppet looking for a laugh. I did not have a good shot at Bess and I did not want to turn my back on the guy at the end of the hallway.

Bess was going to slit Rajan's throat. I moved to them and slid my arm under Bess's. I put my hip into him and levered him off Rajan. Rajan fell. I had control of Bess. I spun him around so his back was to the end of the hallway. His friend down there shot him in the back.

A PKK man came from behind and shot that goon.

Rajan took a long look at me. I wasn't sure what it meant. "You are a very confident man," he said. He kicked Bess aside and we entered the study.

The safe was open. Two body bags were inside. They were unzipped and newspapers spilled from them. I stood there like a drunk at the racetrack staring at discarded tickets, knowing it was useless to inquire. I dragged them out anyway and dumped them onto the floor. Five copies of the same paper from 2005 spread out. On the front page, a photo showed candidates for the Iraqi Parliament sitting unhappily at a long table. Bannion had stuffed the bags long ago. Not a single dollar bill fell out.

The safe did not interest Rajan. He went across the room to the closet. That door was locked, but he was not going to shoot out the lock. Two of his men came in. They reported that the premises were clear. Five dead and the man wounded in the knee. They looked at Bess. Six dead. I asked if Bannion was among the dead. Rajan had to describe Bannion to the men. They shook their heads. He asked them if they found "it." They shook their heads. Another PKK man came in and said they had secured the offices. Rajan asked him about "it." He shook his head.

Rajan asked one man to open the closet door. The man carefully examined the lock. Satisfied, he took the butt of his pistol and knocked the doorknob off. He turned the lock with his fingers and opened the closet. "Everything is ours," Rajan said and held his gaze on me until I nodded.

The computer server was inside. This was their goal, more valuable than money. It held the security details for hundreds of locations in the north of Iraq: electronic and human assets. Rajan took a long look at me to make sure I was not going to try to stop him taking the server. I had no orders to get involved in that and no intention of taking that initiative. I shook my head to let him know I was not interested.

Disgust soaked me. No Bannion, no Victor, no money. And no good next move. The men were rolling the server out of the closet. The wheels got stuck on the doorknob on the floor. One guy picked up the doorknob and tossed it into the safe against the back wall.

It made the wrong sound.

Everyone turned. I ducked and stepped into the safe and picked up the doorknob. I hurled it against the rear panel. The wrong sound: lively and thin when it should have been dead and solid. "Don't lock me in," I said. I pushed the back panel. It swung open.

Rajan ordered the others to take care of the server. He followed me down the stairs into a tunnel. The glare from the one lightbulb hanging midway through the tunnel obscured the other end. The walls were plasterboard. The floor was dirt. We moved slowly, weapons ready. I pressed lightly on the boards as we progressed. There were no side passages or cutouts. We reached a staircase and went up.

I pushed open the door at the top.

The room was bare, no windows and a tiled floor. An overhead light fixture was turned on. On the left, a door was partially open. I stood next to it. The room was dark. I caught a glimpse of a window and a chair. I pushed open the door, and before I walked in, a shot came through the window. A heavy load hit the floor.

"Close that door." It was Bannion. I closed the door and rushed over to kick the gun from Bannion's grip. He noticed Rajan behind me.

"I see you brought help, Mr. Hewitt. Good for you."

"Who is out there?"

"It's Victor," he said. "One of my boys."

I was glad for the darkness so he could not see my expression. I wanted Victor much more than I wanted Bannion. I moved close to the window and peeked out. Cars and trucks lined the dark street. Victor would have an easy time with me if I went out. I did not think I could appeal to our past together. I ached to get him, but the mission was clear: Bannion was the goal. Victor would have to wait.

"He thinks I have millions of dollars on me," Bannion said.

"Isn't that what you wanted everyone to think?"

He chuckled. "You know me too well, Mr. Hewitt."

"We must go," Rajan said.

I took hold of Bannion. "Call me Rollie."

Bannion did not want to escape. He did want to chat, though. The old days, the days of undeclared war and glory: Central Africa, Central America, anywhere a general or a despot got the idea that training his cannon fodder would prolong everyone's agony, Bannion found money and a temporary home. He had grown up operating on his own, much as I had, homeless by the time he was fifteen. Eventually, he found his way into the British Army and discovered that he was good at telling people what to do and teaching them how to do it. So he struck out on his own. Free from the constriction of the Army, Bannion combined his talent for villainy with his talent for organization and training. "People love being told what to do," he said. "As long as it is something they think will give them an advantage. But the next step, Rollie, they seldom know how to take the next step. They continue to need me to tell them what to do."

He wanted me thinking about his story and his wisdom and not thinking about the reason he was cooperating and why he wanted to cross the border into Turkey. I thought I knew. I just did not know how he planned to get rid of me. I expected it would involve an offer.

"What does 'DS' stand for in DS Security?"

"Nothing anymore, I imagine. My boys are killed, most of them, anyway. And the rest scattered. My plans failed. I've disappointed so many who depended on me."

He could have been the reincarnation of Dan. Meaner, more lethal, equally devious. I was part of his plan. I did not know my role.

"What was the plan?" I asked.

"You don't expect me to confess, do you, Rollie? Have you ever confessed?"

"I never staged a coup."

"I will tell you, though, that you were wrong about something at dinner. Defending the oil fields is a better position to be in than attacking them. Those defending the fields control the flow of the oil and therefore the flow of the money."

We reached Dohuk around sunrise. Like Erbil, Dohuk was booming, construction sites every way we turned, and next to them old, tired, low structures begging to be included in the makeover. Rajan gave the orders without explanation and was never questioned by his men. I did not want to question him either. He might have been grateful to me for saving him. He might have just wanted to see Bannion out of the country. He might have been using us as bait. A PKK man drove us and pretended not to understand English. Bannion occupied the backseat: the grand poobah in his carriage. I turned to face him so I spent much of the time looking for followers. I did not spot anyone. The threat of Victor nestled in my spine like an irritating parasite. And I did not think Gill was finished looking for me.

We stopped in an industrial area for about ten minutes, just parked alongside the four-lane road. A panel truck passed us, slowed down, and we followed it for about a mile right into a warehouse.

It was a coffee and tea warehouse if anyone asked or gave it a quick look. It was a liquor warehouse behind the fake walls and in the basement. Liquor was valuable in the Kurdish sections; they were brimming with energy and the taste of freedom, and the PKK needed money. Smuggling the booze across from Turkey gave them access to bribed border guards and the chance to smuggle guns and bombs, too.

Rajan was waiting in the small office. He told us we would start out again in the late afternoon. I could not use my passport and they did not trust Bannion using his. The Asayish had put up roadblocks and was guarding the border crossings into Turkey. The Peshmergas were out in force, too. I asked Rajan about the news reports.

"They want you. They want me."

"What's the fallout from the assassination attempt? Is there a political change?" He shook his head. "What about the oil fields? Any violence there?"

"I haven't seen any reports of that," Rajan said. "I have men who work at the Ain Sifni fields. They're at work this morning."

"Who is guarding the fields?"

He said he would find out.

We started out toward the border in the panel truck. After an hour, we pulled over. Bannion and I were put in the back, snug among the rugs for export. Two hours later, we arrived at a mountain cabin built of stone, a crumbling place. A stream trickled past on the left, and a stone well sat just a few yards from the porch. Again, Rajan preceded us.

"The border is too hot right now. Perhaps in a few days it will calm down. Like a fever."

"And if it doesn't."

"Maybe you'll become a shepherd." He swept his arm across the barren mountainside where no sheep were ever going to live. We were in a hollow, surrounded by crags and cliffs and slopes. No view, not easily viewed.

I slept through the night and deep into the morning. Rajan was gone. Two of his men remained. One was cooking on a propane stove and the other sat outside on the porch with a rifle. Rest had wiped away the fog shrouding Bannion. To understand Bannion, I only had to ask myself what Dan would be doing if he were in Bannion's position.

Bannion wanted to get the money. I was enabling his getaway. He would be my new best friend until I was maneuvered to the edge of a cliff.

The vehicles were gone and that suited me because it gave us a feeling of time stretching without end, which I hoped might exhaust Bannion. Dan always arranged an out, a pressing appointment, a not so secret assignation, and most reliably and most fantastically, the demands of being a single father. I had never seen Dan stranded in this way, so I had an extra reason to look forward to my sessions with Bannion.

Though he was big and a bit blubbery, Bannion was hardy. Uphill did not make him breathless enough to stop his storytelling. I did not tell him I wanted the money; that admission would give him too great an advantage. I assumed that he assumed the money was my interest. I inquired, instead, about which Americans were involved beyond the two generals I had met.

"I started out with a dream, Rollie. A dream of controlling this vast untapped pool of oil. Me, a boy of the streets. But I needed partners. Always look for partners with power. That's the rule, and it meant dealing with the Americans. I admit that their eagerness to join was something of an astonishment. They mistrusted their own government even as they risked their lives to serve it, even as they bragged endlessly about it. It was never a matter of betrayal for them. They convinced themselves they were merely extending the policy and serving their country's interest. Their own profit was an unspoken fact of life. Like self-abuse."

He wanted me to laugh, so I did. He wanted me to tsk-tsk, too, so I did. He spewed names. We stopped and sat on flat rocks and I wrote down the names on a pad I found at the cabin.

"They were generals and colonels, big shots one and all, diplomats, too, and they thought that since they spent years giving orders, they could begin a new empire, blaze a trail, but they were followers one and all, Rollie. They ended up taking orders from me. I just had to lie low and let them pretend they were in charge. But you understand this, Rollie. I can tell. You view them the same way I do. You knew General Garner, didn't you?"

"Did I?"

"We should have been partners."

I knew what to do, but I hesitated. The lifetime of Dan proximity mandated that I reply, "I don't think that partnership would work."

"Close the door partway. Leave it open a crack," Dan would say. "That sliver of light thrown into the hallway is magnetic, Rollie boy."

But did Dan magic work on Dan? It was always easy to hate him, easy to marvel, easy to absorb the lessons and employ them to survive. Easy to work on everyone else. But Bannion had all the knowledge. He had engineered a project far larger and more ambitious than anything Dan had ever imagined. Bannion would recognize my moves. I hesitated, not sure if I did so fearing success or failure.

"I don't think that partnership would work."

"If I had you with me from the start, we would be kings by now." I didn't answer. "You know it's true."

"I know that we can't go backward. Who did you have in the diplomatic corps?" The rule: Change the subject to make him stick with it.

The names of diplomats meant nothing to me. I wrote them down as if they did. "Tell me who you work for now, Rollie. This is hardly a fair exchange."

I spewed a bunch of plausible lies describing a DIA agency similar to SHADE. I called it PLG for Post Liberation Group. I said they chose me for my language skills.

"I should think they chose you for many reasons, perhaps some of the same reasons I would choose you." He widened his eye to exclaim his admiration and his roly-poly cheeks rose with his smile. When he let go, everything fell at once like a popped balloon. "I had a man in the U.S., a Colonel McColl, quite a capable man. Did you know him?"

Only well enough to kill him. But Bannion did not suspect that yet. He wanted to know if I was aware of the buried money. "His name was mentioned," I said.

Below us, a truck labored up the rough track toward the cabin.

We walked back. A PKK man was unloading supplies from the truck. He ignored Bannion's questions about how long we would be there. After dinner, we sat on the porch, watching the darkness slide across the mountainside. He was shameless enough to say he had "reached for the stars." I was being wooed.

"We go into these conflicts with goals. But it's the goals that hold us back. It's like this: You see a beautiful woman and you decide you must have her phone number and you set out for that. But what if you could have gotten more, so much more. The mission defines your limitations. It holds you back if you allow it to. Think of the Americans stopping in the first Gulf War. They could have changed the world if they had just followed their noses. In Bosnia, I saw opportunities to make millions. Not lawfully, mind you, but opportunities nonetheless. And it was my responsibility to face the truth. If I hadn't, I never would have been able to help the Kurds. I never would have met Maya."

He paused and made sure to hold my eyes. He wanted to see if I had slept with Maya. After a while, he said, "I won't ask what went on between you two. It was over for us long ago, long ago. I don't think it could have been any other way. She was attracted to me as someone who was seizing opportunities, and to satisfy her, I would have had to spend all my time seizing her. If she likes you, then I take it as a confirmation of my assessment of you. She is not a woman to spend her passions frivolously."

It was like eavesdropping on Dan and his guests. Opportunities missed, wistful regrets, lessons learned. And just as I was expecting the proposal, he stood and said, "Don't like talking important matters with these fellows listening in. Zealots, you know, can never be trusted." His timing was perfect. He went inside. I sat there letting the endless questions pop and sparkle and fade like the stars.

The morning was a duplicate of the previous day: clear and cloudless. The PKK man said we would not be moving out for hours, at least. Bannion and I hiked the same route. I asked how long he served in the Army. I overpraised my current job as a way of showing my doubts. He mentioned timing as the key to making a decision to go civilian.

When we reached the flat section, he said, "You must know about the money."

"The buried money? That was a good plan."

"It was. It was."

"Yours? The plan, I mean."

"Safe haven, that's what I thought. I must have a safe haven for these riches we found. Remember, I snuck into Erbil before the war started. Finding that money was a top priority from the beginning. They all pretended it was found by accident. They were like kids searching for hidden Christmas presents whenever the folks turned their backs; it was the only thing on their minds. But the generals did not know how long the war would last. They couldn't say how long we would have to hide it until the moment came to put our plan into action. They could not trust each other, though they never said that out loud. Suggesting the U.S. as a safe haven solved everything."

"I heard it's all been found. All the graves located."

"Have you?"

"Maybe you waited too long."

"Do you know the most difficult thing in the world, Rollie? More difficult than cold-blooded murder. More difficult than restraint or patience. Or sincerity." He stopped and seemed to consider what else was difficult in life. His eye darted around, checking each corner of the world for something left behind. "It's knowing what you really want."

"You mean it took you all those years to decide how to spend the money?"

He stopped the gangster, fake friendliness. His voice became a naked growl. "I think you know exactly what I mean."

I did. I knew because there could be only one answer, and I was the only pupil in the class that had been taught this lesson. Bannion had betrayed everyone. The plot to take over Kurdistan was a decoy, a still photo for the cover of the brochure. The ambitions and dreams of the military men and the diplomats were turned against them, used as a leash to parade them and then tie them to the porch. Bannion knew the secret: They would not go out without that leash.

The money was always for Bannion and only Bannion.

"They helped you hide it and you had until the U.S. pulled out to perfect your exit. Most of what you had to do was wait. But knowing what you really want is harder than patience."

"The best plans evolve. Time is an ally." He read from The Book of Dan, chapter one.

Time was an ally, and I worked for time. The story that McColl or someone else spilled the locations took the pressure off Bannion. He would not have to face the moment when his partners faced rotting corpses where they expected crisp hundreds.

"You must have been delighted to get rid of McColl."

He looked at me for a long time and I thought I had revealed too much. Did he already know I was the one who had busted McColl?

"McColl was a problem from the start. He had no business digging up that grave in Oklahoma. Just impatient. And by accident he picked the one that some other guy had looted. Someone I never heard of. Bad luck for him, bad luck for McColl."

"Good luck for you." I was struck by a previously unknown urge to brag about Dan, to claim the connection and tout his brilliance. I resisted, though it bothered me to hear him relegated to anonymity. I know Dan would have said it was an advantage. But this was vanity: A diminished Dan diminished the luster of my hatred and fascination for him.

Just as the day before, we saw a truck bouncing up toward the cabin. Neither of us moved.

"How many graves did McColl know about? Graves with money in them."

Bannion shrugged. "Let's just say the odds were good that McColl would have found a body rather than dollars. Considering his obsessive behavior, I would not have enjoyed dealing with that situation. Instead, that behavior led to his demise."

I waited. He waited. I tried counting up the graves claimed, the money found, tried tallying how much might be left. To reassure him of my ignorance, I would have to act as if I thought I knew it all.

"Only three graves have been dug up with any money. That leaves plenty of millions still in the ground."

"Knowing what you want, Rollie, that's what it's all about in the end."

On the way down to the cabin, I asked about the kidnapping and the million dollars.

"Oh, the million was a nice bonus and a chance to get to know you. Just made up on the spot. You were a gift. The PKK was the

missing piece all along, and you delivered them to me. The fake assassination plot came late. The generals and others were pressing
for action. We needed a fall guy."

A quick scam inside the larger scam. No opportunity missed.
Threads that could never be unraveled.

He went on unprompted. "I made some arrangements, set
some contracts with certain officials of the Regional Government
that said if there should be a national crisis, my company would be
hired to oversee the oil fields. It was that simple. Who guards the
fields controls the flow."

"Who is going to take it over now?"

"Your friend Mr. Gill thought he might. Not my problem now."

"What does the 'DS' stand for?"

"Oh, partners I had."

Rajan was waiting for us.

27

Rajan handed me binoculars so I could take a look at the Habur Gate, the border crossing to Turkey. Barbed wire protected the sides of the road leading in, and if you got past that, rolling brush stretched far enough to give even the worst marksman time to make the shot. The approach was more than fifty trucks deep, clogged by the line of rifle-toting Peshmergas doing the slow search.

"I just wanted you to see it in the daylight," Rajan said. "Tonight there will be a diversion. Guards are bribed. You'll get through. From there, it is not far to the U.S. base at Adana."

"You coming along?"

"I am saying good-bye. I cannot go near the gate."

We shook hands and I thanked him. We both looked at Bannion sitting in the truck.

"Why did you help me?"

Rajan laughed. "Karkukli's servants liked the way you handled Zoran."

"They were working for you." I admired him for seeing that the

King did not have to be eliminated; he could be utilized. I waited for more.

"Besides, I was in need of an American friend," Rajan said. "You saw the alternatives. Call it a long-term investment."

I watched him as he got into his car. He was the opposite of the King, of royalty. Though he had plenty of chances to lecture about the glorious empire he would restore, I never heard a word about it. He and the King shared a lot, though: They both had what they really wanted. The King wanted an audience for his endless rap about his dream, about his quest, about his destiny, and so on. Rajan wanted to fight.

Two rifle-toting Peshmergas met us at the Marsil Grill in Zakho, just a few miles from the border crossing. Maybe they were bought and paid for, maybe they were Kurdish patriots. They conferred with the PKK men who were driving us and went out. Bannion and I sat alone in a back room over tea and kubbeh hamusta, a sort of dough and meatball in a soup.

"Once we cross the border, I'll have about an hour before my boss makes contact and I'll have to turn you over. I'll be out of this."

"We'll stop in Switzerland first," Bannion said. He smacked his puffy lips together as he chewed the meatballs.

"No Switzerland. No stops." Even the name of the country sounded made up coming from his mouth. Nothing he said could be trusted.

"To see my child. Perhaps for the last time." He tried to imply that he missed the kid.

I almost laughed. "I can get us into the U.S. I can arrange IDs. I can help you get out with cash. But you have to give me some reason, now, why I think I'm going to see some money."

The waiter brought a bottle of wine. He struggled with the corkscrew. Bannion took it from him and pulled the cork. He handed the bottle back and the waiter poured two glasses. There were three tables occupied in the front room, but the place was quiet, as if we had it to ourselves.

"You have me cornered, Rollie. Cornered and wounded. Well played. The money is, indeed, in the U.S. but spread all around. Many locales. Many spots."

I shook my head. An inch of squirm room would turn into a yard, then miles.

"You can hardly expect me to hand over a bloody list now, can you?" I did not answer. "Of course not. But I will tell you something, Rollie, something you already know, I'm sure, but will be appreciated nonetheless." He looked at me as he slurped up the soup, then put down his spoon and dabbed his chin. "Sometimes people are looking at the answer and need only realize it. Say you've broken into a home, and the jewels aren't in the safe and they're not in the jewelry box. Well, what's the biggest mistake you make in that situation?"

"Calling the police?"

Bannion did not smile. He was a relentless clue giver, but when he pointed to one, he wanted an answer. He pushed his food away and looked around the room even though we were the only ones in it. One PKK man lounged just on the other side of the partition to the main room.

"I wonder if it will be cold in the truck. Could be in there for hours." He sipped his tea. "I can't blame you, really. You have a job and whatever security comes with it. The villain life is not for everyone."

"What does 'DS' stand for?"

"The worst thing you can do in the situation I described is to become impatient. You're probably very close to the jewels. You have to stay calm and believe in the information and the instincts that brought you to that point." He smiled, let it deflate, then smiled again: a two-faced mask. "You are interesting, Rollie. And I don't believe you went to Columbia University. Not at all. You know too much."

"I don't know enough."

"I've told you all I can for now. You make your decision. I'll live with it."

Another Dan moment: the surrender to victory. But I was excited because I had the better hole cards. I had Major Hensel, who I knew would let me give Bannion all the rope I needed.

We stepped outside. The Peshmergas were loitering down the street, toward the border. The PKK men looked like mirror images, in the other direction, but closer. Cigarettes left brief tracers as the men gestured and talked. Across the street, the light from a TV flickered in a second-story window. We stood still in a wide-open parking spot freshly painted with MAHJOUZ, reserved. Headlights bathed us and a car raced right toward us. It skidded to a stop diagonally in the parking spot.

Two doors slammed. From the driver's side came a tall figure with a bent posture: Zoran.

"John Bannion! Stop there." That was the King.

Bannion turned to face them, but the headlights blinded him. He moved to his right, ignoring the King's order to stop. The PKK men stood upright and ready. Another cigarette flew through air.

The gun looked like a prop in the King's hand. It was hard to imagine anything more deadly than a speech coming out of it. His suit was ripped at the shoulder. He came around the front of the car as Bannion moved out of the light toward the rear. Zoran kept his gun on me.

"Your Highness, what a relief it is to see you," Bannion said. "We were just speculating on your whereabouts and hoping for your safety, weren't we? Are you coming along with us?" This was pudding for him. The delivery was perfect, but the stark lighting and the surrounding silence flattened the seductiveness of his tone.

Maya got out of the car, and Bannion greeted her, too. He wanted to keep the chatter going.

The King shouted, "Stop! Stop!"

It was not clear if he meant stop moving or stop talking. The PKK men were frozen. I saw one of the Peshmergas speaking into his radio. He and his partner looked behind them. Far down the road, in the direction of the border, headlights appeared. They were high, as on a truck or military vehicle. The Peshmergas hopped quickly into their car and drove away.

Bannion went on, "This is good luck, though, isn't it? We have safe passage arranged. Plenty of room for you, and Zoran and Maya, of course. Plenty of room. In fact, we've made great strides these last days. Peshmergas on our side and now the rebels have joined us, too."

The King was shaking. Bannion edged closer to him.

Zoran faced Bannion and shouted for him to stop. I plowed my fist into Zoran's jaw. The bone cracked. I turned my body and my right sank into his gut. He bent forward and I kneed him in the face. He hit the ground. I picked up his gun.

The PKK men ran. The big vehicles coming toward us were close enough for their headlights to irritate.

I said, "King, put the gun away. If there's shooting, we're all in trouble. Maya, too. Look, here come the Asayish. Please." I looked to Maya, hoping she would chime in, but she, too, seemed frozen.

Bannion started again. "We have new interest. From the Chinese. The Great Game is on for them, it seems. They particularly asked about you."

I was behind the King, but I could see him trembling. I slid to the side to get a better look. He glanced briefly at me. The headlights accentuated his silent film star looks: the thin dark lips, the circles under the eyes, the animated eyebrows. And he had run out of words.

"Put the gun away, King. No one wants to hurt you." I was sorry as soon as I said it because it pointed to his insignificance.

The vehicles were close.

Bannion went on. "That's right, Your Highness. Put the gun away and no hard feelings. I certainly bear you no ill will. We're going to Switzerland. To see young Aza. How long has it been?"

The King straightened himself up and said, "Who are you? You adventurer. I allowed you in my presence . . ."

Bannion laughed at him. "Indeed you did."

I could see Bannion's expression harden. The caginess had been spent. The tough villain roared.

"You allowed? You allowed me a lot more, I'd say, than your presence. And in return you did damn well off me. You're lucky I kept you along for the ride. Go inside and ask for a job as a waiter and see what they say . . ."

"Shut up, Bannion." That was me.

Two vehicles arrived, pouring more false light on the scene. Neither Bannion nor the King glanced at them. The two men looked like museum figures in a staged confrontation: waxworks. A car came down the street toward the border. It slowed, then sped away. Silhouettes appeared in the upstairs window where the TV flickered.

"Bannion is finished," I said. "I've got him." The King turned to look at me as if he had forgotten I was there. Bannion rushed him and grabbed the gun. But the King held the gun steady and when it went off, the shot hit Bannion in his belly. He staggered backward against the car. The King shot him twice more. Bannion put one hand on the car and eased his way to the ground. He sat, legs out, against the car door, looking like a worker taking his lunch break in the shade.

I held my gun, but I did not want to use it. What could I get from killing the King? He stood there stupidly looking at Bannion.

"Put the gun down. Please." I spoke softly. He ignored me.

Plainclothesmen jumped from the vehicles, holding rifles and pistols. Behind them, a mammoth climbed down, and the vehicle sighed its relief. I grabbed Maya and yanked her toward me. The King looked at the men and raised his gun toward them and said, "Halt." He said it delicately, the way he would order a servant to stop pouring his coffee.

They killed him.

Maya gasped and ran to her father. I dropped my gun on the ground. My interest was Bannion. He was struggling to breathe. His eye closed and opened over and over. He knew what I wanted.

"Smart boy you are, Rollie. Dead Soldiers. DS. Dead Soldiers." His shirt was soaked with blood. The eye opened wide and Bannion looked terrified. He gripped my hand and the look faded. "Look out for Maya. And the boy. And the boy."

His fat lips wanted to work more, but they stuck together. The effort inflated his cheeks for a brief moment. The eye stopped flickering.

I stood up and faced Gill, who stood close over me. "What did he say? What did he say?"

"He told me you were a stooge for the Asayish and a stooge for him. That you thought you were going to retire and run his security operation, but that was a joke to him and he laughed about it with the others. The thought of it was a riot to them." I wanted to hit him and I did not mind the beating I would have to take. I pushed him in the chest and got ready for him to start. The Asayish behind him were pointing their guns at me.

Gill turned to them. "Wait here. Get this cleaned up." The Asayish men hesitated. They hated him openly. A fat man with a mustache seemed to be in charge. He cradled an M16. I thought for a moment he might point it at Gill. He didn't. Gill pushed me toward the door of the restaurant. "Come inside."

I helped Maya up. "She comes, too." He did not argue. Maya did not resist coming along. Her expression hardened as if she had prepared for this moment. As we entered the building I said, "When he isn't looking, escape out the back."

She said, "Okay."

Gill ordered the proprietor to clear the place: three tables' worth of diners rushed outside without question, leaving their partially eaten meals on the tables. A bottle of wine and a corkscrew on one, the same wine Bannion and I had ordered; a family-style falafel plate; bowls of stew.

Maya positioned herself away from us, toward the partition. Gill looked her over, deciding if he should worry about her presence. He shrugged and began talking.

"I'm going to give you a chance to tell me what Bannion said. You know where he hid the money. Tell me, and you and Maya cross the border and this ends. I sweated for this for too long. Ask her. Ask her." But neither of us looked toward Maya. "I did not torture you. They did. I held them back. I don't know who you are or what you want out of this, but I am going to have Bannion's money. I've been after it too long to let you stop me. You know where it is."

"Yes."

"Tell me. Tell me now. Don't put yourself through this. You have money. You don't need it. You're going to tell sooner or later. Don't put yourself through it. I have nothing against you."

It was as if he had been tortured and wanted to spare me his experience. But he had not been tortured. He had been tantalized, and the wait and the prospect of failure, the certainty of failure, humiliated him. He thought that was torture. But threatening torture makes no sense. It forces the other person to fight much harder. I could not see any reason to wait. I was going to kill him.

I reached back with my right hand and picked up the wine bottle and swung it at his head. He ducked. My momentum turned me around. I smashed the bottle on the marble tabletop and reversed, coming at his right side. The jagged edges of glass dug into his cheek and eye. He snatched the bottle away and slammed it down. I kicked him in the groin, then the knee. Blood ran down his face. He swung wildly at me, but I faded away from him and kicked him again, hitting his hip. I was near the wall to the kitchen.

Gill lifted a table, a table with a marble top, a table I would have a hard time pushing, and rammed it at me, backing me into the wall. I kept my hands up and pushed back, using the wall for leverage. But Gill was too strong.

Shifting my hands higher, I used my forearms against the pressure. That was not going to help for long. I slid my right forearm across the marble, next to my left. The imbalance sent the right edge crashing against the wall and opened the left side. I slipped out.

Gill dropped the table.

Behind him, the door opened. The fat man carrying the rifle, and two other Asayish men, came in.

Gill wiped blood from his face. I kicked. He caught my leg and lifted and I crashed hard on my shoulder amid the broken plates and glass and the food. Gill looked at the men behind him. "I told you to wait," he said with unmasked disdain.

I palmed the corkscrew and hopped up. Gill swung. I ducked. I hit him in the gut, which was as useful as throwing a match into a puddle. But it got me in close. He blocked another right, caught my arm and twisted. And with my left I jammed the corkscrew into his neck.

He sneered at me as if I were a driver who cut him off. "I want to know . . ." He might have lived an extra couple of minutes if he had left the corkscrew in, but that wasn't Gill's style. The blood spurted. He fell to his knees and onto his face.

Maya was still at the partition. The steak knife she had snatched clattered when it hit the floor. I stepped back from the spreading blood.

The Asayish stayed near the door. The fat man tossed his cigarette onto the floor. "Do you have any money?" he said. "The owner will want compensation for the damages."

The King was dead; long live Aza Karkukli Bannion. First stop was Incirlik Air Base near Adana in Turkey. The squadron commander of the 39th Air Base Wing Communications Squadron welcomed us in his office and told a story about how Major Hensel had introduced him to his current wife. Of course. He called in a sergeant and ordered him to show Maya the apartment we could use until our flight was ready.

Army Colonel Homer Hoyle invited Maya and me to dinner along with his wife, Lauren. I got to know Colonel Hoyle in Afghanistan, where he worked in Army Intelligence in coordination with DIA. He was a bright, dedicated officer who tried to understand things as they were rather than the way his bosses wanted them to be.

We went to a restaurant off base and sat on the patio. Three men, all in their thirties, all wearing sport shirts that were not tucked in, entered just after us and were seated a few tables away. They did an awful job of pretending not to watch us. Colonel Hoyle was subdued, not at all like the gregarious, opinionated man I had known. I thought maybe the change was due to the presence of his wife, though I did not sense that she was some kind of shrew. We reminisced a bit. They spoke about their kids and their lives in Turkey. After dinner, we took a walk through the town. The colonel nodded to his wife and she pulled Maya into a shop. We kept walking. The colonel guided me across the street to a small park, just trees and a few benches, and a plaque I could not read. When we reached a dark corner, he stopped.

"It must have been tough in Erbil," he said. I shrugged. When he saw that I was not going to open up about it, he went on. "The three men in the restaurant were CIA. They wanted to interrogate you. I told them I would be debriefing you. But they're on the warpath. You'll be seeing CIA around lots of corners."

"Thanks for the warning."

He had more, but it was not coming easily to him. There was no one else in the park. I was looking for the CIA men. "Maybe we should get back," I said.

"Wait." He looked all around, too, and took a deep breath before he spoke again. "I knew. Last year, two of them approached me. General Howland and Colonel Vollhardt, Air Force, and they talked about me joining in with them. It was all pretty vague. They were just testing the waters. But I figured out what they were getting at. I knew."

"It was your job to listen to them."

"It was my job to follow up and report them. I didn't do it."

I hated my job. Colonel Hoyle was a good man and he expected himself to be perfect and the rules expected it, too. He stared at me, and though our faces were shaded, I could see how tormented he was. I already had their names. "I'll add their names to the list," I said.

"And mine." By his tone I knew that was an order.

"Yes, sir."

The flight to Ramstein AFB in Germany left at 0600 hours. Maya and I spent a chaste night. She talked a little about her son, worrying that she hardly knew him, hardly knew how he would react to the news. She got out of bed and looked out the window for a while.

"Do you think Johnny was evil?"

"Are you worried about your son?"

"Are you like your father?"

Dan and Bannion, I had seen both of them die. Both were perpetually in motion and motion gets attention, especially when it carries the threat of disaster. Both left me clues as they died, and the clues served the same purpose as money left in a will: It poured gas on the fire of my hatred and made it flame out. "I think John had the gift of being able to see people as they really are, stripped down . . ." I paused. She leaned forward, hanging on what I said. "And he saw himself the same way, so he thought he had to act first."

She smiled. "You're just talking about yourself."

She asked me to hold her and I did until she fell asleep.

At Ramstein, I asked Maya to rent the car in her name. I found the flight coordinator and booked myself on the next flight to the U.S., going to Lackland, as Rollie Waters. I was not going to board the flight. I booked a commercial flight from Frankfurt to New York as Robert Hewitt. I was not boarding that one, either. All this was just a precaution to keep Victor off my tail until I was ready to deal with him.

The school was set in the foothills outside Geneva. Iron gates, bigger than the iron gates at the houses in Houston, gave way to a bricked drive that opened onto a huge courtyard. We had to show ID to the security men at the gate. I think I saw a stray leaf on the bricks, but it might have been a fake, some student artwork. The first building was wide and beige, three stories with a mansard roof and two wings. We left the car and walked toward the door in the middle section of the building. A burly security man in a red sport coat and gray slacks watched us from a kiosk. Another one watched us from the foyer, but he did not open the door for us. There were plenty of security cameras.

The secretary seemed used to this kind of intrusion. She checked a schedule and told us that Aza was in French class, which would end in twenty minutes. She offered to call him out immediately, but Maya told her we would wait.

The terrace overlooked a swimming pool. Below lay the lake, wide and dark blue. Geneva was visible to the left, partially blocked by another three-story building. The red clay tennis courts were on the right. The soccer fields were beyond. And behind us, bulging high above the building, were snow-covered Alps.

It reminded me of a resort where I once spent the night in Colorado with a woman who insisted it was better to spend all our money at once on something really nice than spreading it out over time in crummy places. She was right. We spent the rest of the trip sleeping in the car or on rocky spots beside the road, but the resort was worth the money.

"Are you going to keep him here?"

"Johnny insisted on a Swiss school. He mistrusted the English schools. 'They grow up to be people I dominate,' he said. 'The schools can't be any good.' Besides, this is probably the safest place." A sailboat appeared on the lake, too small and far away for any of the crew to be seen. Three birds lifted off and flew toward the town.

A small, thin boy with wavy, light brown hair emerged from the building on the left. He saw Maya and waved and started to run along the path.

"Don't tell him," Maya said.

"About his father?"

"His grandfather. I don't want him to know yet that he'll be king."

Aza ran up and hugged his mother, then broke and waited politely to be introduced. Maya introduced me as Rollie. He shook my hand. He kept his suspicions in check.

"Your father asked Rollie to come here to meet you. They're great friends."

We sat down, and Maya asked Aza if he was happy with the school and about the food and his teachers. Everything sounded okay. He was neither sullen nor forthcoming. He was waiting for the purpose of the visit to be revealed. He had already learned that no one ever dropped in to see him just because they missed him. And my presence settled the matter quickly for him. I recognized the situation. He assumed, of course, that some disappointment would be involved.

I often imagined some stranger arriving and telling me Dan was dead. I imagined faking pain at the news, or just demonstrating my indifference, or using the sympathy to run away or even to nestle in if I were staying with Lita or one of Dan's other girlfriends who smelled nice and treated me well. But the strangers always disappointed me.

I was about ten, around Aza's age, when I was either kidnapped or left as collateral; I never found out which it was. A couple, Ollie and Marvin, knocked on the door so many times that I finally let them in. Dan was out. Ollie sat on the couch and pretended to watch TV with me while Marvin searched the apartment. Then he joined us with a big drink of Dan's booze. Pretty soon I could not hear the TV because they were arguing about whose fault every-thing was. Ollie told me to go to my room. But we were in my room; I slept on the couch in that place. Marvin's phone rang and he went in the kitchen and did some loud swearing. Then they told me to put on my shoes because we were leaving. Of course I told them I would not go. They started bribing me with offers of food. I made them promise to take me to the putt-putt place I had often seen from the car.

They took me to a crummy hotel and bought McDonald's burg-ers. I put the pickles under the covers for a surprise for them later. The arguing got worse. They argued in a way Dan never did; they did a lot of name calling. Dan's girlfriends or business associates called him plenty of names, but Dan never talked that way. Pre-tending he liked the people he was arguing with was an essential component of his act.

Ollie told Marvin he was a moron, and Marvin did not take long to accuse Ollie of sleeping with Dan, which I'm sure was true. He called her a slut. Marvin's phone rang, but they did not hear it, so I took it in the bathroom and answered. It was Dan. That was one of the few times it was pleasant to hear his voice. He was so calm and relaxed. I knew that overplaying things would not help with him, so I did not claim that they hit me or anything, only that Marvin was drunk and all they did was fight. Dan asked if I could sneak away. I told him I could. He said he would pick me up. I did not know where I was and the wastebasket in the bathroom said Red Roof Inn, but I had no idea which one. Dan decided I should just get out and run and, first chance I got, go into a restaurant or gas station and ask to use the phone and call him. I said I would find my own way home and Dan said, "No, pal, can't go back there for a little while unless you want to go back to the Red Roof Inn, too."

I threw the phone in the toilet. Marvin and Ollie had lost a little steam and it was not long before Ollie demanded Marvin call Dan again. While Marvin searched around for his phone, I positioned myself near the door. He made Ollie help him look. As soon as he found it, I turned off the lights, pulled the chain off the door, and ran out.

I don't think they chased me. I heard Ollie yell, "Oh, forget the fucking kid." I caught a bus and rode all night without calling Dan. I was still young enough to think he might worry about where I was.

Maya suggested Aza take me on a tour of the school while she spoke with Mr. Labiche, the headmaster. When she left, Aza said, "Are you dating my mother?"

I said yes because I knew he would take no as a lie. I was going to lie to him later. He had his grandfather's manners, a courtly ten-year-old. The building we were in was for the upper school. Aza was eager for the chance to wander through there with protection beside him; this was forbidden territory for a boy from the lower school. Security cameras checked our movements, and security men appeared around corners. They did not smile or nod or acknowledge us at all and it seemed that the students did not notice them. The students did not notice Aza, either. There were probably more legitimate kings attending classes there.

Aza showed me his dorm room, which he shared with two others. He had a view of the mountains. No bunk beds here. Each bed was tucked into a small alcove. Each boy had his own closet.

We left the room and walked outside toward a cafeteria where some students were hanging around. "Do your roommates steal from you?"

"The older boys come in and steal. They treat it as their right."

"What do they take?"

"Someone took my watch. My father gave it to me. And someone took Nigel's Kindle. They don't take phones, at least."

"What about the envelopes that come from the banks? The ones you save for your father?"

"Oh . . ." He was about to answer but caught himself because he had been told never to mention those envelopes. I could see Bannion taking Aza sailing or fishing, a special outing, just the boys, initiation, and explaining about secrets and their importance, and how the men of the family must keep their secrets from everyone, that it was secrets that made the man. Secrets were holy. And, if Aza kept the envelopes secret, there would be many more days like that one, with better secrets to follow.

Maya was approaching. Aza looked at me and said, "I have not seen my father in almost a year."

Maya and I talked for a few moments about how beautiful the school was and how much I wished I could have attended a school like this. Aza watched me and I could feel the mistrust. If you're going to be King of Nothingistan someday, you might as well learn to be mistrustful at an early age.

Maya and Aza went off together. It was time for the bad news. I went back to Aza's room and found the paperwork I wanted from the banks, in a wooden box at the bottom of his closet. A security man was down the hallway when I came out of the room. I walked straight to him and told him Aza's father had died and grandfather, too, and that there were political implications that the kid was unaware of. It was possible that enemies might come around to take advantage of the situation. Extra security was essential. He thanked me for letting him know.

Aza was crying and looked like he meant it. Not a big hysterical show, just tears flowing down while Maya held his hand on the terrace. He was a rich, spoiled kid living at this luxury resort and would someday parade around the world calling himself royalty and I could talk to him, sympathize with him, care about him. But confronted with genuine tears at the news of his father's death, I was flummoxed, could offer no genuine consolation. I did not know how he felt. I sat next to them and said nothing.

I was taking the riches his father had left him and leaving him with his grandfather's legacy of delusion: the delusion that royalty existed as anything more impressive than a ribbon or a medal that could be bought at the art supply store. The King's patrimony was a perpetual Halloween.

Rather than one of the grand Geneva hotels, we stayed at Hotel de la Cigogne, a small hotel where Maya had stayed with Bannion early in their marriage. We walked through the old city, which felt abandoned at nine P.M., and ate dinner. On the way back, Maya said, "I know you laugh at my pretensions, at the Kingdom of Kurdistan."

"Does it matter if I laugh? Do you want me to believe in it?"

"Imagine if I let it go. If I pulled Aza away from it and he dropped it and never mentioned it to his children. In a short time, it would disappear, disappear forever. And we would never know if it could have happened. Never know if the kingdom could have been restored."

"I don't mind the idea of a united Kurdistan. Means nothing to me. As for kings, if the boy is going to be one, it's from his father. You were married to one."

She took my arm. "You could at least pretend to believe in royalty."

"Why?"

"Then I would not mind liking you so much."

We made love, affectionately this time, slow and easy. That was probably the last time. I boarded a plane for Los Angeles in the morning.

T he stewardess is cute. Send back the wine so I can see what
      kind of personality she has."
      The flight was Dan time. He belonged in first class
much more than I did. I told the stewardess the wine tasted wrong.
She said, "I agree. I was waiting for someone to notice." I don't
know if she meant it, but her personality was fine. My mind was
leaning toward corpses and royalty. I took the envelopes from my
bag. Each came from an investment house in the U.S. Each one
started with some version of "JB Limited in cust for Aza Karkukli
Bannion." The first one I opened listed a current balance of about
forty-two million dollars. The next was twenty-six million. The
last was thirty-nine million. Aza was a nine-figure man.

"It's a great feeling, leaving money to your child," Dan said.

The stewardess asked, "Are you okay?"

I had choked on Dan's comment. I reassured her. She brought
me water.

*"It would have been more fun to take it away from the kid if he
knew it was there."*

"You mean if he knew it was gone," I said.

"Do you think Maya knew about the money?"

"I'm sure she did not know the boy received the envelopes. Bannion would never have let that out."

"But she knew there was always money. Those rented mansions in Houston. Bannion's large staff of his boys. The supposed effort to obtain the throne for her father. She was around, had to hear talk of Saddam's stolen stash."

"But if she knew, she would not have looked to me to help get money for the King. She would have just wanted Bannion killed."

"Well, then."

Dan did not deliver bad news. Dan allowed bad news to ripple naturally, through silence, preferably in his absence. I did not like thinking that Maya saw me as a potential assassin from the start, though it might have been the case, whether she knew about the money or not. As part of my self-indulgence I had assumed "savior" meant something noble. I was infatuated with an image of Maya, and an image of myself.

Consoling me, Dan said, *"She didn't carry on when Bannion died. If she thought she would be coming into all that money, she would have pretended that his death devastated her. Besides, no one knew but Bannion that the money wasn't in the graves. He loved her. But that's different from trusting her."*

I did not care if she knew or not. She was going to have to pretend that it was all legit money when the legal moves to recover the money hit her. She would consider it her sacred duty to fight for the treasury of United Kurdistan. I settled back in my seat, thinking of the curses and hatred that would be launched in my direction.

"Bannion's only mistake was relying on the consistency of the King. But it was hard to figure that guy would choose martyrdom."

"If Bannion lived, I had him."

"Did you? Dead Soldiers? Clever boy? He was going to take you for a tour of grave sites around the country. Oh, look, here's a million dollars. And here is a corpse. Maybe the money was removed. So sorry. And soon enough, you would be distracted enough for him to slip away. You know he had a plan to slip away. And if you handed him over, he would have melted his jailors in the palm of his hand because he would offer them a couple of fruitful graves he had not given you."

"Stop." I knew Dan would see it Bannion's way. "I would have gotten to the kid though I might have been too late." Why argue with him? I sat back and let the voice of one great artist explain the work of the better craftsman.

"I have to admit I'm envious, Rollie boy. I was there. I was there and I let it pass me by. Bannion must have had fun. He must have seen early on that once he pitched the plan to plant the money, everyone would relax their watch. I would bet he pulled a lot out and spread it around as mad money, maybe tens of thousands per, to make them feel big. Everyone had his eyes on the handouts. Then it became a matter of confusing the issue. Twenty-five million in the grave I dug up, and maybe one other, but lower amounts in others. It hypnotized even me. I saw one and closed my eyes to the possibility that there were others, many more. Half the graves that McColl or Frank had marked for money had bodies or who knows what. Same for your DS graves, you'll see. That way, if he had to give some up, he wouldn't lose big numbers. He had a private jet, lent it generously, of course. All the generals felt important. But when they weren't using it, Bannion loaded it up with cash and moved it to Switzerland. And from there to the U.S."

"Some left in Switzerland? Some to burn in case he had to give it up?"

"Certainly."

I started thinking about how Dan and Bannion thrived by starting ventures that must come to a bad end. No one could accuse them of being optimists. It wasn't visions of rosy futures that drove them. They were sensualists: slaves to the pleasure of deceit on a scale large and small. They found it irresistible. The inevitable pain was a lightning bolt at the horizon; there was no sense in running inside while the sun still shined.

Dan interrupted, moaning about the opportunity missed. *"I was there. I was there and I did not see the possibilities. I was stealing iPods."* Dan had gone to hell.

"But you walked away with twenty-five million dollars. More than anyone else besides Bannion."

"If it were about the money, I would have spent it. And so would you. And so would you."

received VIP treatment upon landing. An official from Immigration and Customs Enforcement, an ICEman, wearing a badge on his short-sleeve blue shirt, came on board and asked if he could carry my bag. We were first off the plane. One of his equally sour coworkers met us at the end of the ramp and they escorted me down many long corridors to a small room, a private room. I was allowed to enjoy the facilities for two hours. Free. Two different ICEmen came in and asked all about my trip.

"Have you ever seen the Citadel in Erbil? They say it's been inhabited for six thousand years. You really should go," I said. "Unfortunately, I forgot to take pictures."

ICEman One said, "Your passport stamps indicate that you entered Russia six months ago and China twice in the last three months. Can you explain this?" He mumbled it, as if he were nervously intruding on a stranger. His face was sallow and thin, and his belly fought with the buttons on his shirt.

"They must have stamped it when I entered there."

ICEman Two said, "Who are you?"

"Whatever it says on my passport." They looked at each other for a signal on how to take that. "Look, guys, I know you'd rather be scaring some old woman from India coming in to visit her grand-children or stopping a couple from Africa from enjoying their va-cation. I'm sorry to keep you from your fun. So why don't we agree that you tried your best, but I was uncooperative. And you can go about justifying having an assignment in this air-conditioned air-port instead of the Nogales border station. Meet whatever quota you have for tears and fears. When you get the word that it's okay to release me, come and get me. Okay?"

"What did you mean when you said your name was on your passport?" ICEman One asked.

ICEman Two looked at him and stood up. "C'mon. Let's get out of here." Then to me. "Someone will bring you water."

ICEman One wasn't sure. ICEman Two waited at the door. ICEman One said, "I hope they keep you in here for days."

That was the key to everything for that guy. He was stuck there and he wanted everyone else to share a piece of his misery and he hated them because they would all get out before he would. There was no use in rubbing it in. He knew.

Pongo and Perdy, Patterson and Pruitt to the Marines, met me when I came through customs. They were still MPs, still big, and still in uniform. Pongo carried the suitcase I had left behind in Erbil. If the Major intended to draw attention to my arrival, he suc-ceeded.

"Major Hensel arranged for it to be sent," said Pongo.

"Am I under arrest?"

"Do you want to be under arrest?" That was Perdy coming as close to a smile as he could.

I had not seen them since my last mission, when I learned that a baton pressed across my throat made a convincing argument, but I felt like I was reuniting with old friends. They called me Lieutenant, and with that I could feel Robert Hewitt fading into the background. That was fine, but the tension between soldier and spy welled up. Soldier felt like a cheat because in peace, at home, nothing was easier. And ease was an unwanted visitor. I was afraid of it. Afraid ease would make me wither. At home, time was a nice soft ride on a tram: nap time. Under cover, time became a roller coaster, stretching almost to a halt, careening through fog and darkness, chasing the light. The stuttering current of that life, the unpredictability, was like a puzzle injected directly into my eyeballs. I did not want to stop until I completed it: It could never be completed.

Pongo and Perdy took me to an office building just a few miles south of the airport. I told them what little I safely could about the graves and the money, and they were grateful for the update. I meant it when I said I would try to use them on my next mission.

They ushered me into a room where Major Hensel sat with two CIA men: Thompson and McCoy, late thirties, fit, lean, clear-eyed and ambitious: twins from different mothers. McCoy had a thick head of brown hair. Thompson kept his short. They were the opposite of the ICEmen I had just left. These guys believed they were in a great place and wanted to stay there. McCoy fixated on my bags. "Are those yours?"

The Major made the introductions. We did not shake hands. He ended by saying, "These gentlemen were responsible for your delay at the airport. They felt it was important to meet with you before you slipped away to attend to other matters." He returned his attention to his iPad.

"We'll have to search those bags," said Thompson.

Pongo and Perdy left. Major Hensel looked at me questioningly. I shrugged. The two CIA men searched through my bags, which contained the clothing Major Hensel had bought me in Chicago. From a side pouch, McCoy pulled two matching ski masks and held them up like a cop who found planted bags of dope. "And what have we here?"

"Souvenirs." He set the masks on the desk. "Put them back," I said. I did not mind them seeing the masks. It was Major Hensel seeing them that bothered me.

McCoy smiled at me, knowing he found a way to irritate me. He left the masks on the desk and so did I. Anger was erupting in me. I was looking at the room to plot my moves: kick McCoy, spin, slug Thompson, and so on. They were so easy to hate. But I decided to fight the anger rather than fighting those guys.

They put me on a couch so I sat low, and they pulled their chairs close. The Major sat in a chair on my right. Thompson showed me a small voice recorder he would be using.

McCoy started right in. "We had the situation in northern Iraq well in hand. You have destabilized the region and undone years of our work. The PKK is a terrorist organization. In the last two days, they have attacked a border station and blown up two oil rigs. They are terrorists and designated as such by the United States government and, let me mention, every European government. Hell, even the Australians hate them."

"What do you have against Australians?"

"You will give us all the information you have about the PKK. Full descriptions of everyone you met. Locations. Every word of every conversation you had."

I said nothing. Thompson said, "Start now."

"I don't know where to start."

"Start when you first contacted the PKK."

"I never contacted the PKK."

They looked at each other like prosecutors at their first trial.

"When you first met them."

"I never met them." I breathed deeply and kept my voice calm.

"The PKK assaulted a Regional Government facility and took you with them."

"Was I at a government facility? Was that where they hung me up and electrocuted me?" Time to huddle again. I got up and re-packed my bag. "You guys don't mind, do you?" We all sat down again.

McCoy tried again. "You led a raid on DS Security Services with a group of men suspected of being members of the PKK."

"No one identified himself as PKK in all my time in Iraq."

Thompson groaned and said, "You claimed to have given money to the PKK."

Major Hensel said, without looking up, "That was part of a cover story on a classified intelligence mission."

They went on, banging into the wall of my equanimity at different angles. The anger had dissipated. I felt refreshed. I kept expecting some mention of Gill, but his name never came up, so I gave it a try. "Do you guys know Gill? Big guy. CIA man. Thought you might know him."

They denied knowing him. The Major decided the interview was over.

"This is not over," Thompson said, to prove that he had given up.

Outside, Major Hensel said, "Nicely done. I thought you were going to confess to killing Gill. That's why I ended it."

Will Panos was waiting for us at The Slammer, another sports bar featuring over ten million beers no one will every taste, near the pier in Manhattan Beach. The Major was as careful there as he had been at the French restaurant in Chicago. We sat at a high-back booth in the rear of the restaurant, far from the windows and the view. The TVs could not be avoided. Loud rock and roll from the seventies and eighties overwhelmed the buzz of basketball fans burping their opinions.

Will Panos and I sat across from the Major, whose choice of beer was called Delirium Tremens from Belgium supposedly.

"They only have three kegs in the back and they pour some flavoring into Bud and call it rare."

"Maybe. I've been to this brewery, so maybe I'll be able to tell," he said.

The waitress was young, with blond hair made bright by sun and peroxide or something similar. She was slim, but had chubby cheeks. Her eyes were light blue. Her teeth were white and smooth. At last I felt like I had arrived in Southern California. I wanted to flirt with her. Instead, I ordered a Dos Equis and a hamburger.

I asked the Major about Daisy.

"Casts on both arms and legs. We got her some help. She said she liked working with you."

"Any investigation into Darrell White's death?"

"I'll get to that."

"She thinks you're god," I said.

"She said the same about you. Do you think that devalues it?"

I told the story, only leaving out Victor entirely. The Major opened the bank envelopes and looked over the figures. He put them away without comment.

Will reported that all the goons' names belonged to dead soldiers, but I had already figured that. "One of the graves is at Arlington. Three are in a private cemetery near Bishop." I liked hearing that. "Will these graves have money in them or not?"

"Some will have money, some won't. Can't tell until they're dug up."

Will squinted for a moment. The waitress delivered the beers. Will said, "If most of the graves did not have money, then why did they rush to dig one up right after Frank Godwin was shot? Why go after Frank at all?"

"Every lie needs a partner. The best lies are polygamists. Bannion was under pressure from his partners. Even his boys were tapping their feet. They wanted to start their revolution and they wanted to know when the seed money would reappear. Bannion could hardly say don't worry about the government because the money was never in the ground. He had to pretend he was fighting us for it. Racing us to it. It wasn't enough to kill Frank and say he betrayed us. They had to raid one grave and get caught to prove the government was in control. That way, Bannion could say they could carry on with the millions he wanted them to think he had already stashed in Erbil." I paused to let Will digest that. "What was in that one they tried to raid?"

"Half a million," the Major said.

"Just in case they managed to get away with it. But the result was that Bannion never had to worry again about anyone, someone like McColl, opening a grave and finding a body where there should have been money."

Will said, "So Frank's list was a backup to McColl's list, which was a backup to another list, the DS list?"

"Yes. A big circle. All just in case. I rushed back to Wisconsin assuming Frank gave me bad information. Frank had given me what he had."

The Major went back to Erbil. "When you passed through the tunnel and caught Bannion, why hadn't he run?"

"One of his boys had turned on him. Was waiting outside."

"Why?"

This was the danger zone with Major Hensel: the simple question. My answer had to shut out further questions because Victor was my problem. I was not sharing him. I sipped my beer and took a bite of the burger and stole a French fry from Will. The short truth—money—would be the worst answer. It opened doors. This called for a long-winded lie, the kind that is transparent to people like Major Hensel.

"Bannion had fired him and never got around to paying him off. The goon had stopped by that night to collect and ran into the attack. When Bannion ran, this guy trapped him, not realizing what was really going on."

At least the Major didn't laugh. I hoped he understood: What's the use of hiring a liar if you don't let him lie? I handed over the lists of officers and diplomats that Bannion had dictated. The Major pushed his plate away to look these over. I saw him wince a couple of times. "Carl Haberman is a close friend. So is General Wick."

"With Bannion, it's safe to assume there will be some payback included. Some false leads."

The Major put the lists in the inside pocket of his sport coat. He shook his head. "We have to treat it as real." He was not happy. I told him about Colonel Hoyle, too. Nobody was happy.

The waitress cleared the plates and asked if we wanted fresh beers. The Major ordered another round. I watched her walk away.

Will said, "Kristen is coming down to Pendleton for a visit. With her daughter."

"When?" I was too quick, too tense.

"Why?"

"I might need your help."

The Major changed the subject. "The FBI thinks you killed Darrell White. The secretary identified you. Said you had visited the office. They want you for a lineup. Someone saw the body being carted down the street. Naked, apparently."

"He couldn't decide what to wear."

"Agents Hanrihan and Sampson are going to be looking for you. Expect them. I've managed to make it clear to the FBI leadership that the graves are none of their business. But if you show up at the graves, they will show up and I can't stop them."

I said, "It would help if you went back to Frank's list and dug those up first and left the DS graves for a little while."

He leaned forward and stayed that way and stared right at me. The lights bounced off his glasses, keeping me from a good look at his eyes except to tell they were not moving. I thought he was going to reassign me or order me not to pursue any loose ends. My side of the booth sank a few inches into the concrete floor.

"One of the graves on your fake list was dug up last night. Would that be Victor Kosinski doing that?"

I looked daggers at Will, but he was as astonished as I was.

"Will did not tell me. Was Victor the goon shooting at Bannion?"

"Yes."

"Anything else you want to tell me about him?"

"Not yet."

He sat back and looked at one of the TVs as if he had not noticed it was there before. "If you need help. We do have resources."

I thought about my pledge to utilize Pongo and Perdy, but I was not ready for them. The Major excused himself.

Will and I walked out to the pier. Pigeons strutted and fluttered. Seagulls swooped. Four small sailboats bounced beside the highway of sunlight painted on the water.

"I didn't tell him," Will said.

"I know."

"Victor Kosinski has entered the country twice at the Peace Arch into Seattle. I never have him leaving the country. That's it. Until three days ago. He flew into New York."

"Where was the dig from the fake list?"

"Massachusetts. Pittsfield. What is going on?"

"I can't tell you yet."

"Why did you want to know when Kristen would be down here?"

Will was a careful, precise man. Questions were phrased to elicit the answers he wanted. He was also a single-minded man, and if I told him that Victor Kosinski was the shooter in Montana, Will would insist on helping me go after him. I did not want Will to die helping me.

"Just because of the timing of the search of the graves. You might be busy for a while."

"I don't lie to you." His voice was breathy with passion, a mix of fear and hurt feelings. He slammed his palm on the pier railing, startling two pigeons. His head tilted up while he struggled to control himself and form his next question. He did not look at me when he spoke. The wind took his words and I asked him to repeat what he said. He turned toward me. "Is Kristen in danger?"

The shooter in Montana hit him and missed me, and Will had been wondering about it ever since. Maybe he wanted to believe he had saved Kristen. The shot that killed Sergeant Rios drilled his head and came from farther away. Why was Will hit in the knee? Why was Jim Williams hit in the neck? Will had been thinking about it, just as I had been.

"The shooter wants the money and he is going to want me to lead him to it."

31

Agents Hanrihan and Sampson started following me that night in Santa Monica where I had checked into a motel near the beach. From my motel, I walked over to Ocean Avenue and turned north. The postcard on my left showed the sun touching silvery blue water, a wide beach, two kids standing in the surf, and a sparse assortment of sunbathers. After two blocks, I came across a fish restaurant with a patio in front. Just past the valet parking, a particularly dirty homeless man was sitting against the building. I gave him twenty dollars and pointed out the agents down the street. "Tell the woman I want to talk to her. If the man tries to come in, wrestle with him a little bit, just a little bit. He's an FBI agent, but he won't hurt you."

I took a table on the patio so I could see the action. The homeless guy stopped the agents about twenty yards before they reached the restaurant. Hanrihan was dismissive and started to move on. Sampson listened. Hanrihan had to wait while Sampson dug in her purse to give the guy money. They proceeded toward the restaurant, but as they got close, the homeless guy stepped in front of Hanrihan to block him. Hanrihan tried stepping around him. The homeless guy was talking and putting up his hands the way a crossing guard would; he had a job and he wanted to do it well.

Sampson saw me and I beckoned her to join me. She took a quick look back at her partner, then came over. Hanrihan pushed the homeless guy out of the way and that made the homeless guy hug him from behind to stop him. Hanrihan was extremely unhappy about that embrace. He threw his arms out wide to burst away. He pushed the homeless guy too hard and landed him on his ass. Passersby were watching. Hanrihan brushed himself off and marched over to our table. He sat down next to Sampson and glared at me. He was still brushing himself off. He brushed back his bang with his fingertips, then looked at them and wiped them on the tablecloth.

"You put him up to that. You think that's funny? What the hell is wrong with you?"

I didn't answer. The silence made him self-conscious. He checked with Sampson. She said, "He'll talk to me."

That didn't sink in at first. "Okay. Let's hear it."

"I mean, he'll only talk to me. He'll talk to me only."

Hanrihan squinted in disbelief and his mouth hung open. And the homeless man spoke from the sidewalk. "That's what I was trying to tell you."

Hanrihan stood up fast, as if he were going to chase the homeless man. But he just growled at Sampson. "I'll wait across the street." He went out and the homeless man followed him.

She ordered ice tea. I had a beer. We ordered a seafood appetizer sampler to keep the waiter happy. Sampson waited patiently for me to get started. She wore no makeup that I could see and the small wrinkles near her eyes added to her attractiveness. Her attitude was all business without being abrupt or harsh. "I know who did the killings in Montana, Wisconsin, and Houston."

"That's nice. We think you did a few of them."

"You don't. And neither does your partner. He's just pretending to think it."

"You've lost me." She wasn't cold and she wasn't warm. She kept her tone in that zone that would allow me to keep talking but would discourage huge exaggeration or outright lies.

"You said yourself I didn't kill Frank Godwin. And witnesses know I didn't do the shooting in Montana."

"And Houston?"

I told her about Gill killing Arun. "I have no proof. But the same guy did all the others, even the guy with the flame tattoo."

She sipped her ice tea and looked across the street at Hanrihan, who stood next to a palm and watched us. "He's stupid, but he's not evil," she said. "He works hard. The sexist comments are so lame they're not worth protesting. But he thinks the best approach is to accuse everyone he interviews. He claims he's had success that way." The waiter delivered the appetizer. Sampson turned her gaze on me. "How do you know the shooter is the same guy? And who is he?"

"Your partner is bent."

"Oh, come on."

"How did you know where to find me in Houston?"

She looked at me for about thirty seconds. "We can check hotel records and rental card records and flight records."

"Did you do it, or did he?"

"He put in the request."

My turn to wait. I tried a shrimp. Sipped my beer. She did not rush me. "If you access that request, you'll find that he was looking for Robert Hewitt. That was the name I traveled under. Rollie Waters was not in Houston. The shooter knew I was Robert Hewitt. How did Hanrihan know?"

"I would have to check this out. I can't just take your word."

"When you do that, see if he ever interviewed a Victor Kosinski entering the country from Canada."

"Why don't I just arrest Victor Kosinski?"

"I'm going to tell you how you can do that, too." I explained what I expected would happen over the next few days and the part I hoped she would play. First, Hanrihan was going to be in touch with Victor, letting him know where I was. Then I was going to need Sampson as backup, need her to take Hanrihan out of the mix. I told her we could not meet or talk again and she would have to improvise along the way.

"That's fine. If your story checks out."

"Be careful of your partner. He's stupid, but not as stupid as he looks."

Waiting tried to burn me out on a hilltop in Helmand. It might have been on my second tour, but I can't be sure; waiting time is hazy time. Waiting feeds on congealed hope. Every day in every way, I was getting worse and worse. And I was doing better than most. Randy Jackman, a corporal, hounded me. "How do we know it will ever end? How do we know they'll ever attack? This is hell. We're already in hell. This can go on forever."

"Do you have a dog?"

"What the fuck has my dog got to do with this?"

"Every time you leave the house, your dog thinks he's gone to hell. He thinks you're never coming back. But he waits patiently and doesn't piss all over the house. So try to be a dog, man."

I was a dog, too. But when I realized I did not have to wait for the enemy to attack, I was fine. I did not have to outwait time; I only had to outwait my commanding officers. Eventually, they would send us to find the enemy and on to a slightly cooler level of hell.

I wanted to set up Victor and grab him immediately. I did not want to wait: I had to wait. Will Panos went east to play the Exhumationist, with plenty of backup, enough for Hanrihan to notice. I had to wait for it to look like I had been taken off the case. I had to hang around for it to look like I had not brought any new information about where the money was hidden. I had to wait for Victor to find me and watch me.

Waiting made me a target. My instinct was to hide. I longed to go to Big Bear and work at Loretta's shelter. But if Victor trailed me there, Loretta would be put in jeopardy. That would be an unforgivable sin. I considered luring Victor into the cave in Arizona the way I had done to McColl's men. But Victor was too wary and maybe even too shrewd to fall for that. I had to wait.

One night while taking a walk, I went into a video store and found a copy of *The Criminal*, the Stanley Baker movie that Bannion was so fond of. Baker played a career criminal, a villain named Johnny Bannion. He ran the prison block he was on, and as soon as he got out, he set up the heist of a lifetime. Slick confederates and his ex-girlfriend betrayed him and he was sent back to prison. The rest of the plot hardly mattered; everyone was trying to get Johnny's money. Johnny just loved being a villain, loved playing one enemy off another. He thought nothing of being sent up again. In prison he operated freely, according to the Universal Law of Villainy. But the money was on the outside. He thought nothing of the cost of breaking out.

The two Johnny Bannions shared a need for chaos, which they believed they could rearrange for their benefit. Both men thought they could cheat their destiny, too. The Bannion I knew was a thorough villain: cruel, treacherous, and deceitful. And he was a lodestone. I consoled myself with the thought that there were probably plenty of Johnny Bannions to go around. He would cheat anyone, but, like Dan, he specialized in the vain and fatuous, the men who thought their epaulets meant something, and didn't know they were there only to store their gloves.

"You miss him," said Dan.

"I know what you want me to say and I won't. Not ever."

"You could do the same. You could take his place."

But I knew I could not take his place or Dan's. I saw their ends. I saw the consequences. I was on another track and as blind to my future as they had been to theirs.

During the day, I walked down to Venice and joined in with an outdoor tai chi group. Afterward, I ran into two guys fighting quarterstaff and I paid them to teach me. It was similar to Aikido in some ways: your balance, his momentum. Attacking left you vulnerable. Countering was the way to achieve hits. The staff was about eight feet long, but after about a half hour, it became manageable. By the third day, I could hold my own. We worked out for two hours, then went for a beer.

They were Englishmen who made their living performing at

fairs around the world. The girlfriend of one of them, who was also part of the act, joined us. At that moment, it sounded like the best life anyone ever had. Perform, leave soon, before the dust of responsibility or duty could settle. We talked about the possibility that I might fill in if they needed me. They had always managed to cover expenses and did not worry about the future. One of them talked vaguely about someday opening a school to teach quarterstaff and other similar skills, but the other guy mocked him: "Teaching kids to hit each other with sticks? I'd rather be selling the insurance policy."

Other worlds drifted across the boardwalk until a set of crazy, staring eyes sliced through at the far end. On the Venice boardwalk, that should not have been alarming or notable, but these were unforgettable. They belonged to a man a little shorter than me, a little thicker, dark.

The Englishmen were probably relieved to find out how unreliable I was before we got too involved with one another. I got up quickly and walked in the direction where Victor had appeared. He was gone.

Around midnight, I took a walk. The streetlights painted the night with a pale gray tint, making the clear night feel foggy. I walked south first, below Pico, before turning toward the ocean. The homeless men had already settled into their doorways and onto their benches. I always preferred unlocked cars, parks, and cemeteries; the zombies were protection from all the other homeless men who believed in zombies. Any one of the lumps could have been Victor, ready to pop out after me. I sped up like a gang member crossing enemy territory. Across the road, I went down a flight of stairs and followed a path toward the water until the bike path cut across. Uneven white lines rolled hypnotically off the black screen on my left, just ahead of the grunting snare sounds. A couple holding hands appeared from under the pier and they tightened up as they came near me. The boy shifted to the left so he would be closest to me. I kept my gaze beyond them, but I saw no movement.

I walked under the pier, moving slowly. On the other side, the view expanded and the beach spread out. The pier was silent and the cars above, on the bluff, could hardly be heard. I looked back, hoping Victor would materialize like some demented wraith who I could wrestle in a death match. He did not appear.

In the morning, I drove to LAX, parked, bought a ticket to Phoenix, walked through two terminals, came out and got on the Avis shuttle, and rented a silver Toyota. I did not think I was going to lose Victor; I wanted him to think I intended to lose him.

First, north, then east, past Edwards Air Force Base, north again, into the Owens Valley. Tufts of green stained the wrinkled camel hair hills. This was the Garden of Eden ravaged by its promise. Forced water tribute had left behind plains as dry as a forgotten sponge. Outside Lone Pine, I stopped for gas. Victor did not pull in behind me.

Mountains, gray and frosted, jutted on both sides. Though I had driven through there a few times before, I could never tell which peak was Mt. Whitney. None stood out to me. Bishop has a Sears, a Kmart, and a Penney's spaced along a wide, faded, two-story Main Street that looks like the other stores would be featuring record players with stereophonic sound, and TVs with color and remote control. I snuck in between the pickups in front of the hardware store. I bought a shovel, a pick, gloves, and a lantern. Just off Main Street, I found a mountaineering supply store. I bought an anorak, thick wool socks, two sweaters, and a wool hat. I did not know what kind of shelter I would find. I did not know how long Victor would wait.

Aspens and pines lined the climbing road northeast of Bishop. An unpaved road cut off to the east and wound around a couple of hills. Below on the left sat a small placid lake. The road curled down again toward the lake and stopped at a gate marked DS Lodge. A heavy padlock held the gates together. I considered shooting it out with my pistol, but I used the pick instead and smashed the lock.

The log cabin was big for a fishing lodge, with a big square-paneled wooden door and an ostentatious knocker. I parked facing out. A steep path led to the lake about fifty feet below the house. Yellow and purple wildflowers spread in a meadow toward the hills to the left of the house. Behind the house was forested. Foothills ringed the property, isolating it from the world. I saw no sign of Victor, no sign of Sampson and Hanrihan. No sign of the graves.

I had to knock off the front doorknob and fiddle with the bolt to get into the house. The stone fireplace and chimney dominated the living room. The back wall was blackened, but there were no ashes. Two chairs faced the large front windows. There was no other furniture in the entire house. The kitchen had been cleaned out; not even a spoon remained. There were two bedrooms, one on each side of the living room. They were empty. None of the windows had blinds.

By the time I walked the meadow twice end to end looking for graves, the wind rose and pushed in heavy clouds. I moved through the forest, checking the clear, flat spots. No graves. The path down to the lake had been provided with a few makeshift stairs of stone. It wound left for about thirty feet, then cut right, straight down. The meager shore consisted of big rocks and three feet of dirt. The lake level looked a little low. A peeling, turned-over rowboat was pulled up onto the rocks. No graves. Underneath the boat I found a pair of oars.

By the time I was halfway across, I knew where the graves were. I kept rowing anyway until the boat bottomed on the opposite shore. There the dirt, covered in grass and weeds, ran back thirty feet to the spot where the rocks began to rise.

The headstones were in the shade, near the rocks.

It was after six. It would be dark by the time I got back to the graves with a shovel. I could dig by lantern light, but I did not look forward to opening a bag full of money with no idea where Victor was. I expected Sampson and Hanrihan, too. But they would not show themselves until Victor did. I decided to spend the night in the house. Even if Victor spotted the graves, he would not kill me until he knew whether they held the jackpot or not. At least that was what I told myself.

Bundled up against the cold, I finished the bag of pretzels and the two chocolate bars and one bottle of water. I placed the bag and the crumbled wrappers near the front door, which would not lock anymore, in the hope that I would hear them crinkle when Victor stepped on them. I pulled the chairs together, got comfortable and repeated a few different versions of this mantra: He won't kill me until he is sure there is money in the graves.

The mantra might have worked better if there had been curtains or shades. Breaking into an empty house was a familiar experience for me. I always slept well. But I had never done it when I was bait. The wind and the varmints became the tools of a mad adventurer fixated on me and obsessed with finding money that probably was not there. I moved to the floor and sat in half lotus.

The mesquite tree, the porch, the swing, the sheer curtain jostled gently by the breeze—I lingered on each leaf, link, ripple, and fold. Murmuring came from inside, but I went no farther than the window. I turned back and absorbed the scene from that angle. I sank into the peace. The murmuring was soft music. But I turned toward it again, and I saw the window.

And I thought about windows.

I hopped up and looked outside, but I might have been back in a cave; the blackness was absolute.

Repeat: Victor would not try to kill me until he saw what was in the graves.

I moved the chairs in front of the door, sat on one, put my feet on the other, my gun in my lap, and went to sleep. I don't remember any dreams and I don't know how long I slept. I don't know what woke me.

The eyes were clear and backlit, despite the darkness. Just two feet in front of me. I reached for my gun, but it was not there.

"I have it," he said. But he was not holding a gun on me. He just stood there looking down. I pushed the chair away with my foot and straightened up.

"Sit down, Ethan," I said.

He stood up straight and his eyes got wide and lost the fire. He stepped back. "What did you say? Why did you call me that?"

"Ethan. Ethan Williams. That's your name."

"My name is Victor Kosinski. You know that."

"I gave you that name. You know that. Sit down, Ethan."

"Let's go dig right now. You have a lantern and so do I." The sales pitchman was still there, but impatience had crept in. I wanted him to lose the sugar completely. I wanted him ordering me to buy the goddamn sprinkler system even without the added nozzles.

"We can dig in the morning. Sit down." I kicked the chair in a gesture of my hospitality. It took him about two minutes, but he finally adjusted the chair and sat down facing me. He cradled a pistol. I could not tell if it was mine or his.

"That was a good trick at the airport. I almost lost you. I gotta use that one sometime."

"How did you follow me?" But I thought he did not follow me. Hanrihan had told him where I was going.

"Do you think it's here? The rest of the money?"

"No. I think some of it is here." He seemed to like hearing that. His eyes narrowed a bit and he smiled. "Tell me, Ethan, how did you hook up with Bannion?"

"I told you to stop calling me that."

"You were Sam Simmons when I first met you. Who was he?"

"Why do you care about Sam Simmons?"

"Who came before him? How many were there?" He was looking at the window. I turned and could see his pale reflection. He leaned forward and I did the same. "You've watched me. Studied me, you said. I've watched you. I want to know how you did it. All of it." He stayed there, leaning in. His eye blazing again. "Tell me about Iraq," I said.

"This is one of your tricks. No tricks anymore."

"You have the guns. You know where the graves are."

The wind picked up and sand scratched at the door. There was nowhere for him to disappear to, nowhere for him to send me off to. He could not say, "You go first. I'll wait here." His relentless eagerness had trapped him in the abandoned house. I waited until I thought he felt the trap, until he could rationalize his mistake and deal with it.

"How did you get in? I heard nothing."

"When you were on the lake, I came in and unlocked a bedroom window."

"Smart. Did you kill the NGO worker in Farah?"

"I needed the money. I thought you knew. I thought you hated the NGOs."

"Hated the NGOs?"

He tilted his head and his eyes were puzzled. He had not thought about an answer to that, had never gotten more specific than "hated them all."

"I thought you hated everyone there. The growers and the NGOs and the Marines, too. Lieutenant Spera told me you said everyone was in business together. I asked him, y'know. Asked him to go in with me. He said he wasn't smart enough to get away with it, but you were. But, he said, if I asked you, you'd shoot me."

"He was wrong."

"When you didn't shoot me, I gotta tell you, I thought about it for a long time. You must have had a reason. It was tough getting out of there. But the thought that you had a reason to let me live kept me up. If you saw something, then I decided I better see something, too."

"Thank you," I said. He smiled as if the coach had patted his back.

Inspiration to a lunatic. I tried to reconstruct the moment when I let him go, refigure the calculation. It was not compassion for Victor, I hoped, that influenced my decision. I did not want to think I had deemed him pathetic or helpless, which would have only highlighted how pathetic I was. The picture of handing him over to the Afghan authorities had colored everything. My weakness was in the dread of sacrificing people to procedure, sacrificing people to appearance. Passing Sam Simmons to the Afghans would have turned him into a token. It would have been a mere gesture, not a duty or responsibility. It would have made me want to change my name.

"Tell me about Iraq, Ethan." He was silent. I sat back and put my hands behind my head and crossed my ankles. "You want someone to know. I know you do. Just like I'm glad you watched me."

"I'm not Ethan."

"You shot your old man at the graveside in Montana. I can't blame you. He was pretty awful and he knew you weren't in the grave. You had visited him, hadn't you? Before you knew about the money. Before you hooked up with Bannion. Tell me about that, about becoming one of the goons. You fooled them all."

"The old man couldn't keep his mouth shut. Never could. He was drunk from the day I knew him. I knew when he saw the body in the grave he'd start blabbing and then people would be looking for me."

"And you knew I'd think you were looking for the money."

"Don't worry. I wasn't gonna hit you. I'm a damn good shot.

Only thing the old man was good for, teaching me to shoot. We'd go hunting. By the time I was twelve, I'd have to take the rifle away from him in the afternoon. He'd want to shoot something and I was the only something he could see."

"What about Kristen?"

"Whaddaya mean?"

"Were you aiming at her?"

He moved his mouth, but no words came out. He tried it a couple of times. At last he said, "She didn't know. Unless the old man told her. She was never bad to me."

"She's still your wife."

He chuckled. "I'm gonna have millions. What do I want a wife for?"

I remembered Nita, the waitress at Frank's place who had fallen for Ethan's charms. The story in Farah was that all the female NGOs were taken with him, too. Maybe the TV pitchman tone worked. I did not mention his daughter.

We had hours to go. I wanted it all. Once he acknowledged being Ethan Williams, the rest came easier. He had been an Army sniper at Fallujah with the 325th Airborne Infantry. They were moved out and the 101st replaced them. But Ethan was left behind to support the transition. No one knew him. He saw the strutting Blackwater men flaunting their freedom and money. The rules did not apply to them. The rules were going to get Ethan killed.

"Were you scared?"

"You were scared. Everyone is scared."

"You're right," I said. That concession seemed to satisfy him. He breathed deeply a few times and then he smiled.

"It was such a great opportunity. I hitched a ride with three

Blackwater guys. They didn't know each other at all. They were guarding a shipment of Coca-Cola and chips and shit. But it was overcovered. About thirty other guards were on top of it. These guys had two cases of bourbon in their vehicle. We went back to where they were camped, at the edge of the 101st, who were also just setting up. It was all just coming together. Two of the guys passed out, and the other one got real drunk. Real drunk. And he wanted to come back with me to where I was assigned at the edge of the city. I was due back at 0200 hours. I let him come with me. We weren't there an hour when he stood up. We were on the second story. The windows were all shot out, of course. And he was hit. In the face. It was such a great opportunity."

I knew Ethan had killed that guy, lured him there and murdered him. "Was he Sam Simmons?"

"Nah. He was someone else. Joe Nobody."

"In the grave in Montana."

"I guess. I didn't stay around to check. Maybe they switched the body. Maybe there was money in there. Was there?"

"No."

"I went north. Avoided Mosul. Ended up in Kirkuk. That's where I first heard of Bannion. A lot of the Blackwater guys were talking about him and his operation."

"And the money?"

Ethan gripped the gun and stood up abruptly and walked to the window. "You know, I could have killed you a thousand times and I didn't because of you letting me go. But if you hear all this, everything changes."

'I could tell, but I'd have to kill you': everyone's lame joke, but Ethan's earnestness was absolute.

"You can't kill me. Not until you see the money."

"C'mon. You admitted before that everyone is scared."

"You went north . . ."

"I met the guy you called Gill. He was special forces at the time. Ted Marker. Master Sergeant Ted Marker. Everybody heard about the money. Everybody was looking for it. Gill found some and he took, I don't know, he must have taken maybe two packets, twenty thousand dollars. And some guy is stupid enough to threaten to hand him in. So I killed him. That was Sam Simmons."

"And years later, you looked up Ted Marker and reminded him that he owed you a favor."

"That's how I got in with Bannion."

Bannion, the King, McColl, each thought he was the story, his plans and schemes were the centerpiece around which the world spun. But the toxic concoction of ambition and arrogance bred slime like Ethan, who wriggled below the surface and oozed through the cracks. It was not a play about a schemer or a soldier or a king; it was about a fiend without compunction, a jokester, a demon. And his idea of how to act was to imitate me.

He told me not to go anywhere and he walked into the kitchen. He came back a moment later with a bottle of water for me and one for himself. "It'll be light in less than an hour," he said.

I closed my eyes and pretended to go back to sleep. All I did was wonder how Sampson was going to get to the other side of the lake to help me.

33

We were just two prospectors certain that this time we would hit the mother lode. But we did not have to wait to count the booty to become paranoid fiends. Our calculations in the murder matrix powered the way. Ethan could not shoot me until he was sure these three graves held a worthwhile payday. I would be digging first. If the grave yielded twenty-five million, I was dead. If it yielded only a couple of million, or nothing, Ethan would try to make me dig farther. Failure meant life for me.

The sun, just poking through the pines, made me hold my eyes down as I rowed across the lake, flat and still now that the wind had escaped. I stared at the shovels and the pick on the bottom of the boat all the way across the lake and tried to figure out ways to survive. Mallards honked far off. Ethan aimed a gun at them but did not shoot.

Sampson might arrive on time but it would not matter. How would she cross the lake? Maybe on Hanrihan's back. He would be eager enough to get at the money.

"What are you laughing about?" Ethan said.

"You could dig, too," I said. I held out a shovel toward him.

"You dig. I'll stand nearby holding a gun on you."

"Which one should I start on?"

He examined the headstones for clues the way a sucker plays three-card monte. He pointed to the grave on the left, the one belonging to Neil Bess. I laid the extra shovel and the pick on the middle grave. Ethan sat on the rocks, facing me and the lake. I dug and thought about Ethan Williams, who joined the Army and kept finding opportunities too good to pass up.

He was his own best customer. Every step down to this lakeside graveyard was guided by his faith in the power of hucksterism. The lower it sent him, the deeper its claws dug into his flesh, and the more grateful he was. In his version, I had saved him in Farah Province and Gill had introduced him to Bannion. We were sent by the god of good luck, who wanted him to find the lost city of gold. Gill was dead; I was his only companion. At journey's end, when he lifted the pot of gold, I would have to be sacrificed; that was the shipping charge, the small print. He was so busy selling himself the magic elixir that no one had ever tried the truth on him. Why bother? I had reason to bother.

The silence did not last long. "Why didn't you bring Bannion outside while I was waiting? We had him. We had a deal."

"Maybe I'm not who you think I am," I said.

"You are." Too loud. The sound boomed. Both of us looked across the lake as if someone there might have heard.

"My mission was to catch Bannion, not recover the money. I had to try to bring him in."

"You were always after the money."

"Never. You have me wrong. You just don't get it."

"I know you're lying."

I just kept digging. I hit some rocks and changed the shovel for the pick and worked that way for a while. The sun came over the trees and was directly in his eyes. He moved over to the grave on the right. He was careful not to step directly on it.

"Why are you here, if it isn't for the money?"

"The money isn't here, Ethan." I kept picking away at a big rock. "Bannion put it all in bank accounts. I already gave them over. The money is gone."

"Stop digging."

I kept pounding on the rock with the pick. He repeated the command. I kept working. He fired the pistol at the headstone. The echo died and we both turned to see the Mallards take off. The lake remained a mirror.

"You can't kill me yet, Ethan. Unless you believe me about the money. And you don't. You can't, can you?" I changed the pick for the shovel. "You have some water?"

I hit the top of the box about three and a half feet down. Ethan came forward cautiously. He smiled, showing his small, even teeth, and his eyes lit up. Door number one was going to open; all the prizes were waiting behind it. He commanded me to dig out a bit on one side so the box could be pried open.

"Why do you think this one is any better than the others?"

"Just a feeling."

He treated hope like a lighter, flicking it over and over again to see if it still worked, not understanding that the flame was meaningless. The failed opium scheme was one of hundreds meant to remake him. But his plans were disjointed pieces, notes hit simply to make a noise that went with the previous note. It took about twenty minutes more digging and scraping. I hopped up and leaned on the shovel. "I'll make you a deal," I said.

"You don't keep your deals."

"If there is no money in there, you dig the next one. You can hold on to the weapons."

"No."

"I'll never make it through three in one day alone. We'll have to spend another night here. Do you have enough food?"

"Open it up."

I used the pick on the latches. I used the shovel to pry open the top.

"Pull it out," he said.

I had to lie on my belly and reach in and pull up the bag. It was too heavy to lift from that position and I told him so. He moved next to me and got on his knees to help. I could have made my play, gotten under his arms so he couldn't reach the guns, which were stuck in his belt, and wrestled with him. I decided to wait for a surer chance, betting on Bannion, betting the DS list was mostly fake.

We dragged it out. By its weight it might have been a big stash of money or it might have been a corpse. Ethan stood over me as I un- zipped the bag. I turned and looked at him instead of the contents.

His glowing eyes got small as slits and he scrunched up his nose in disappointment. A corpse was in the body bag where the money was supposed to be. Two rounds left before the show was over.

Ethan held the pistol on me for about a minute. I didn't move and neither did he. At last he said, "Is there any money in these graves? Just tell me."

"I already told you."

The light in his eyes seemed to flicker. To shoot me meant an end to his quest. He would have to start over, admit defeat. "Start digging," he said quietly.

"Which one?"

He set me to the grave on the right, belonging to Roger Clark.

34

Roger Clark, or somebody posing as Roger Clark, was in the second grave. Ethan groaned. I was tired and hungry. I threw down the shovel and sat at the edge of the grave. Our dance was too static. Ethan stayed more than shovel length away.

"Y'know, no one will ever find all the money Bannion put in the ground. I don't know how many graves he seeded, but I think it's a lot. None with big numbers, but I bet it all adds up."

"C'mon, it's gonna get dark."

"I'm just telling you because I want it on the record that I'm not digging them all."

I went to work on the middle grave. Ethan became quiet. The coming decision was weighing on him. Just standing there and watching had to be tiring him out, too. The sun had rolled across the lake, so Ethan moved with his back to the hill, facing the lake. I slowed my pace. I wish I could say it was some brilliant strategy, but it was really dread. I did not know what was going to be in the grave. I did not know what decision Ethan would make.

"There's no money down there, Ethan. Let's bet on it."

"Why should I?"

Why should he?

Ethan watched. The sun and the lake seemed perfectly still. I was the only thing moving. After a while, Ethan said, "Where do you think we should go next?"

"Bannion gave me lots of names, Ethan. We could stay busy for a long time."

I decided to go faster and I hit the top of the box in just five minutes. Ethan hopped up at the sound of the shovel striking the wood. He wanted to come close to get a look, but I glanced up at him and that made him cautious.

I didn't mind, because I was looking at Sampson and Hanrihan standing above him on the hill.

Sampson walked ahead of Hanrihan, which I did not like to see. When she was just a few feet above Ethan, she spoke up. "Drop your gun. Do not turn around."

Everyone played their part in the dance: drop gun, hands up, drop shovel, turn around. I pointed out to Sampson that Ethan still had a gun in his belt. Sampson and Hanrihan came down to flat ground. Sampson picked up the gun Ethan dropped and put it in her belt. She came behind him and reached around and took the other gun from him. That move looked wrong. Ethan let her take it too easily. I was not happy.

Hanrihan noticed it, too. Sampson moved away from Ethan and said, "Which one is his?"

"The Beretta," Ethan said. "Marines . . ."

"Who is this guy?" Hanrihan said. I was very unhappy.

Sampson looked at the gun in her hand, put it in her belt, took the other gun out, transferred it to her right hand. I watched it all. Hanrihan watched it all. It was the last thing he ever watched. She shot him in the head. Hanrihan staggered before he went down. His left foot stepped sideways and into the first grave. His other foot stayed out. His body lay across the grave like a broken plank. His gun fell from his hand on the ground on the strip between the graves where I stood.

"Why'd you bring him here?" Ethan sounded like a husband who just found out the neighbors were coming over for drinks.

"The lieutenant had to shoot him. And he has. Hello, Lieutenant. Surprised?"

"Surprised."

"You guessed right and you guessed wrong."

"We fooled him this time," said Ethan. He went up to her and kissed her on the cheek and took one of the guns from her belt. He turned to me. "We didn't know you would help us like that, telling Amy where you were going."

"Amy." Ethan had a way with women. "So all you had to do was let Hanrihan and me dislike each other and that gave you an excuse to track me."

"That's it," she said.

"But why bother with me at all? Why not take it in a different direction that could never lead back?"

"That was Victor's idea. He thought that FBI pressure would help him turn you."

"Every little bit," Ethan said.

"Get Hanrihan's gun. We have to kill him with that one so it looks like they shot each other," Sampson said.

"First let's see what's in the box," Ethan said.

"We can open it ourselves, without him."

"We don't shoot him yet. We might need him."

Sampson looked at him and took her time about her answer. She was as deliberate and thoughtful there beside the graves, holding a gun, as she had been questioning me in an office or hotel room. "I don't think we will need him. If there is money in the grave, then we've got what we want and we don't need him. If there is no money, it's safe to assume there is no money in any graves. At least none that we can get to. The Marines are digging up graves right now. They're way ahead of us. This is pretty much it."

She was right. I wished she would have spent more time explaining it so I could figure out a way to grab the gun near my feet.

Ethan did not like the argument. He shook his head and grimaced. The decision was being forced on him. "I don't know. There's definitely more. He even said so. Didn't you?"

"I did. There is."

"C'mon, Victor," Sampson said. He was Victor to her.

"Ethan, you two keep discussing this, I'm going to starve to death."

"Keep quiet."

"I'm going to start digging, Ethan."

Sampson was puzzled. "Who is Ethan?" she said.

"Ethan Williams. Didn't you know?"

"Dammit."

Sampson was controlled and methodical and she would get to that later. "Pick up the gun and let's kill him and get going."

"No, let's wait on that," Ethan said.

Sampson said, "I'll do it." She took one step and Ethan shot her. She fell and she shot him. I dove for Hanrihan's gun and faced Ethan first, but he had dropped his gun. He was wounded in his right arm. Still on the ground, I turned and kicked Sampson's gun from her hand. She was alive, but had been hit in the gut. She tried to speak but couldn't make anything more than low sounds. Ethan was moving to pick up his gun. I shot next to him. He stopped.

I hopped up and faced him. This time I was not going to let him get away. "Get in the grave, Ethan. Get in. Now."

"C'mon. What for?"

Sampson's eyes were still working and her hands tried to contain the damage, but the blood was too juicy and kept spreading.

"Get in, Ethan. That's where you're going to be until you rot. No one is going to dig this grave up again. Get in." He didn't move, so I shot next to him again. He moved slowly to the first grave and squatted down, staring at me the whole time. When he finally looked down, he did not like what he saw: the open body bag and the rotting corpse.

"This isn't right, Lieutenant. I let you go. We're supposed to be partners."

"That's your new partner. Get in."

He stepped down onto the corpse and it crunched. Ethan was terrified. He kept looking at me for some sign of reprieve, but I felt no mercy, no sympathy. I was putting him where I wanted him. I wanted him buried.

"Lie down, Ethan. Stretch out in that coffin."

He slowly lay down. He shivered. "Are you gonna bury me alive?"

"Do you think I'm cruel, Ethan? I'm not cruel. I'm going to shoot you first. Not for your sake. For mine."

And I would have. But from behind me I heard, "I don't think you really want to do that, Lieutenant."

It was Pongo, or Perdy. And the other stood on the rocks. Neither held a weapon. One shrugged and then the other shrugged.

"I do. Very much."

"Nah, Lieutenant. That's not you."

Ethan opened his eyes. I moved away from the grave and the MPs moved down.

Before we left, when Ethan was all bundled up and ready to go, he looked back at the graves and said, "Lieutenant, I really want to know. Please."

Pongo and Perdy were willing to pull up the bag. I shook my head. They took him away.

35

I offered to break the news to Kristen, but Will wanted to face her himself. She and her daughter, Eva, were visiting him at Camp Pendleton. Will wanted to know what kind of sentence Ethan might be facing. I said I thought the Army had him on desertion for sure. And maybe murder. And the civilian authorities had him for the murder of Agent Sampson, bent or not. Maybe they could convict him on the other murders, too.

Will had already taken his visitors to Disneyland and Sea World, so I took Eva to the races at Del Mar. Dan used to take me there quite often. Sometimes he would leave me at the paddock or behind the track at the stables with grooms and jockeys. The first time I asked to bet, Dan bought the ticket. He said, "If you want the horse to win, pat your head and turn around three times." I did that. "Now skip across the walkway and whistle." People were staring at me, but I did it. The horse lost. Dan had already torn up the ticket. "Now you know, Rollie boy, what betting on horses does to a man. Makes you a fool. Sometimes people keep their nonsense hidden inside, but if you're watching carefully, you'll learn to spot it. Learn to watch the people here, not the animals. The people are the ones who will make you rich."

Eva wanted to bet on the four horse in the fourth. I didn't tear up Eva's ticket, but I told her about Dan's lesson and let her watch the race if she promised to find at least one person twisting themselves around as if that would make a horse run faster. She lost, of course. I had a terrific time showing her how to tell the people who were regulars from the amateurs, the ones who needed the money from those who just wanted it, the hustlers from the hustled. I think Eva enjoyed it, too. And only once, only once, did I wonder what it would be like if the daughter of Ethan Williams met up with Aza Karkukli Bannion later in life.

I had a few weeks' leave, so I drove up to Big Bear. Loretta was in the bakery. I had not seen her since I left the money behind in her closet. She didn't mention it at all, but she tugged at my shoulder so I would bend down, and she gave me a peck on the cheek. I did not hug her because I was so relieved to see her I would have crushed her. The unsteadiness from the MS was about where it was before.

The runaway refuge looked in good shape. Eight kids were there. She had them rebuilding a gravel walkway. She let me help them and then I got to work on fixing the crumbling stairs along the path up to the kitchen and main building.

We all ate dinner together. Loretta even let me cook a couple of times. Some of the boys wanted to know about being a Marine. I tried my best to paint an accurate picture, but it was hard to tell what they were hearing. In the evenings, Loretta and I sat on the porch or on the couch inside and talked. She told me about the kids who had been coming through, the local politics, the efforts to oust her.

She wanted to hear about me. I told her the Victor Kosinski story, the Afghanistan part.

Loretta was quiet for a long time. I could not see her eyes because we were on the couch and I had my arm around her and her head was on my shoulder. Finally, she said, "You should have killed him."

"Right there on the mountain? Unarmed?"

"No. More recently. When he came back and you had another chance."

I had not said a word to her about the further adventures of Williams/Simmons/Kosinski. "How did you know that?"

"You wouldn't have told me the story unless there was a follow-up to it. That's why it bothers you."

I would have done anything for Loretta then, and I still would. Anything.

I stayed awhile more. The night before I left, I was sweeping out the kitchen when she said, "You look terrible, you know. Whatever you're doing, you should stop."

"I'm going to stop," I said.

She pushed me angrily. "Damn you, don't you patronize me. I'll kick you out of here."

"Ask me when."

"When?"

"As soon as it's too late." I dropped the broom, picked her up so her feet were off the floor, and hugged her and twirled her around while she cursed me. Kids were peeking in at the windows.

Major Hensel asked me to join him for dinner again. This time we went to a Greek restaurant in San Pedro. He had ordered Pongo and Perdy to follow me after my cell phone told him that I was heading for the private cemetery. I thanked him for that. It had taken him some effort to clear me of the Houston deaths. He did not want to involve Daisy as a witness. But the FBI had backed off, even though Ethan had not confessed. The CIA was going to be a long-term problem, he said. "It's partially my fault. I don't want to share any information with them." So I dined with a senior officer who said the words "my fault." Sometimes the world just tilts a little.

As many graves as they could guess at had been dug up. A total of one and a half million dollars was found in two graves.

"Does that include the middle grave up near Bishop?"

The Major smiled, delighted I asked. He stared at me, as if he wanted me to guess. "That body bag contained ten million dollars. Worth killing for, maybe."

"I don't know," I said. "He might have wanted to let it ride. I don't know." And I thought the matter of Ethan was settled.

"There is still the matter of the masks, though," the Major said.

I told him exactly where I got them.

He shook his head. "You had him, wounded and unarmed, and you were going to kill him. You might want to explain that."

I had told Loretta the story freely. But confession is terrible for the soul and I would never recommend it. Confession is destructive. I considered bargaining with the Major: Tell me who you really are and I'll tell you the whole Victor Kosinski story. Instead, I shook my head. He didn't argue. He asked for the bill.

After the waiter went away, the Major said as calmly as if he were describing why he preferred scotch to vodka, "If he were dead, it wouldn't matter. There's going to be a trial. Maybe a few trials. If your past with him comes out, I may not be able to help you. If I know what happened, how you first met him, I might be able to steer the prosecutors away."

Cornered. He made no comment at the end of the story. I don't intend telling it ever again.

He told me he did not need me right away, but to stay close. And to watch out for the CIA.

I did not feel like returning to Camp Pendleton, so I drove north without a plan. The cozy traffic rolled along slowly as if it were a destination in itself. A middle-aged woman driving a silver BMW jumped in front of me, then jumped back. She cut me off three times and I kept tempting her to do it again. Each time she changed lanes, she held her cigarette out the window and flicked the ashes.

Dan waited until we were passing LAX before he started telling stories.

"I knew a guy named Cookie. He was not a good guy, but he had a good thing going with Fran, a woman who ran a sales operation. You gave your product and her people got to work on the phones. Fran was big on counting: I gave you this, you give me that. And Cookie had what she wanted after a long day making sure her team never put down their phones or stopped their tongues from spraying sugar water.

"Cookie decided he had more to give, or extra, anyway, and he found quite a few willing recipients. Fran began noticing that Cookie's affections were less robust and she asked me what I knew about that topic. I was in business with Fran at the time—we were selling land in Nevada, up north—and I knew the answer I had to give her."

"Whether it was true or not," I said.

"Coincidentally, it was the truth. Cookie blamed me, though.

Hounded me. Threatened in a very believable way. Followed me. I decided to disappear. Had to leave you behind."

"But you came back." He always came back. He was still coming back. Coming back was an important part of keeping people off balance.

"Fortunately, some fellows who had been looking for Cookie, related to another matter, found him. Cookie went away. I never knew if it was voluntary or not, but right to the end, I kept looking around corners for him."

I had enough of whatever I was getting on the freeway and turned west on I-10 for the connection to the coast highway. Dan let the story sit and cool and firm up. I said, *"After I testify, Ethan will be in jail for a long time."*

"That's good. People don't like the people who testify against them. I tried to stay away from juries, but sometimes they get it right. That's what I heard anyway."

I had never been near a jury and had not thought much about how unreliable they were. Ethan would have to win twice, though, in military and civilian courts, a tough parlay. If he did, I would get another chance to make a choice regarding him.

Maybe I knew all along where I was going, but I did not admit it to myself until I was passing Point Dume. The farmhouse where Dan had hidden the money, where I had taken my mother to hide her, where I retreated into meditation, whether for peace or puzzles, was set above a Buddhist monastery at the edge of Ojai. As I passed Oxnard, I considered stopping to see my mother, Kate, another time. But I made no promises.

I parked in the dark lower lot at the monastery just before midnight and walked up toward the main buildings. Two young monks appeared beside the chapel. One of them recognized me. They guided me to lama Gyamtso's room. He asked them to bring tea.

While we waited, he said, "Kate came back here about two months ago. She asked to go up to the house. She spent about three hours."

I had brought Kate here to escape McColl and his men, but I never mentioned the money to her, and she ran away before I ever made it up to the house. I guessed she had broken up with her boyfriend and that made her rethink her conviction that Dan could not have left anything at the house because he never had anything.

But the lama did not care about Kate; he wanted to bring up the subject of the money. I told him I returned all the money to the government.

"Was that difficult?"

"I could probably find a way to get hold of money if I needed to."

The lama smiled and said, "You sounded just like your father when you said that."

But Dan would have said *"Yes, it was difficult."* Because he would know that was what the lama wanted to hear.

We talked for a little while about the monastery and how popular it was becoming as a corporate retreat. The lama worried that he was taking the monastery in the wrong direction. Then he said, "You can stay here. There is a room for you if you like. Always. But the house is for you, too. I think you might prefer that."

He offered to have the gates opened so I could drive up, but I preferred to walk, so he took me outside and showed me a path that took me to the house without having to climb the fence.

First I sat in the swing. A half-moon floated off to the left. Each leaf on the bent mesquite tree stayed fixed as if stapled in place; the air seemed to have settled in for a rest. The chains holding the swing emitted small, pleasant squeaks and soon, in between the noises, I heard Dan's voice coming from inside the house.

"*So you have some time off now. Might consider putting the time to good use. You don't have to dig up any graves yourself. You just sell the information. So much for the DS list, so much for Frank's list. You could even sell your fake list.*"

"*I could make up more fake lists.*" That was another voice, which sounded like mine.

"*You could sell each one quite a few times, to many buyers. You tell them there are no guarantees but my father did find twenty-five million in only one grave. Nothing sells like the truth.*"

"*How about selling access to the future King of Kurdistan? I could probably marry his mother if I wanted to and become regent.*"

"*Regent is good. Did I ever tell you about the heiress I knew in Georgia? Dalton, Georgia. Carpets, it was…*"

He went on. He was a goblin, a djinn, and an indispensible nuisance. I admitted that he had set me in the right direction, leading me toward the PKK partnership. He had forgotten more than I ever knew and I was condemned to dredging all of it up. It was treasure.

I sat there on the swing long after Dan's voice faded away and the moon rolled behind the house. Just as dawn made its first threat, I went inside.

ABOUT THE AUTHOR

DAVID RICH has sold screenplays to most of the major studios and to many production companies in the United States and Europe. He wrote the feature film *Renegades*, starring Kiefer Sutherland and Lou Diamond Phillips. The author of *Caravan of Thieves*, he lives in Connecticut.